Dear Kate

a novel

Dear Kate

HANNAH DUGGAN

CROSS
HILL
PRESS

ISBN 0692246819
eISBN

Printed in the United States

PRAISE FOR *DEAR KATE*

"I was hooked; literally unable to put it down. The reader become involved in the story, really caring about the characters. From beginning to end plot twists keep the readers on their toes."

-Katrina

"Full of surprises. It made me laugh, cry, gave me shivers, and…even had me holding my breath."

-Camelia

"Exciting! A fast-moving book. I enjoyed every page!"

-Lynn

"Dear Kate is a page turner, full of action, adventure, and mystery. I enjoyed every minute!"

-Candie

PRAISE FOR HANNAH DUGGAN

"Hannah is a wunderkind. A prodigy. She is an up-and-comer with remarkable talent."

-Pastor Ben Courson
Applegate Christian Fellowship

"I've read *From the Flames* & found it to be a fascinating read! I was not only extremely impressed, but equally blessed by Hannah's words. The Lord's hand is upon this young lady!"

~Pastor Mike Stangel
North Shore Christian Fellowship

"I loved having Hannah as a leader because she's young and fun and always positive and she's just an amazing influence on us."

~Peyton
Age 13

"It gives me hope, knowing that there are young people, such as Miss Duggan, who truly care about spreading the truth."

~Angela
Amazon Reviewer

For Camelia, Elizabeth, Nicole, and Bella:
As He calls us each by name,
may we keep our eyes above the waves
as we leave the harbor.

"But now thus saith the Lord, that created thee, O Jacob:
and He that formed thee, O Israel,
Fear not: for I have redeemed thee:
I have called thee by thy name, thou art mine.
When thou passest through the waters, I will be with thee,
and through the floods, that they do not overflow thee.
When thou walkest through the very fire,
thou shalt not be burnt, neither shall the flame kindle upon
thee."

ISAIAH 43:1-2

CHAPTER 1

I'd always imagined myself having peace at this moment, when I knew there was nothing more I could do, when I knew I would die. The terrified panic that consumed me was not what I had planned, but then, nothing in my life ever had been.

"Kate!" James said my name over and over from the cliff far above me, barking orders that made no sense to my frantic mind. What had I been thinking? When I jumped from the cliff down to the crumbling ledge several feet below, I had been sure it would hold. Now the only thing keeping me from plunging hundreds of feet to the deadly rocks below was the weakening grip of my burning fingers. Even if my grip could endure to the end of time, the ledge would not, and my life was not the only one in danger.

I heard a crash as the unstable portions of the ledge broke loose and plummeted downward. We didn't have much longer. I gathered the strength for one last effort, pulling myself up far enough to thrust one hand forward and claw my fingers into the dirt. I steadied my grip, then plunged the other hand forward as well. If I moved quickly enough I could walk my hands forward and pull myself up inch by inch before the ledge or my strength gave way. I started the slow process, and by the time I had pulled myself far enough to see over the ledge, I could go no further.

The earthen shelf around us was crumbling. James was above us on the cliff's edge, still screaming commands that didn't matter anymore.

I looked at the little girl on the ledge in front of me. She looked back. Swallowing the taste of dirt and blood in my mouth, I searched for some shred of hope, some word of consolation. "I'm sorry," I gasped, hating myself for having attempted to be a hero. In the end, I was simply dragging her down with me that much faster, just as I'd done to everyone I loved my whole life.

She crept forward on the ever shrinking ledge, and set her tiny hand on mine. The tranquility on her face astounded me. That was what I wanted, what I had envisioned myself looking like at this moment. I saw in her dark eyes the knowledge that we were both about to die, yet she seemed unafraid.

Her quiet strength awakened something inside of me. I couldn't give up. Not now, not when she needed me.

My arms quivered with fatigue. My fingers were numb and about to give way. I began to kick my feet back and forth. The movement jarred the ledge, and it disintegrated faster. My left foot found a hold, and I pushed myself upward. I felt a thrill when my knee slid onto the ledge. I tried to stand up without causing another shift, but was unsuccessful. As I got my footing, a cracking noise sounded. I reached down to snatch up the little girl, but before I could, the ground beneath her came loose and collapsed. She screamed and I frantically grasped the air, catching the back of her dress. I heard the fabric ripping as I tightened my hold. With a deep breath, I drew her slowly upward and into my shaking arms and watched as half of the ledge crashed downward and exploded into a cloud of dust on the rocks below.

"James!" I shouted to my cousin, who hadn't for a moment left cliff's edge above me. Having read my thoughts, he was already down on his stomach, arms outstretched, ready to catch her.

I hurled her upward with all my might, weak with relief when his massive hands closed around her tiny ones and he pulled her up over the edge. His face disappeared for what felt like an eternity. Was he walking the girl all the way back to London?

"James?" I called, pressing my back against the cliff behind me. Sweat poured down my face as I searched the cliff for anything to grab onto. There wasn't so much as tree root.

"Kate!"

Looking up, I saw James, on his stomach, his hands open and waiting for me. I leapt up and our fingertips touched. He leaned far beyond the cliff's edge, but couldn't grasp my hand. When I fell back to the ledge, the outer rim of it dissolved, tumbling downward. Fighting to regain my balance, I looked up at my cousin. I could see the frightened tears in his eyes, and his lip trembled slightly.

"Try again!"

I gave a shaky nod and jumped. His hand caught mine, but the sweat from our palms loosened his grip. His fingers curled around mine until I thought all the bones in my hand would snap. He started to lift me up, but the slightest movement caused my hand to slip from his grasp, and I dropped.

"No!" he cried as he lost his grip.

When my feet hit the ledge under me, it surrendered to my weight. I scrambled forward toward the cliff side, pressing myself to the wall of the cliff. I scrunched my eyes shut, waiting to plummet downward. When I didn't, I glanced down and saw that the ledge was now only a tiny foothold under me. It wouldn't forgive one more failed attempt.

My heart drummed in my ears. "God," I gasped, the prayer springing from the habit of my childhood. "God, please." Looking up, I saw James' face, watching me in horror. One last time I crouched on the foothold and sprang from my spot. Our hands connected and held. I looked down and saw the last of the ledge crumble into pieces, falling to the rocks below, and shattering into oblivion.

The moment I was dragged onto safe ground, I crawled as far from the cliff's edge as possible before collapsing, my face pressed into the warm, sunbaked earth.

I listened to the wind moan above me. Everything throbbed. My cousin's voice, which hadn't stopped since I had jumped down to the ledge, was asking question after question.

Yes, I was hurt. No, I was not all right. Yes, I knew how close I had come to dying. But I couldn't verbalize any of those answers. All I could do was breathe. I was alive.

I felt a hand reach down, brushing away the dark curls that blinded me. I thought it was an oddly thoughtful gesture for my cousin, but it wasn't him at all. As I looked up, I saw the wide eyes of the little girl. Her lips were pressed together like the clasp of a jewelry box. She wasn't crying, and I wondered if she understood what had just happened. She was so small yet her dark eyes flashed intelligently.

Sitting up, I tried to ignore the pain pulsing through every muscle. I turned to look at the cliff's edge on the side of the road and shuddered at the thought of its fatal power. While this girl had kept her life today, she had lost much. I was reminded of the sick feeling that took hold of me as I tore down the road after the runaway carriage. I had rounded the corner only to find that the coach had gone over the cliff. This girl had been thrown from the carriage, landing on the ledge. I wondered if she understood that she was the only survivor. I spoke softly, as though she would run if I startled her. "Was that your family in that carriage?"

She nodded, the clasp of her lips still fastened shut. Her eyes pooled with tears, and her lower lip began to tremble.

I reached out to lay a hand on her shoulder, but she turned and scrambled into my lap, wrapping her arms around my neck, sobbing into my dirt-stained dress. I looked to James. He was as helpless as I was. Without the slightest idea of how to comfort her, I set a hand on her back and stroked her hair. "It's all right," I murmured, my voice weak with emotion. "It's all right." The lie stuck fast in my throat. Nothing was right. Her family was gone. Her life would never be the same. My words were so futile. What could I offer? Numb with shock, I rocked the child back and forth. "What's your name?"

She gasped for air between sobs. "Emily."

I felt the tears slipping down my cheeks. "Emily," I whispered, fighting back tears of my own. "I can't bring your mother and father back, but we're going to help you any way that we can. I promise."

"We'll take you home," James suggested.

I sent my cousin a look.

He shrugged, wondering what he'd said wrong and ignored me. "Where do you live?"

She tightened her grip on my neck, the sobs shaking her little body.

I glanced at him. "Not now." I shifted her in my lap, and felt something crinkle inside her dress. Reaching down I felt the hem of her course black skirt. I ran my finger along the inner edge and felt a texture that didn't belong. Turning the hem over, I stared in disbelief.

It was paper sewn into her dress with black thread. Despite being smudged with dirt, the parchment was unharmed. "Look at this," I said to James as I took the corner and began to tear it out of her dress. Thread snapped and parchment ripped until I was holding in my hands a sealed letter folded from all four sides. The seal caught my attention. It was a leaf, surrounded by Latin words and decorations, most of them too tiny for me to make out. I knew that each mark, however small, meant a great deal to the seal's owner. I searched for a family name and found nothing. Flipping the letter over, I hoped to see an address of the intended recipient. There was none. I broke the seal, unfolding the letter. As I did, several coins spilled into my lap. Confused, I stared at the message. The salutation made my heart pound in my ears.

Dear Kate,

Gasping, I dropped the letter, as if it had been a snake.
"What's wrong?" James asked.
"I—I don't know," I stuttered, reaching for the parchment
again. I picked it up, reading further this time.

Dear Kate,

*Your services are required to escort Miss Emily
Blake to Barrow-Haven. You will be paid for your
services upon arrival. Please accept this initial
payment for your traveling expenses. If you find
yourself confused, know only that the reputation of
your work among the flock precedes you. Your utmost
discretion is appreciated in this matter. Thank you
for your assistance, and please take good care of my
little girl.*

Sincerely,
Simon Cephas

CHAPTER 2

"What does it say?" my cousin asked.

Unable to reply, I handed him the letter. He skimmed the contents, then stared down at Emily, still curled up in my lap. "Where did you get this?" His question sounded more like an accusation.

She looked to me for help, but I could only offer her a blank stare. Turning back to James, her lower lip trembled. "Mother sewed it..." She took in a shaky breath. "In my dress."

"But who is it from?" he cried.

I felt a tremor run through her little body. "James," I reprimanded. "She doesn't know." I glanced back at the letter. *The reputation of your work among the flock...* An icy chill settled in my stomach. That was impossible. No one else knew.

James took the letter from me. "Perhaps it was written to someone else. It must by an accident."

I shuddered, letting my gaze sweeping over the landscape. "Do you think any of this was an accident?"

When her cries had quieted I set the little girl on the ground beside me and pushed myself to my feet. The world began to blur and spin. Taking a few deep breaths, I waited for everything to return back to normal. My legs shook under me as I took a few steps. How would I ever walk back to the tavern? I wondered at every moment if my legs would hold me up, focusing on the road in front of me.

"Please."

The strange voice made me halt. It hadn't been much more than a whisper.

"What's wrong?" James asked.

I glanced around. "Did you hear that?"

"Please!" This time it had been nearly a shout. I turned to my right where the voice had originated and saw only the shrubbery.

James had heard it too. "Who's there?" he called.

"Please don't leave me here." Stepping around Emily, I pushed back some of the foliage and caught my breath. There in the shade of the undergrowth was a man. He gasped for air, gripping a red stain at his side. He squinted at the light. "Please don't leave me," he hissed.

James bent down beside me trying to examine the man's wound, but he protested. "No. In the light. You need to see it…in the light."

My cousin placed a firm arm around the man's middle, and dragged him onto the road. As James set him down, a venomous stream of cursing spouted from the stranger's mouth. I gripped Emily's hand in my own, instinctively feeling the need to hold onto her.

"I tried…" the stranger coughed. "I tried to save it."

"Were you the carriage driver?" my cousin asked.

The man nodded. "I thought I could save it, but the brute threw me under the wheels." A volley of coughing proceeded, showing a few blackened teeth.

James looked at me. "Kate, run to the tavern. Get help."

I turned, wondering if my legs would carry me that far.

"Wait!" The plea came from the injured driver.

He was looking at Emily with a strange gleam came in his eyes. He reached a hand out to her. "I'm so sorry, Child. I tried to save them."

I expected the girl to shy away, but slipping her hand from mine Emily took two steps forward, watching the stranger. I noticed a black stain on his wrist behind the thumb as he reached up and set a soiled hand on Emily's arm. His black eyes glinted and he flashed a smile that I saw too late.

In one swift movement, he reached for her throat as if to choke her, but instead hooked his forefinger in a chain around her neck and wrenched her toward him. The necklace snapped, the force jerking Emily to her knees as he unsheathed a knife with the other hand and raised it above his head. I dove for the girl, snatching her backward. James caught both the man's wrists, pinning them to the ground. The driver struggled under my cousin's strength.

The stranger stared up at James and let out a shriek. "This isn't over, Cephas! Scot may have lost the key, but you lost so much more." He gave a sharp cry, then fell silent.

Still clutching the girl, I watched James, not daring to breathe. His jaw was tight as he stared at the stranger, prepared for any further movements, but the stranger was still. His breathing came to a ragged halt. Slowly, my cousin released one hand, then the other.

"James?"

"He's dead."

I realized I'd been holding my breath, and loosened my grip on Emily.

James looked up at me. "Get her back to the tavern. I'll take care of this."

I nodded, taking Emily by the hand, but she wouldn't move. She gazed at the dead man. Stepping toward the body, she knelt on the dusty path, retrieving her necklace. Then she stood and walked toward the tavern without looking back.

· · ·

I watched the little golden head toss back and forth on the

pillow, long after her breathing was steady and peaceful. I'd listened to her cry herself to sleep, not asking any questions, just listening as she fell into a dream haunted sleep. Occasionally she would whimper, thrashing beneath the blankets. I knew all too well the nightmares she was facing, but could never bring myself to wake her up. Anything she was struggling against in the dream world was only a shadow. The true cruelty would have been to awaken her, flooding her with the harsh, cold light of reality.

Hearing voices outside the door to our room, I picked up the candle and crept into the dark hallway to see James and Master Owens, the owner of the tavern. They were exiting a store room when I saw them, but they didn't notice me.

"But the man said he was the driver." James didn't hide his agitation as he followed the owner down the hallway.

"Men often lie, Master Elyot," Master Owens said with an air of superiority. He opened the door that led to the empty dining room, shaking his head. "You learn these things when you're in my business."

I knew James was holding back a snide response, as he entered the room.

My cousin took a deep breath. "Then he wasn't the driver?"

Master Owens shook his head, heading for one of the long wooden tables lit by a single candle. "If you think I'd let anyone like that come week after week, bringing other men of his kind into my tavern, you've lost your mind. The body you brought to the store room wasn't the driver. The driver of that carriage was Jeptha Morgan, and he ran a clean business. In fact, there was a time—"

"But you said you *did* recognize the body," James interrupted, stepping forward and letting the dining room door swing behind him.

I caught the door as it swung toward me and I slipped through. James already disliked Master Owens for one simple

10

reason. My cousin was not one to mince words. Master Owens was.

The owner took a seat at the table, disappointed not to finish his story. He gave a slow nod. "He was in here this morning by himself. I never did see him leave. He must have sneaked aboard that carriage or paid the driver a handsome fee. Jeptha Morgan didn't let men of that kind on his carriage. As I said, he ran a clean business." A reminiscent look came into his eyes. "In fact, one day when he stopped in here there was a man who—"

"What do you mean by 'men of that kind?'" James interrupted again, sitting down across from Master Owens.

The tavern owner rattled off a list. "Street rats, thieves, sailors." He shrugged. "Jeptha Morgan's carriage was for the more refined. That's why I enjoyed his business here in my tavern. Why once he brought a woman in who—"

"How do you know this man was any of those things?"

Master Owens' shoulders sagged visibly as the realization dawned on him that there was no way James was going to let him divert from the subject. "Did you see the mark on his wrist?"

"I did," I said, surprised at the sound of my own voice.

For the first time, both of them noticed me.

"It was a black stain, wasn't it?" I mumbled, stepping forward to stand behind James.

Master Owens gave another slow nod. "It's the mark of a sailor. They get them from the islands of cannibals and head-hunters. Those that make it out, that is." The pool of light from the candles felt suddenly eerie as Master Owens raised an eyebrow at me. "It's an ancient heathen practice known as Tatau. They scrape away the skin and pour in a black powder, with all sorts of wicked designs and drawings. You don't want to know the stories I've heard of what goes on in those islands."

"No. You're right. We don't." James was adamant.

"Could the mark tell you anything else about him?"

"Why do you care?" The crestfallen tavern owner scratched his fingernail against a divot in the wooden table.

My cousin gave a heavy sigh, and stood to his feet. "Just curious, I suppose."

"Ferox," Master Owens muttered under his breath as James turned to leave.

"What was that?" James asked, turning back.

"Ferox," he repeated. "The word on his wrist was Ferox."

"What does that mean?" I asked.

"How should I know?" Master Owens grumbled.

James' patience had reached its end. I could tell he was not interested in playing Master Owens' guessing game. "Thank you for your help," he said, turning to leave.

"Funny," the tavern owner mused, as James planted his hand on the door. "No one knew these roads better than Morgan. He's run that mountain road once every seven days for the last twenty years. It seems odd to me that he would lose control like that."

I glared at James. He hadn't told the tavern keeper the whole story, but my cousin refused to look at me, staring instead at the closed door in front of him.

"You two aren't from here, are you?" Master Owens asked.

"No." James irritation charged the air with tension.

"So where are you from?" he asked, as if it were a breezy summer afternoon, and we were making simple conversation.

"London," he replied, without turning around.

"London?" The man was astounded. "You're a far cry from there. Are you here on business?"

The muscles in my cousin's neck were tense as he nodded.

"London's a two-week journey south of here. It must have been important business."

James sent me a reproachful glance. "Not anymore."

Before one more word could be spoken, he shoved the door open, and disappeared into the dark hallway. As the door swung back toward me I took hold of it, but the tavern owner hadn't finished.

"Funny. I served that sailor a drink this morning."

I turned back and was surprised to see Master Owens staring right at me, as if searching me.

"Said he was from London, too."

CHAPTER 3

"You didn't tell him everything, did you?"

James shrugged. "Does he need to know?"

"Someone should." I shuddered. "Someone needs to know what I saw."

James leaned his back against the heavy wooden door speaking in hushed tones to keep from waking the little girl. "Honestly, Kate, do you even know what you saw?"

His doubt stung. "I know you don't trust my judgment, but just this once—"

"That's *not* what this is about," he said, stepping around me and reaching to stir the fire in the hearth.

If I closed my eyes, I could still see the figure jumping from the carriage window, and leaping for the driver's seat before it turned the corner. Master Owens had been right about one thing. The driver hadn't simply lost control.

"You didn't tell him about the letter either, did you?"

"I didn't see that it was any of his business."

I turned to face him. "Perhaps not, but if we don't tell the whole story we'll never understand what's going on."

He glanced over his shoulder at me and gave a condescending sound of disgust.

I glared back at him. "What is that supposed to mean?"

He stood to his full height, and turned to me, his arms

folded across his chest. "Really, Kate? You don't already know what's going on?"

I set my shoulders back. "No, and neither do you."

"Look around. Are you telling me that none of it seems familiar?"

Turning to look at Emily, I saw the simple, black dress made of fabric that I knew all too well. I felt my throat constrict. "I don't want to talk about it."

"That's fine with me, but you're blind if you can't see who these people are. I knew it the moment I saw her family in the tavern."

Don't say it, I silently pleaded with him.

"They're Puritans." There was a darkness in his voice.

"You don't know that." I stepped toward him, my voice shaking.

"Yes, I do. And you know it too. You just won't admit it." He let out a long breath. "This was a terrible idea. We're going home in the morning."

"James," I started.

"No." He turned, setting his hands on my shoulders. "No more. It's got to end somewhere. We're done."

"We just started."

He turned back toward the fire. "We never should have left." His fists clenched. "Why did I listen to you?"

"Because you hated London as much as I did."

"But at least we had a roof over our heads. At least we had work. We gave all of that up, walked all the way here only to find out from some old man that your inheritance has been gone for more than ten years."

I gazed into the flickering hearth. "It wasn't about the money."

"So we're just up here to see the sights?"

"We're here to find our home."

"I should have known better." He shook his head. "I should have known you weren't ready for this."

His condescending tone made me furious. He was hardly a year older than me.

I struggled to keep my voice controlled and even. "I'm seventeen years old. Stop mothering me."

He glanced over his shoulder. "Someone has to."

His words pierced through me. "I had to do something." My voice was low. "I had to get us out of there. I hated London. I hated working at the Seven Stars Tavern. And I knew if it was up to you we would be there forever because you are afraid of absolutely everything!"

He recoiled at my words. I could see the flash shame and anger in his eyes. I had gone too far. I had wanted to say it for months, but now that the words were out I regretted every one of them.

"James, I'm sorry." I put a hand over my mouth. "I didn't mean..."

He looked back into the fire, his jaw rigid. "We're going home. That's final."

I nodded, trying to keep back the tears stinging my eyes. I looked at the little girl asleep in the bed. "What are we going to do with her?"

He shook his head. "The letter says Barrow-Haven. That's on our way."

"It's not that simple."

"Why, because you want to stay up here?"

"There might not be a home in Barrow-Haven," I said, ignoring his comment. "Even if that's where she's from who would take care of her?"

"Do you have a better idea?"

"No," I sighed. "I just don't see why she's our responsibility."

He looked at me for a long moment. "Do you remember what it was like to be no one's responsibility?"

I felt the knot rise in my throat. "This is different." My anger melted into cold fear as I stared at the helpless little girl.

"James, I can't do this again." Tears pricked my eyes. "What if something happens to her? What if we can't do it? I don't think I could bear it if—"

"Stop worrying," he grunted. "It's a two day walk to Barrow-Haven. Nothing is going to happen."

The discussion was closed. His mind was made up, and nothing I could say would change it.

• • •

I lay awake in the dark. Every time I closed my eyes all I could see was the carriage tipping over the side of the cliff, or the sailor unsheathing his knife.

After hours of tossing back and forth, listening to the rhythmic breathing of the little girl beside me and the snoring of my cousin, asleep in front of the hearth, I sat up and lit a candle.

I picked up the letter. The sight of my name sent chills down my spine. True, Katherine was not an uncommon name. Yet there was something about it that made me shiver.

Maybe it hadn't been meant for me, but here it was in my hands.

Take good care of my little girl.

In the flickering light I looked at Emily and felt the familiar, sickening dread. I couldn't do it. I couldn't be what she needed. After all that had happened she needed someone who would love her and mother her and make her feel safe. I was not the one for the job. I was not ready to be hurt again.

Turning back to the bedside table I noticed her necklace. It wasn't really a necklace at all, but a ring suspended on a chain. I picked it up and examined it closely. It was a signet ring, used to press an original symbol into the wax seals of documents and letters. I compared it to the torn seal on the letter beside it. The ring held the same leaf symbol as the wax seal. The leaf was made up of two letters. An S swooped delicately down to form the stem and one half of the leaf. The C was tucked into the lower curve of the S to form the other half. S. C. *Simon Cephas*? I tried to think of a way that it would make sense, an angle that would make everything come together. *Simon Cephas.* The sailor had said that name with his last breath, telling him it wasn't over. *What wasn't over?*

James was right. There was no question. They were Puritans. The very word made my heart quicken. Puritans defied the Church of England's authority. They moved the altars in their church. They didn't observe the King's book of games. I had seen the way they violated all of these laws. I had also seen the price they paid. It was everything we were running from, everything we'd left behind, but what if it had caught up with us?

I glanced at the sleeping child beside me. It was more than just her family's convictions that frightened me. I'd witnessed her parents death, seen them as they were ripped away, and watched it dawn on her that she was completely alone.

The ghosts were too real, the memories too fresh.

When I looked into her eyes I wanted to run as fast as I could in the other direction because I knew. I knew the fears. I knew the griefs. I knew the terrible emptiness. I had lived this terrible nightmare before, and I had been exactly her age the day it began.

. . .

I was six, nearly seven, the day we left everything behind. I could feel the strength and warmth of my father's hand as we walked to the docks. I glanced around my father to James wondering if he was as excited to ride a ship as I was. He wasn't. He was afraid.

Adventurers. That's what my father had called us. It was like all the stories he'd told me as I sat in my mother's arms. He told me stories of how the world was changing, how ships full of people sailed for a New World somewhere across the ocean. He said that we were leaving home for the same reason, so that all of us could find a better life, especially Mother, whose health would not have sustained her through another harsh winter in the north. Unlike the party of settlers our destination was the Southern Coast of England, but our ship never reached its port.

The first explosion tore through the ship, knocking all of us from our feet. There was a blinding light from behind the door. I knew I was screaming, but I couldn't hear myself. I could feel the searing heat, see the light, hear the thunder. I watched Father gripping the door, trying to open it. The door burst into splinters, knocking him back. A man in singed clothes stepped through debris, snatched up my cousin and I, and began running with us.

My hands gripped the rung of a ladder like claws as I scrambled up. When the three of us reached the top, another roar coursed throughout the ship. There was heat all around me as the ship began to sink beneath the surface. I watched the hatch in the deck, waiting for my mother and father to emerge from the hull, but they never did. Hands pulled me from the embers of the deck and tossed me overboard. I flew through the air, plunging into the icy water, grasping, choking, unable to surface. As I was dragged down, I could see everything beneath the water, lit up by the burning glow of the ship.

My parents and the captain had been the only casualties suffered that day. James and I had been lifted into the longboats by the same man who had rescued us from the ship.

I remembered asking him over and over where my mother was, and when my father would come to get us. He had only looked at me saying, "I'm so sorry, Child."

No matter how sorry he was, he, like everyone else, didn't wish to be burdened with us. We were given to the first person who would take us, Fortune Cole, the old woman who lived in the cabin on the River Medway.

CHAPTER 4

The chilling downpour soaked the two fresh mounds of earth, as tears mingled with rain on the little girl's cheeks. I wondered what was running through her mind. I had never had this moment. My parents' only grave had been the ocean that had claimed them. James and I watched her from several steps away as she bent beside each grave. It was a poor excuse for a funeral, but we had nothing else to offer her. We had heard all of it, knew every platitude by heart. In the end it was the silent company of one another that had consoled us on the darkest days.

She looked at me, and I felt my heart convulse. Unable to bear the sorrow on her innocent face, I looked away. I had lived without hope for so long. What hope could I offer her?

"It's time to go," James whispered.

I nodded.

He turned and walked toward the tavern, and I watched him go. None but me would have noticed the subtle limp that had plagued him since childhood. I fought back shameful tears when I thought of my words the night before.

With a deep breath I turned back to Emily. She left the came to stand behind me. As she looked up at me, her dark eyes were brimming. "I miss them."

I swallowed back the tears. "I know." I reached down to

stroked her hair, but stopped myself.

No. I had to draw back. I could already feel the way she tugged at my heart, and knew I was becoming dangerously close.

We kept a slow pace as we walked silently back to the tavern.

"Do you think they miss me?"

Her voice startled me. "Of course they do," I managed.

We walked in silence for several moments when she looked up at me. "They got to see Him first."

"Who?" I asked, confused.

"Jesus."

I stared straight ahead, unable to answer.

"Do you think He told them I'm all right?"

"I'm sure He did," I said in an emotionless voice as we neared the tavern door.

"What's wrong?" James asked when we met him in the room packing our few belongings.

"Nothing," I answered, releasing the little girl's hand. "I'll go pay for the room."

"Are you sure?"

"Yes." I cleared my throat. "Please, just take her."

He poured the coins into my hand, trying to search my face.

I ducked into the hallway. Seeing that it was empty I leaned my back against the wall, putting a hand over my mouth, trying to forget her haunting words.

• • •

The coins clinked in my trembling hand as I stepped up to the long wooden counter. We had agreed to use the coins from the letter to pay for our room and buy food for the journey ahead. "I'm here to pay for our room, Master Owens."

The tavern keeper looked me up and down. "You'll have

to wait a moment." Picking up a plate of food, he stepped around the counter in front of him to deliver the meal to a bearded gentleman seated by the window. I found myself staring at nothing in my exhaustion.

"Right, then." Master Owens dusted his hands unnecessarily on his work apron as he came around the counter. "Now forgive me if I'm mistaken, but I was told by Master Elyot that he would be working for me to pay off the room. I don't usually accept payment of that sort, but the circumstances being what they are I…"

"The circumstances being what they are, our plans have changed," I interjected.

Master Owens was attempting to detain us, still holding out hope that James and I were going to turn out to be murderous pirates, and of course, he would have the joy of being the one who suspected all along. It chafed me knowing that I was only one more exaggerated character in a tavern keeper's endless stories.

Plastering on a pleasant look, he nodded. "Yes, of course. I never could deny a pretty young lady anything she wanted."

And it certainly can't hurt if the pretty young lady has a handful of pretty gold coins. I thought to myself as I counted out the fee.

"Do you see that man by the window?" Master Owens whispered right next to my ear, startling me and causing me to drop the coins. They clinked onto the counter and several clattered to the floor. As I bent to pick them up, several heads turned, including the bearded gentleman by the window whom Master Owens had served previously.

After retrieving the coins, I placed them back on the counter starting to lose my patience. "I see him."

"Reverend Howe. He's an old friend of mine. A scholar and a cleric. As the story goes, he wanted to raise money for a church, and his congregation said to him, 'Yes. But, Reverend, *how*?'" Master Owens exploded into laughter, apparently not deterred by my less-than-amused expression. He wiped his eyes and continued. "When I saw him this morning, I was surprised. He usually doesn't come on Saturdays, the next day of course being Sunday, but—"

"Is this the right amount?" I questioned, motioning to the coins.

"Yes, yes." He waved away the coins. "He was in this morning and I said, 'Reverend Howe, what a pleasant surprise!' And do you know what he said?"

"Master Owens," I interrupted, my patience reaching its end. "Does this story have the slightest shred of importance?"

He leaned an elbow on the counter. "Oh, no. It's of no importance really. Just an old man babbling on."

I nodded, shoving the coins toward him.

"Unless, of course, you want your question answered."

I folded my hands in front of me on the counter to keep from scraping my nails down the wood. This was usually about the moment when James would point out that my nostrils were flaring. "I don't recall asking you a question."

"Well you did, and I took your question to Reverend Howe and he says it means 'Wild.'"

I began to wonder what would happen if I screamed in the middle of that dining room. His roundabout methods were going to destroy any hope of sanity I still possessed. "What means wild?" I measured out every word.

He laughed. "You know, for someone who is always in such a hurry, you're rather slow. Any reason you'd be trying to escape my establishment so soon?"

Unable to take it any longer I leaned forward until I was eye to eye with the tavern owner. "I do not appreciate your suspicions, Sir. Nor, do I enjoy being treated like a criminal." I took a deep breath and a step back. With a sigh I thanked Master Owens for the accommodations and turned to go.

"Ferox."

The word made me freeze.

"It means wild, courageous, or defiant."

I looked back at the tavern keeper and managed a grateful nod. "Thank you, Master Owens." With that, I turned and left the little tavern, wishing I had never entered it.

. . .

The rain hadn't abated by the time we set out. Emily asked question after question about life and death and Heaven and her parents. Neither of us possessed the answers she was searching for. I reminded myself that it was only for two days.

We descended the hill by midday and entered the farmlands, leaving behind us the place of our childhood. The hills were disappearing from sight when I turned to have one last look. I stared long and hard at them, wondering if there would be any last hint of my father's laughter or my mother's embrace tucked into the sight of the familiar green hills cloaked in mist, but the landscape was silent. My mother had had a saying about those hills and the mist that shrouded them, but after ten years her words had slipped from my memory. The hills stretched upward like sentinels guarding the past.

I had told James we were traveling north looking for an inheritance. I had told myself that we were trying to get away from London. In truth I had come here in search of my parents, for some memory or hint of them that I could carry with me always, but I had found nothing.

I looked down at the solemn child walking beside me. I had found something, but as was often the case, it wasn't what I had been looking for.

I tried to ignore the rush of fear that surfaced whenever I considered what we had gotten ourselves into. I felt trapped. We were part of this now. There was no turning back.

I looked from the girl to James, who was staring at the road ahead. Neither of us could stop what was about to happen any more than we could stop the mist pouring down the hills.

24

CHAPTER 5

He screamed. He pleaded. She would hear none of it.

I pressed my ear against the paper-thin walls cracked with age and listened.

"Worthless!" I heard a slap, and his sobs grew louder.

"Waste!" Something crashed on the other side of the wall, probably one of her bottles. By the sharp cry, I knew that he'd been cut by the shards of glass.

"Useless!"

I wanted to back away, to clap my hands over my ears, but I couldn't move. Though the sounds of the beating were frightening, it was silence I dreaded. The tears coursed down my cheeks as I listened.

We had to run. We had to escape, but that was why he was getting a beating in the first place, wasn't it? There was nowhere to run.

My eyes shot open. I was staring at the unfeeling gray sky. Where was I? I shivered, the cold reminding me exactly where I was. In the middle of nowhere, asleep on the cold wet ground. I looked around, shaking off the nightmares as I did every morning. Mist crept along the freezing ground. The eastern sky was lightening, but an hour or so from sunrise. I glanced down and saw Emily curled up next to me. Sitting up, I folded back the cloak that had served as my blanket and laid it over her. She shivered in her sleep and a wisp of her hair slipped down over her nose, and I couldn't help but smile. I reached down to sweep back the strawberry curl, but stopped.

No.

"Why do you do that?"

James' irritated voice startled me.

I turned to see him sitting by the ashes of last night's fire. "Do what?"

"Draw back like that."

I felt the ache in my throat. "I'm afraid."

"Of what?" he asked.

I looked back at the sleeping child nestled beneath the cloaks. "Of loving something so fragile."

"You know, she doesn't understand that."

I pushed myself to my feet. "Well it doesn't matter, does it? After all, it's only a two day journey."

He rolled his eyes and stared into the dead ashes.

"Two days, James," I repeated. "How many days ago did you say that?"

"Four."

"Five," I corrected.

He continued to stare into the fire pit. "I don't want to talk about it."

I stepped through the dew covered grass to stand in front of him. "We've been walking for days. Our provisions are gone. How much farther is it?"

"I don't know!" he cried. "I don't know how much farther it is. I don't know why it's taking so long. I don't know."

He'd said Barrow-Haven was just across the Hull River, but after five days of wandering through the woods the river was nowhere in sight.

Taking a deep breath, I turned away, not ready to be

arguing with him this early.

"I'm not afraid of everything," he muttered.

I turned back. "What?"

He was still staring into the ashes. "I'm not afraid of everything."

"This is about what I said at the tavern?" I asked in disbelief. "I said I was sorry. I didn't mean it. I just wanted you to…" I stopped, knowing he wasn't listening and took a deep breath. "I know that you want to keep us safe, but I can't spend the rest of my life in the back room of a tavern, hiding from everything that happened."

"Why were you always the brave one?" he asked without looking up.

For the slightest moment, I caught a glimpse of what he had looked like as a child, and it broke my heart. I walked toward him and settled myself on the ground next to my cousin, staring into the same pile of charred wood and ashes.

"Do you remember the night we ran?"

He nodded.

"I was terrified," I continued.

"But you kept running," he said. "That's what I mean, Kate. Even when you were afraid, you kept running. It didn't matter how many times we failed, you always had a new plan."

I turned to him, realizing that my anger had dissipated. "I'm not the one who took the beating for it, though."

He cleared his throat, glancing upward.

"Why did you always take the blame?" I asked softly.

He shrugged. "Fortune Cole drank away any heart she had. She would have killed you."

"Like she nearly killed you?"

He waved away my comment as though I was exaggerating. I wasn't. "James, you took the blame and the beating for every one of my schemes. There's nothing cowardly about that."

I could see him considering my words. Then the relief of it broke on his face, and for the first time in days I felt the tension release.

He turned to me and his calm vanished.

"James, is something—"

"Quiet." He was pale, staring directly at me, as if afraid to look away.

"Did I say something?"

"I said be quiet," he commanded in a hoarse whisper. With a deep breath, he continued. "Call Emily."

"She's asleep."

"No she's not." He shook his head. "Call her."

I started to turn, but he gripped my shoulder. "Don't turn around. Just call her over here."

I tried to catch a glimpse of her out of the corner of my eye. "Emily, come here." I glanced at James, who gave me a nod.

She was at my side in moments. James had refitted the broken chain, and the ring was once again hanging around her neck. For reasons I didn't understand, I tucked it inside her dress.

I watched James for a signal, but he was wearing an unconvincing smile. He stood and stretched. "We should start moving." There was an urgency in his almost carefree voice that no one on earth would have noticed, except me.

Standing, I brushed the dust from my skirt. "I'll get our cloaks."

He put an arm around my shoulders, leaning down to whisper in my ear. "Leave them."

I stared at him. "What?"

"*Leave them.*" He guided me away from the fire pit and into the mist-bound trees.

I followed him, tempted to glance back. What had he seen? The fear in his eyes was as undeniable as the biting cold. I reached down for Emily's hand and noticed James had glanced behind us, his horror was undisguised as he turned to me.

"Run," he said under his breath. He reached down and snatched up Emily. "Run!" He gripped my shoulder and shoved me forward.

As I stumbled, trying to keep my balance, the tree beside me exploded. Shattered bark flew everywhere, the impact knocking me to the ground. I scrambled on my hands and knees, trying to regain my feet. Glancing behind me I saw a man standing in the middle of our campsite. A cloud of smoke surrounded him, his pistol trained on us. I finally got to my feet and caught a glimpse of the tree beside me. It was blackened and riddled with holes. I froze at the realization of just how close the shot had come to me. James gripped my hand and wrenched me forward, Emily clinging to him as we raced through the trees. I was short of breath, my heart pounding in my ears when I noticed that James was taking sporadic, random turns. He still had no idea where we were going. Another explosion sounded farther behind us.

"Don't stop!" James called.

The trees appeared endless. Everywhere we looked the landscape was exactly the same. The branches above us blocked out the early light. It was like so many nightmares I'd had. No matter how far we ran, it didn't feel like we were moving. We were going in circles. I gasped for air, trying to control my panic, when a sound caught my attention. "Do you hear that?" I called.

James didn't slow down. "It's the wind!"

"No." I stopped, listening.

"What are you doing?" he asked, turning to look at me.

"It's this way!" I shouted, veering to my right, and plunging down a steep hill. I glanced behind to make sure James was following me as the sound grew louder, and louder.

"I hear it!" James yelled from behind me.

Through the tree line, I could see the white frothing river.

The torrential waters stretched endlessly, disappearing into mist so thick that I couldn't see the opposite bank. The deafening roar of the waters told me it must have been miles across. I was so amazed to have found it that I halted. James sped by me. We weren't out of danger. I pounded behind him, desperate to keep up. At the foot of the hill, we reached the river, and James stopped for a moment to study it. It was running right to left. James turned, running downstream along the river, toward its ocean outlet. Following behind, I glanced over my shoulder and saw our pursuer crest the top of the hill. When I looked forward again, I saw that I'd fallen behind James, and fought to close the distance.

My vision blurred as the wind stung my eyes. I glanced back to see if we were still being followed, but saw no one. I turned forward too late and plowed into James, who nearly lost his balance. He teetered on the edge of a rock ledge, about a man's height from the ground. James regained his balance. Even when he had steadied himself, Emily clung to him, burying her face in his shoulder. If I hadn't run into James I would have gone straight over the edge. The miniature cliff jutted down to the rocky river bed beneath us.

I glanced behind us again, but saw no one. Setting Emily down beside him, James jumped to the shore below, the stones crunching beneath his feet, and turned to Emily with his arms open. His expression offered strength to the frightened girl. "I'll catch you!"

She glanced back at me, then turned to James, and jumped. He caught her and set her on the stony ground. He turned to me again, and held out his arms. I jumped, felt the solid grasp of my cousin's hands, and heard the crunch of my shoes on the rocks. I instinctively started running as soon as I found my balance, but James caught my hand.

"In here," he called.

I turned to look at him, and saw that the underside of the ledge we had jumped from was hollowed into a cave. He guided Emily and I inside and we crouched under the low ceiling, hardly daring to breathe. Emily turned to look at me and I saw the tears in her wide eyes. Her nightmares had come to life. I didn't stop myself this time. Placing an arm around her, I held her close, feeling the way her heart trembled.

Pain tingled through my feet as the moments wore on in the cave. I tried to shift my weight backward silently, but dislodged several stones in the process. They rolled out of the cave, clattering along the rocks. James shot me a deadly look. Scrunching my eyes shut apologetically, I scooted back, bumping into something. It wasn't the cave wall. I moved my hand noiselessly behind me, and felt the object I had backed into. It was a rounded, rough, wooden plank. As I moved my hand up and down I found it was not just one, but several planks. It was a man-made contraption.

"I think we're safe," James whispered, starting to stand up.

"James, I found something."

He sat back down, and I reached for his hand. When I got hold of it, I placed it on the wooden object behind me. He looked puzzled and motioned for me to move out of the way.

I moved aside, guiding Emily out of the shadows. I glanced around to assure that we were alone, startling at every sound. James was close behind us, walking backwards, dragging a small skiff. The vessel wasn't anything impressive, just big enough for a fisherman and his trappings. Though from the look of it, the fisherman hadn't been by in some time. Inside were two oars and a coil of rope, which James took out and tossed onto the bank.

"What are you doing?" I asked.

He didn't answer me, moving quickly to drag the boat knee deep in the rushing water. He watched it for several moments, placing pressure on it here and there, then dragged it back to the beach.

"It can get across," he said, unpinning the cloak from

31

around his neck.

"Get across what?" I asked, my throat tightening. "That thing wouldn't make it across a puddle."

He gave me a warning look. "Emily, come here," he called.

The pebbles crunched under her feet as she made her way over to him. With a warm smile, he wrapped his huge cloak around her. "Are you warm enough?"

She nodded.

"What are you doing?" I asked, trying to keep my voice calm.

"You have to keep her hidden. Keep her at your feet, or under the seat of the boat."

"No!" I struggle to keep my voice from shaking as the icy tide of panic rose inside me. "I can't do it."

He glanced at me sharply, then turned to Emily. "You need to be very quiet." He rested his hand on her head, then scooped her up into his arms, laying her in the bottom of the boat. She looked like a pile of clothes, wrapped in his cloak. "Hold still. You'll be home in no time."

"It will never hold the three of us," I babbled on, still trying to dissuade him.

He straightened and turned to look at me, his arms crossed in front of him. "It's not going to hold three of us."

A shock went through my body. "No, no, James. You know I can't do this." James knew that water made me go stiff with terror.

He took a few steps toward me.

"You know! You know I can't." I felt dizzy. "Please don't ask me to. I can't even see the other side. It could be miles. I can't do it."

He came closer.

"I won't leave you behind. Please, James. You can leave me here. I'll meet you in Barrow-Haven. You two go and I'll find another way."

"Kate." He gripped my shoulders in his strong hands. "There isn't another way."

In the distance I heard shouting, and horses' hooves. I thought we had lost the man chasing us, but it was clear now. We were being surrounded. "No, James. Not the river. Please! We shouldn't have done this."

He cupped my chin in his hand. "You need to listen to me."

I closed my eyes, trying to hold back the hot tears that slipped down my cheeks.

"You take care of that little girl. You get her to safety. Then you get home. Do you hear me?"

My jaw trembled so fiercely I could hardly speak. "James, I can't. I can't do it."

"Kate, I need you to be the brave one right now. Emily needs you."

I crumpled into his arms, feeling the strength of his embrace encircle my shoulders. "I'm sorry." My voice was muffled in his shoulder.

He pulled back and I saw the tears glistening in his eyes as his voice shook. "This isn't your fault. Do you hear me? It was never your fault!" He stiffened, stepping back and I glanced behind me.

More than half-a-dozen men running toward us, through the forest. A few aimed pistols in our direction. I turned back to James and met his gaze, giving him a determined nod.

I turned and raced toward the boat, but before I could reach it, my foot caught on a stone. I hit the ground, my hands scraping against the rocks. I scrambled forward on my hands and knees, when the ground in front of me exploded, shards of rock flying everywhere. My ears rang from the noise as I tried to see through the cloud of smoke. Rough hands gripped my arms and pulled me upright. He twisted me around, and I saw that two of the other men had pistols leveled at James. "What do you want?" my cousin asked evenly, watching the men as they circled him.

"We've got a ship to catch, so I'll get right to the point." Their leader scratched several days growth on his chin, as he stepped out of the trees. "He wants the key." His words slurred together.

"What key?" James tried to keep the man's attention on him, but didn't succeed.

The man's gaze landed on me. A wicked grin spread over his features, as he shoved one of his men aside and staggered toward me. "Aren't you a sight?" His breath was foul with the stench of ale as he leaned over me. His expression grew mockingly mournful. "Oh, now, don't be frightened. I'm known as a man who treats gentle creatures like you with utmost respect. You're safe with Brice." He ran a filthy hand over my hair. Not even fear could mask my revulsion. "Come now, Harris," he said to the man who gripped my arms. "I'm sure she'll be cooperative." Harris released me, but didn't move far away. The leader flashed his sickening grin again. "Where is the key? Scot knows the girl has it. There's no use in…" He paused, looking around him, as if something was wrong. "Where is she?" He leaned over me, his confusion darkening into a scowl. "Where is she?"

I stared at the ground, an idea forming in my mind. "Floating in the river," I answered, my voice breaking. I didn't have to feign the tears.

"What?!" He took a step back.

"I tried to stop him, but he wouldn't listen. He threw her in the river." It wasn't difficult to sound hysterical as I motioned to James.

Brice turned to his officers, ordering four of them to search downstream. To my relief, one of them was the man standing next to me. When they had gone, their leader turned back to me. "And the key went with her, I assume?"

Glancing at James, I scoured my brain for a clever response. "I…"

The sailor leaned closer. "Where is it, Love?" Then his gaze traveled passed me, landing on the skiff. "What have we here?"

Panicked, I turned to the boat.

The leader caught my left shoulder, and spun me back to face him. With the momentum from my turn, I brought my right fist around, catching his jaw. He recovered without missing a moment and caught my right hand in his, twisting it around behind my back. I shot my left elbow back toward his midsection, but he caught my arm and held it.

I was out of options, praying James had taken the opportunity I had given him. I heard an earsplitting shot and knew he had. The leader threw me to the ground, the rocks grating on my palms which had already begun to bleed. I glanced behind me and saw that James had the leader on the ground. This was my only chance. I snatched up the oars, tossing them into the boat and jumping in behind them. I looked back just in time to see James drive his fist into the man's face.

The leader stopped struggling.

James scrambled toward us and lunged for the boat. He fell to his knees, the other men close behind him.

"Don't stop!" he gasped, giving the boat a shove off the rocks and into the icy river. An explosion sounded behind him and his eyes went wide. Clutching his shoulder, he fell face down on the rocks. Behind him, a cloud of smoke cleared, revealing the leader's shaking pistol, still aimed.

"No!" I cried, watching helplessly as the three men surrounded him. He didn't resist. He didn't move. The riverbank disappeared as the veil of mist closed around me and he disappeared from sight.

CHAPTER 6

I couldn't move. He was gone. I was alone.

At my feet was a little girl who trusted me with her life, and rushing beneath me, trying at every moment to swallow me up, was my greatest fear. The river roared like a starving beast. It was the only sound I could hear, besides the thrashing of my own heartbeat. The outline of my vision began to turn black and my chest ached as I gulped in air. I couldn't breathe. My hands lay in my lap, balled into tightening fists. Every muscle was rigid with fear. We were going to die in this river.

Don't think. Move.

The words were so real, so forceful, I glanced around to see where they had come from. Around me there was nothing but rushing water and walls of white fog.

Don't think.

That was the only way I would ever have the strength to get across the river. Thinking led to fear, fear led to panic, and panic would swallow me up just like the ravenous water.

Don't think. Move.

I reached for the oars in my lap and set the paddles in the water. Emily whimpered at my feet, her cries reminding me that I could not fail. I had to keep going.

I exhaled, relieving my aching chest, and went to work. Though I couldn't see the shore, I knew the current must have already dragged us some distance from the rocky bank. How far was it to other side? What if I simply couldn't make it? Where would the current drag us then?

Don't think.

I gripped the oars, straining to move as much water as I could with every stroke. My efforts were pathetic. If James had been at the oars, the boat would have soared over the water. He should have been the one to take skiff, not me. Why couldn't they have taken me? It would have been better for everyone.

Voices. I could hear voices. I lifted my head to search the shoreline, but all I could see was the white fog. I glanced around me frantically. The voices were close. Where were they coming from? I felt the deep endless river dragging us downstream every second.

A dark shadow emerging from the mist. I watched it for a moment. It was getting closer. It stood like a tower in the middle of the river. Then the prow of a ship pierced through the fog. The river was dragging us toward the vessel at a terrifying speed. Sailors shouted futile warnings from the deck. I rowed frantically, but my efforts were useless in comparison to the river's raging pace. I gave one look at the ship, and braced myself for the collision.

Crack!

The jolt threw me forward and nearly out of the boat. Emily was screaming. The oars went flying from my hands, landing in the water. I gripped the sides and held on with what little strength I had left, throwing myself over Emily.

Crack!

The boat scraped against the hull of the ship. I looked down to see a gaping hole in the side of the skiff. Water poured through the hole as though the current beneath us had clawed its way in. The ship's crew watched from above. The frigid water soaked my feet. Throwing aside the blanket, I snatched up Emily, holding her in my arms. "God, please!"

The skiff's edges were sinking beneath the waterline. She clung to me, her arms around my neck, as the boat slipped beneath the current. "I'm sorry. I'm so sorry."

I could hear her whimpering in my ear. "Please, Jesus. Please!"

A splash caught my attention. I saw a man swimming toward us. The boat was slipping out from under me. He would never reach us in time. When I tried to get another breath, water choked me, and my head went under. Emily's arms encircled my neck, her grip fastened tightly around me, but I was only dragging her down faster. In my last effort, I untangled Emily's arms from around my neck and pushed her upward, toward the surface, toward the air. The current dragged me down, the icy water was swallowing me up, the way it had in all my nightmares. My heart nearly pounded out of my chest. I struggled and kicked, my efforts only dragging me downward. My chest burned, screaming for air. The cold. The darkness. The silence. They all began to meld together. Everything was ending. I couldn't stop death. I had cried, and once again God had not heard me.

Pain shot through my left shoulder. I pulled away, but the pain pressed in harder, growing tighter. Suddenly sound was everywhere. I opened my eyes to the light. Air filled my burning lungs. Beside me, there was a man, putting an arm around my waist in attempt to keep me up. Suddenly, something brushed my arm under the water. It was a hand.

Emily. I gripped the tiny fingers, trying to pull her to the surface and succeeded for only a moment before the extra, thrashing weight dragged both myself and my rescuer down. He fought to get us up, but the weight of two people was simply too heavy. I tried to slip my arm around the little girl's middle and was relieved to feel her struggling against the waters. The current pulled us down. We surfaced for a moment.

I heard him shout a name before we plunged beneath the

icy depths again.

Emily went limp in my arms. I couldn't let go of her. Not now. I felt two strong calloused hands close around my arm, find Emily, and pull her away from me.

My head reached the surface, and I gulped for air. When I looked to my right there was a young man holding the little girl's head above the water as he fought the current, but she didn't move. I struggled to keep my head up as I was drug toward the ship through the icy current. I couldn't think. It was hard to breathe. The arm around me was too tight. I tried to pry it loose, but it may as well have been made of stone. I was so cold, so tired. *No.* No, I had to stay awake, but sleep began to engulf me. Right now, that was all I wanted...soft, warm, endless sleep.

· · ·

The rigid face above me was dripping. He was shaking me. Why was he shaking me? The face disappeared and I was staring into a cold gray sky, but the shaking continued. Then I realized, I wasn't being shaken. I was shivering. My muscles convulsed without my consent. A heavy weight, like a blanket was thrown on top of me. It smelled foul. I couldn't feel my hands or feet. Why wouldn't I stop shaking?

"Please help me," I managed through chattering teeth.

No one answered.

"I'm so cold." My words were garbled. I was so tired. Everyone around me moved so quickly. What was I doing here? Who were these men? Why weren't they helping me? Where was James? He would help me. He would stop this dreadful shaking. This had to be a dream. This was all just a terrible nightmare. I would wake up back in the London tavern, safe and warm. That was where I was now. This was just another nightmare.

Hands gripped my arms, sitting me up. I felt my back

resting against something hard. I stared straight ahead, unseeing. I couldn't make my eyes focus. My mind scrambled as I tried to remember what was happening. Where was I? Why couldn't I remember? Was I losing my mind? Nothing looked familiar. Should I know this place?

I needed to focus. If I could find one thing, one object, one face to focus on, maybe something would come back. As I searched for one thing to focus on, I saw men in dark caps working together like the little black ants that stormed the tavern kitchen. They were all gathered around a railing. Sailors. They were sailors. I was on a ship. They were retrieving something from the water.

A face appeared over the railing. The sailors all worked to help him onto the deck. His face looked familiar. He was tall and lank when standing, but dropped to his knees just after his feet hit the deck. He was hunched over an object in his arms. His sharp jawline shook with the cold. He was pale, his hollow cheeks a dull purple color. He laid the object in his arms on the deck in front him. He seemed desperate but unable to speak. I followed his gaze and saw the pale little face.

Emily.

"Sh-she's not breathing. Where's Newman?"

I threw aside the heavy overcoat that was covering me and tried to drag myself forward. My limbs trembled and gave out. My cheek pressed against the cold, grimy deck. I watched the young sailor place a rough hand on the little golden head. There were tears in his eyes as he mouthed the word *Emily*.

She was so still, her lips a deadly blue. I had to get to her. Putting one hand in front of the other, I began to drag myself toward the little girl.

"Where is Newman?!" the young man shouted. He saw me out of the corner of his eye and everything gentle and compassionate about him vanished. His black eyes flashed with anger as he shouted at another sailor. "Keep her away!"

Hands gripped my arms, holding them behind my back

and pulling me to my feet. The sailor's grip was the only thing holding me up. Yet, even the vice-like grip trembled. I looked back to see that he was the same man who'd pulled me from the river. He too was shivering and dripping.

A man stepped through the gathering crowd, and knelt next to Emily. Removing his coat, he wrapped it around her. "We need to get her below!"

The young man scooped her up in his arms and tried to stand, but stumbled, nearly dropping her.

His friend bent down next to him. "Jack! You're freezing. Give me the girl."

His grip tightened on Emily.

"I need to get her warm," his friend insisted.

The young man handed her over.

They were taking her away. No. She needed me. I struggled against the man that held me, fighting desperately to free myself. Feeling my struggle, he gripped me tighter, pulling me close. I flailed and kicked when my hand, still held behind me, brushed against something tucked into the man's belt. It was exactly what I needed. A distraction.

Slipping it from the belt, I lunged my shaking arm upward. I broke his grasp for a moment the pistol clutched in my freezing, fumbling hand. I pointed it straight up in the air, hoping the noise would give me the distraction I needed. The sailor behind me grabbed my forearm, wrenching it downward. The force caused me to pull the trigger, and the shot fired straight in front of me. Erupting in a cloud of sparks and smoke, the crack of the shot made my ears ring just as the door closed behind Emily. I was too late.

The man behind me gave my hand a violent shake, causing me to drop the gun. It must have clattered to the ground, but I couldn't hear it. After the shot, the world had gone silent, with nothing but the ringing sound reverberating through me. The man ripped my arm back behind me. When the smoke cleared, every eye was on me and I felt the air hiss out of my lungs. One face stood out from all the others. The young man who'd helped Emily. His eyes were twice their normal size as he stared at a gaping hole in the barrel beside him, mere inches from his head. The young man fixed his eyes on me with such a look of hatred that I wanted to sink into the floor. Sound crackled and buzzed in my ears, as my hearing returned and the ringing abated.

Nervous laughter burst from one of them men. "Time to pay up, Jack! I told you that was no lunatic fisherman in the river. You were wrong. Admit it!"

The young man didn't smile, or look away. "I was only wrong about the fisherman part. I'll pay you half."

Several of the men laughed, but his furious gaze was fixed on me.

Without warning, the laughter stopped. Every face grew suddenly fearful, even the face of the man I'd nearly killed. All of them were staring at something behind me. I turned to look, but whatever had them terrified was blocked from my view by the mainmast behind me. The silent terror lasted only a moment before every sailor was rushing to a position. The man behind me let go and I fell to the deck, unable to even remain standing. He snatched his pistol from the ground, cursing me one last time.

Every sailor scrambled to form an orderly line. When the line had formed, everything was silent, and every man still. One set of heavy footsteps pounded with emphasis like fateful methodic execution drums. The men in front of me had gone from careless sailors to rigid crewmen in a matter of moments. Unsure of why, I pressed my back against the mast, wanting to simply disappear. The fear in the air was palpable. I watched out of the corner of my eye as heavy black boots pounded into view. A dark coat was all I could see of the man as he walked down the line of sailors, looking over each one. Reaching the end of the line, he turned on his heel and for the first time, I saw his face. I suddenly knew why his men trembled at his stare. It was terrifying. Gray eyes pierced through every crew member as his gaze swept over them one last time.

"Jackson." His voice was nothing more than a low rumble, like echoing thunder.

The young man they'd called Jack stepped forward. His sharp jawline was tight as he stared straight ahead, unable to restrain his shivering. "Yes, Captain?"

The heavy boots plodded closer to the young sailor, who looked like a frightened child standing in front of his captain. "I'm going to ask you two very simple questions." He took in a deep whiff as if smelling something unpleasant. "Why are you soaking wet?" The line of sailors braced themselves as the captain neared the young man. "And who fired a weapon on this ship without my orders?"

No one answered.

"I will find out!" he cried as he leaned forward, mere inches away from the young man's face. "And you had better hope to glory that it wasn't you, Reverend Jack!"

"No, Sir," he replied, eyes fixed straight ahead.

"Captain." The stocky, sun-darkened sailor who'd tried to restrain me moments ago, stepped forward, also dripping and shivering.

The captain looked back at him. "What is it, Connors?"

"We've acquired a passenger, Sir," Connors said, tilting his head toward me.

The captain turned slowly, seeing me for the first time. His eyes struck through me like lightning, draining me of any courage I had left. I could feel him searching me, finding my every weakness and fear. When he'd found all he needed, a confident smile crossed his face. It was the smile of a man who knew he had won before the fight even began. I straightened, still terrified, but desperate to prove him wrong. I didn't know why, but his arrogance made me set my shoulders back defiantly.

"Explain this to me, Jackson," he said, without taking his

gaze off of me.

"She was sinking, Sir."

"Drowning," the stocky sailor added.

The captain very deliberately turned around to look at his men. "That explains my first question. Now, who fired the shot?"

"She did, Sir." The young sailor swallowed, the knot in his throat bobbing up and down.

I glanced up in time to see the captain's eyes widen ever so slightly and land on me. He examined me a second time, as if he had miscalculated, then looked back to his crew. "I see no weapon."

The stocky sailor called Connors held forth the empty pistol. "It got away from me, Captain. She's raving mad."

The slow fateful drumming of the captain's footsteps began again as he moved toward Connors. When the heavy black boots stopped in front of the sailor, the captain held out his hand. The man placed the pistol in the palm of his superior. Without warning, the captain closed his hand around the weapon and swung it upward, driving the butt of the gun into the man's forehead. The sailor's head shot back as the captain shoved the pistol back into his hand. "Step back!" he ordered.

The sailor obeyed, blood soaking between his fingers as he clutched his forehead.

"What possessed me to make you second in command?" Turning on his heel, the captain gazed down the line of men. "Let me see if I understand." The drumming began again. "The crew of The Defiance..." He met the eyes of every man. "...was outwitted, outmatched, and outgunned..." He reached the other end of the line, and the drumming ceased as he turned around. "...by a half-drowned, female lunatic." A look of shame permeated the crew. "You're cowards. Every one of you." Folding his hands behind his back, the drumming began pounding up and down the line. "Perhaps you have forgotten the code by which this ship operates! Perhaps you have forgotten that the Defiance has no cowards. She carries no deserters. They will be eliminated one way…" he paused turning to look back down the line of men. "…or another. Is that clear?"

"AYE, SIR!" they all answered in unison.

"If this insubordinate behavior continues, you will all suffer for it. Back to your posts." He looked disgusted as the men began to march back to their positions.

Jackson stepped forward once again. "Captain," he said, choosing to stare straight ahead rather than at his superior.

"What is it?"

"The girl, Sir. What do you suggest we do with her?"

A cruel smile played on the face of the captain as he stared down his nose at the slight young sailor. "Let me see. She's disruptive, insane, and tried to kill you. What do *you* suggest we do with her?"

"Secure her in the hold, Sir."

"Brilliant," groaned the captain. "Is this the way our fight for freedom begins?"

The young man stared at the ground, ashamed.

The captain gave a sound of disgust. "Give me a reason not to leave you in London." He turned and the drumming faded as I lost sight of him.

"Harman! Taylor! Secure her below." As Jackson called the crewmen he pointed them out, and his shirt sleeve fell away, revealing a dark stain on his wrist. My heart thudded. The stain looked familiar.

I turned my attention to the two sailors approaching me. They neared me cautiously, as though I were an unidentified insect.

"Is that how you control a prisoner?" The young man had transformed into a thinner, shivering version of the captain. The same hard lines reddened his forehead, the same clenched fist pounded in the palm of his hand. "On your feet!"

It took me several moments to realize he was shouting at me. Before I could respond the men gripped my shoulders and began to drag me toward a door. I was too weak to resist. Staring down in defeat, I saw the iron hands that gripped me. They too bore the mark, the word I would never forget.

Ferox.

CHAPTER 7

The world was cold and dark. I opened my eyes, but darkness smothered me. It didn't matter if my eyes were open or closed. It was a darkness I could feel. I couldn't move. I was too afraid. Fear choked me. It was an eerily familiar feeling. It had paralyzed me in the boat. It had kept me awake so many nights. It had nearly killed me once before. It was panic. When I was afraid, when I could find no hope, something in me froze. My mind began to race at an uncanny speed. I had to get up. I had to scream. I had to cry, but I couldn't. I was gulping in air and tried to force myself to exhale. What had rescued me from this feeling of darkness before? What shred of light had I clung to?

James. He had rescued me. He was gone. That thought brought one warm tear to my eye. It slipped down my cheek. James. He was all I had.

I was alone. This was my worst nightmare. I had always had James, even after the accident that took my parents, even after Fortune Cole, even after my darkest night.

I wanted to die. If he had left me there was no reason for me to stay in this horrible dark world, but something tugged at the back of my mind.

Emily. Where was she? It was then that I remembered. The ship, her pale little face, the pistol. Emily. Was she dead too? I had to find her. I lifted one hand, and it sank back to the floor with a rattling sound. For the first time I became aware of my surroundings. I could see nothing. Had I gone blind? I couldn't remember. The aching in my back told me that I was sitting against something hard and couldn't move my hands. They were heavy. Every time I tried to lift them, they would crash back to the ground. Stretching my fingers out as far as I could, I felt them brush against something cold and hard. Chains. The thought crashed through the fog of my thoughts and I started to thrash, pulling, with all the strength I had, against the condemning bands of metal. My feet were shackled together, but I scrambled away from the wall, dragging the chains behind me, unable to lift my hands from the ground. I felt the chains snap tight. They were secured to the wall behind me. I fought and struggled, the fetters biting into my skin. This couldn't be happening.

I sank to the ground, curling up in defeat. I was in chains, in the dark, all alone. It was my worst nightmare, and it was everything I deserved.

"God." I laid my forehead against my fettered hands, feeling the sobs that shook my body. "Why? If I've done so much wrong in Your sight, why let me live? Why did You let James die, when it should have been me?"

The response was a screech like the screams of tortured souls. I sat up. There was a flickering light in the distance. The sound of plodding footsteps made me draw back, wanting the solid wall behind me. My mind raced as I cowered in the corner. I had no way to protect myself. The candle moved toward me, until someone was right above me. I was too terrified to even look up. "Please. No," I whimpered, trapped and terrified.

"Is that really all you can say?" asked a gruff voice.

I opened my eyes. A face looked down at me lit by the lone candle. I recognized him as the stocky sailor who'd pulled me onto the ship.

He shook his head in dismay and looked away. "I give up. 'No.' 'Please.' 'Don't.' Seems to be all you can say. You really are mad, aren't you?"

I swallowed my tears. "No," I gasped, then realized that was one of the three words he'd just mentioned. "I mean, I'm confused."

He leaned forward. "So you *can* speak."

I nodded, fighting to control my emotions and appear somewhat sane. "Where am I?"

He straightened, towering above me. "You're aboard the Defiance."

I looked around, unable to comprehend my surroundings in the dark. "Am I a prisoner?"

"For attempted murder." His face was as compassionate as a stone.

I remembered with overwhelming clarity how I'd pulled the trigger and come within inches of killing someone. "It was an accident."

"Right." His jaw slid to the side. He didn't believe me. "You don't have to pretend. You're not the first one to have a shot at the Reverend Jack. Took a crack at him myself once." He looked toward the door and I feared I'd lose my chance.

"Emily!" I blurted her name. "Where is she?"

His face darkened and he looked at the ground, unwilling to answer. "There's some food left in the galley. The cook wants to know if you'll eat it before I bring it. He doesn't like to see his hard work vomited all over the floor."

"Please. I need to know," I begged. "Is she alive?"

"That's enough!" His outburst made the flame shudder. "If you're going to survive on board this ship you're going to have to learn to keep your mouth shut and your eyes down. No more questions."

His thundering voice made me tremble.

"Do you want to eat or not?" he asked, placing a hand over his eyes.

I shook my head, unable to answer.

He turned without a word, the candle lighting his way as he moved toward the door. The terrible screech of metal against metal echoed through the cavernous darkness. He stopped in the open doorway for a long moment. Then without turning to face me, he spoke as though to himself. "She was asking for you tonight." The door clanked shut behind him, and I was once again alone in the dark.

. . .

"Two years, and this is how you greet me? I expected an army. You have underestimated me for the last time."

I opened my eyes in time to see the door to the hold slam shut. I blinked, trying to remember where I was. That had been the captain's voice. Who had he been talking to? A dreary light surrounded me. I must have slept at some point and rolled over in my sleep because I was staring at everything through of veil of my dark hair. Boxes, barrels and crates towered over head. I couldn't tell where the light was coming from. I shuddered remembering the horrid darkness of the previous night.

She was asking for me. Was the sailor lying to me, in an attempt to weaken my will? If so, he didn't realize what an easy task that was.

I curled up tighter on the rough wooden floor in defeat. This was such a mistake. If only I had recognized that when James had tried to tell me. I cried until I could hardly breathe. James was the only person in this world who loved me. He had stood by me, even when I was nothing but a burden to him. Why was I the one that lived? He wouldn't have shot that pistol the way I had. He would have kept his senses on the ship and given Emily the help she needed. He wouldn't have acted like a lunatic. He would have been able to keep her above the water. In fact, he wouldn't have lost control of the boat in the first place. He would have rowed her safely to the other side of the river and taken her home.

The metal hinges shrieked as the door on the other side opened. The stocky sailor who'd spoken to me the night before shoved another man in ahead of him.

"We should be undisturbed in here," one of them muttered.

I recognized the other man as the young sailor who I'd nearly shot. I scrunched my eyes shut as he turned to glare at me, not wanting to see his icy stare.

"What's worrying you, Jackson? She's contained quite nicely."

"She's insane."

"She's asleep. Better keep a hand on that pistol, just in case." The man's mock solemnity frustrated the young sailor.

"Do you think this is funny?" he asked the other man.

"I do. You have such a way with women."

The young man didn't laugh.

"What's wrong with you, Jack?"

"Nothing, Sir," he answered.

I dared to open my eyes in time to see the stocky sailor, seat himself on a nearby crate. He was facing me, his eyes fixed on the younger man, whose back was turned to me. "Oh, I see," said his superior. "Nothing. Is it the nothing of being shot at yesterday? Or a seven-year-old nothing that has you wrapped around her little finger?"

The young man turned his back on his fellow sailor, and I caught glimpse of his face. "She's working for Cephas."

The older man nodded slowly. "Oh. *That* nothing."

The young man let out a forced laugh, turning back to face the officer. "After two years he still can't leave it alone. When is he going to accept that this is my life? This is what I want."

"Then you're not going back?"

"Never. If working under you has taught me anything, it's

that this is the best life there is. Deep in my bones I know I'm meant to be on the sea. I'm a sailor."

"Or just an idiot." The officer glanced up at the young man in front of him. "The fact is, Jack, all I've done since we left port two years ago is beat you harder than I ever beat any cabin boy on this ship. I've called you plenty of things in the last two years, but a sailor was never one of them."

"You showed me that I can make it through the storms and the raids and that I can earn the respect of any man."

The superior let his gaze drift downward. "Maybe that's true. But do you want to?"

The young sailor straightened with pride. "Yes, Sir."

"Then you're more of an idiot than I thought. Are you really letting them take you to Devil's?"

"Why shouldn't I? After two years without setting my foot on land, I'm ready for a little celebration."

The stocky sailor let out a sigh. "I always assumed that it was your choice to stay on board."

"It was a great choice, wasn't it?" the young man scoffed. "What did it get me? A lot of lonely nights, and a name to live down."

"Then your mind's made up?"

"Yes, Sir."

Pushing himself to his feet, the officer turned and headed for the door. "Then, I wish you fair weather."

"What does that mean?"

Turning back to Jackson, he shook his head. "It means good luck."

"But Sir, aren't you—"

"How clearly do you need it spelled out, lad? I'm deserting." The older man started to turn.

"This is a test, isn't it?"

A smile crossed the deserter's face. "No, Jack. This isn't a test to see if you'll turn me in. I'm leaving."

"Why?"

The officer looked at the sailor with a perfectly frank gaze. "The sea has been my whole life, but I've never found what I was looking for."

"You think you'll find it by leaving?"

The older man shook his head. "I've already found it."

"I hope she's worth it."

Connors groaned at his ignorance. "It's nothing like that."

"Did you fall into some money?"

Again, the officer shook his head.

Jackson leaned forward. "Now I'm just curious. What would a man like you be looking for?"

Connors met the young sailor's gaze again. "Peace."

The young man appeared stunned into silence.

"Been after it for a while now," Connors continued. "And I'll tell you the one thing I've learned. It isn't on this ship."

When the young man didn't reply the officer turned to go, but stopped once more. "Don't let Captain Scot poison you, Jack. Cephas isn't after you anymore."

"And what makes you say that?"

"I met him."

The young sailor tensed as he stared accusingly at his superior. "So that's it. That's what this is all about. You're being paid off by him too. Why am I not surprised?"

The officer turned with unbelievable speed, catching the front of Jackson's shirt in his enormous fists. "I've had enough of you! What makes you think that a man like Cephas would waste his time on you? Are you just that important? Do you really think he can't go on without your help? He's been at it for two years. He doesn't even know where you are."

"How much is he paying you to say that?" Jackson asked with an accusing grin.

His officer shoved him back and Jackson crashed into a stack of crates that tumbled down behind him.

Connors stood above him, ready to ward off any resistance, but the young man appeared too smart to attempt anything. "Want a surprise, Jack? I didn't just talk to Cephas. I prayed with him."

"While I had tea with King Charles and Bishop Laud," Jackson smirked, standing to his feet and dusting himself off. His cock-eyed grin faded when his superior didn't back down. "Come on, Connors! Do you really expect me to believe that the First Mate of the Defiance set foot in a church?"

Connors didn't reply, but continued to stare the young man down. "A few years back, this ship procured a cabin boy. He was put under my control. I hated him. Not just because he was he was scrawny, and awkward, or because the captain favored him. I hated this one because he was pious. Not that there hadn't been a few of those on board. But I'd never met a man who wouldn't turn after a few weeks under my authority. This one wouldn't though. I beat him. I starved him. I punished him for things I knew he hadn't done. He still wouldn't turn. I was obsessed with his torment. I would drive him to the Devil like I had a hundred other cabin boys." The mate's huge hands were balled into fists as he spoke.

"And what happened to him?" Jackson asked, as though he already knew the answer.

"Oh, he turned like all the rest. Not because of anything I did, but because he became a favorite among the men. He never was a good sailor. He tried to pretend like he belonged here to impress the other men, especially the captain. But I always had hoped that somewhere inside that weak second-rate sailor was the same cabin boy who pointed me in the right direction." The officer took another step forward, until he was right in front of the young man. "And if he's half the man I think he is, I'll see him in London."

"What are you planning?"

First Mate Connors smiled. "Ask the little girl. She has a special job for you."

Jackson flinched as his superior officer set a hand on his shoulder. "Remember one thing, Jack. Cephas may not be after you, but Scot is, and he's going to use you until he can use you no more, and then he's going to kill you."

Jackson swallowed hard and averted his gaze. "I'll take my chances."

"You do that. But you're going to talk to her first."

He glanced up defiant. "And if I choose not to?"

The older sailor took a step back. "Then, I'll have to make sure you're not in any condition to turn me in."

Jackson held up his hands in defense. "I should at least say goodbye to her."

The officer smiled. "Good idea. Make it quick."

With that, both men turned and left the hold, slamming the door behind them.

• • •

He had said her name. I couldn't get that thought out of my mind. I had watched him as he bent over her still, pale little body and said the word *Emily*. How had he known her name? He was nothing more than a heartless sailor. What could he possibly have to do with her?

She trusted me so blindly. My stomach turned and twisted. Would she trust anyone the way she trusted me? What if they lied to her, or turned her against me? What if they had told her I was dead? Then again, they might tell her I had abandoned her, which would be worse. The worry made the shackles feel tighter. I had to get out of here! I had thought nothing could be worse than fearing Emily was dead, but knowing she was alive and helpless had awakened hundreds of new fears in me.

What had happened to me? I had tried so hard to hold back. I had refused to care. I had promised myself that my heart would not be broken again. Now it had shattered just as I knew it would.

I would go insane before we docked in London. I scraped

at the shackles around my wrists, pulling them to their limit.

Another jolt of fear overtook me as a new thought crept in. The mark on the young sailor's wrist matched the mark of the man who had tried to murder Emily. *Ferox.* Everyone I'd seen on board the Defiance bore the mark, and it chilled me every time I laid eyes on it. A memory stirred in the back of my mind. *Ferox.* Master Owens had told me what it meant. My mind raced as I sought to remember.

"Wild." The sound of my own voice made me start. "Wild, courageous, or…" There was one more. I scrunched my eyes shut. *Defiant.* I didn't have to say it out loud. That was the meaning of the mark. The word signified the sailors of The Defiance.

He had said her name. Not only that, but every worry, every fear, every ounce of love I felt for Emily had been reflected in his face when he held her in his arms. I knew he hated me. I had seen it in his eyes, heard it in his voice. But I had also seen the tenderness with which he looked at the little girl, and the familiarity with which he had said her name. He loved her, and no matter what he thought of me, perhaps he would be Emily's escape. I would beg him. It was all I could do. I stopped trying to drag my chains or tear them apart. I surrendered the hope that I would ever see the light again, that I would ever leave this hold, but maybe I could still save Emily.

The door opened some time later. First Mate Connors set a plate of food in front of me without even looking at me. One might have thought he was simply misplacing the food instead of delivering it. It was as if I didn't even exist. Being unable to lift my chains from the floor for any length of time, I was forced to crouch, shoving the food at my face like animal. The hard, flat bread was riddled with mold, and the salted beef was so tough I had to swallow most of it whole, choking it down with sour, brackish water. When I had finished eating, the ship swayed back and forth, and the wretched food threatened mutiny before it even reached my stomach.

The day wore on and the hold began to darken. At first I thought that night was drawing near, but the ship began to toss in the waves. We were leaving the river mouth and heading for the ocean. The water rumbled as if a beast had the ship's hold in its claws and was trying to crush the life out of it. This was what my nightmares were made of. At any moment the claws of the vicious water would crack the hold and the beast would devour me. Lightning flashed, lighting up the darkness and illuminating the terrifying shadows. It was followed by a crack of thunder that shook the vessel.

"You wanted to speak with me, Captain?" a voice echoed through the cavernous hold, making me start.

I sat up searching frantically for the voice's owner. I could see no one.

"Yes. Close that door," ordered a different voice.

Lightning flashed and for the briefest moment white light shone through several cracks in the ceiling. The voices continued to drift through the cracks from the deck above. I could hear every word echo through the hold.

"Have you any idea why I've requested to speak with you?" I recognized the second voice as the captain's.

The other man didn't respond. I hardly dared to breathe, trying to hear the slightest sound.

Footsteps drummed slowly, methodically, back and forth above my head as he continued. "Did it ever enter that thick skull of yours that I might want to know that Emily Blake is aboard my ship?"

There was a long silence.

"Answer me!"

"I knew that you had other pressing matters, Sir, and I didn't think it was worth your time."

"You would do well to let my time be my own concern." The fateful drums began again. "Just when did you plan on telling me she was on board?"

"When…" The young man's voice cracked and he cleared his throat. "When the opportunity presented itself."

"And why didn't it present itself yesterday?"

"It slipped my mind, Captain."

"Why would you do this to me?"

"I don't know what you mean, Sir."

The captain groaned, as if exhausted. "After two years, you're still on their side, aren't you? I rotted in prison for years, suffering for the crimes that he committed, and you're still on his side."

"No!"

"Oh, that's right. Go ahead. Prove your loyalty."

"I have nothing to prove. In two years, I've been nothing but loyal to you. I have handed over every rumored mutiny, every breath of treason!"

"Until now. I know when I'm being betrayed! Tell me your heart didn't soften at the sight of that little face, that your blood didn't quicken when you saw that you'd pulled your own cousin from the river."

The young man didn't answer

"The day you stepped on board this ship, all I saw was a miniature of him. After two years, I was finally convinced that pathetic copy of him was gone. You were finally…" He searched for a word.

"A pathetic copy of you," Jackson answered.

There was a long silence before the captain cleared his throat. "You will not stand in my way."

"Nor do I intend to."

There was a sigh from the superior. "Get out of here."

The lighter set of footsteps started, then stopped. "She's just a child."

"That's where you're wrong, Jack. She's the key."

"She'll never help you find him."

"As it so happens, I don't need her help to find him. I already have. Why so sad, Jack? I thought you were nothing but loyal. No, I don't need her help finding him. But she's going to be ever so helpful in persuading him."

My heart thudded.

"You can't do this. I won't let you!" Jackson cried.

"And just how are you going to stop me? Offering yourself in her place? That would be an uncharacteristic surprise. You can't stand against me because you're not strong enough. You can't mutiny because you're all alone. And even if you had enough gall to sell yourself to me in her place, it would be useless. Because, Jack, I already own you. The day you made your choice, you sold yourself to me for nothing, and I will own you until the day you die. And if you get in the way of what I am about to do I will kill you and the girl. Understood?"

The pause was long. I could picture the lean, young sailor standing nose to nose with the broad-shouldered Captain. I was holding my breath, waiting to hear his answer.

A crash, followed by pounding footsteps made me jump. "Captain!" a new voice called.

"This had better be important!" Captain Scot thundered.

"It's Mate Connors. He's gone, Sir, with one of the longboats."

"What?!" The drumming started double time and I waited for the sound of a slamming door.

"Captain, there's more." The messenger's voice was timid. "He took the girl."

CHAPTER 8

The screeching of metal sent a jolt through me, as the storm raged on all around us. I hadn't been able to sleep. Where was she? Was she safe?

In a flash of lightning, I saw the figure of a man dragging something at his feet.

"Captain doesn't favor you so much now, does he?"

I recognized the slurred, whining voice, but it took me several moments to remember why. He was the drunken sailor who'd caught us on the riverbank, the man who'd shot James. He lugged the object he was dragging into the hold and gave it a sharp kick. "Should have learned your place in the beginning, Jack."

The door screeched shut behind him, and my gaze traveled to the man piled in the middle of the floor. He struggled to sit up, and as he did I caught a glimpse of his back. His shirt was soaked with blood. His breathing was ragged as he grasped the side of a crate and pulled himself up.

"Why did You abandon me here?" he asked, his voice reverberating off the walls. His coughing rattled his whole body as he leaned back against the wooden box. A cold, gray light leaked through the cracks in the ceiling shining directly on his face. Beads of sweat fell from his forehead mingling with his tears. He wept like a child, as if he'd lost all hope. I watched in silence I was sure he too had forgotten that I was there.

"This is your fault, you know." His weak voice echoed off the walls and ceiling, as he stared up into the light. I assumed he was talking to himself until he turned his head to look directly at me. His dark eyes were burning. "You brought her here. Why? There are so many places to go, so many holes to hide in. Why did you bring her here?" He looked up again. "Didn't Cephas warn you?"

I didn't have an answer. I couldn't explain where it had all gone wrong. I wasn't even sure I knew.

He turned to stare into the light again. "It was all starting to work out. I was finally starting to forget. Then you came, and brought her here." His features twisted in agony as he shifted his position. "Now Connors and Emily are gone and Scot thinks I know where they are. Cephas is trying to catch me. Scot is trying to kill me." He glanced at me. "And you're doing both at the same time."

"What?"

"You're working for Cephas, and then you tried to shoot me." He gave a bitter smile. "Has he finally realized I'm hopeless?"

"I don't understand," I said.

His weak laugh pained him. "I noticed." A troubled look came over features. "And that's another thing that doesn't add up. You truly don't understand." He shook his head, as if I were the confusing one. "So why did he pick you?"

I watched him several moments more and saw a tear slip from his eye. "I didn't think he would do it. Scot's the worst captain any man could have, but I honestly didn't think he'd kill me. He tried to tonight. He's never whipped anyone like that. He can't kill me, you know. I belong here. I will prove it to both of them." His lip curled. "So tell that to Cephas when you crawl back to him."

"Why?" I couldn't stop the question from coming, as I

stared at his obvious suffering. "Why would you stay here under Captain Scot?"

"He's my father."

I felt the blood drain from my face. He watched me until I had to look away. I knew he was waiting for a response. "I didn't know."

There was silence for quite some time as the light from the cracks grew brighter. I didn't know why, but I had to say it. The words weighed heavy on me. "I was never trying to kill you."

A wry smile spread across his face. "Next time maybe you should. You wouldn't be the first."

• • •

They came to retrieve Jackson from the hold just a few hours at dawn. We hadn't said anything more to each other, but I had watched him at every moment. He puzzled me for so many reasons. He didn't seem to belong in a place like this, yet he was fighting to stay.

It was the longest day yet. At what must have been noon, Jackson brought me a plate of salted beef and hard, stale bread which, though still repulsive, gave me strength. He was the same rigid young man I'd seen the day before, as though our conversation in the night had never happened. He looked at me with such contempt that I couldn't bear to look back at him. He hated me, but it hadn't been for different reasons than I had supposed.

My twisted stomach tied itself into one more knot as I thought of something else. From what I could tell, Jackson was the only one who had access to the hold. Waves of fear began to churn. He could do anything to me. He could kill me and no one would notice any more than if a barrel had tipped over in the hold. No one even appeared to remember I was here. I was chained, with no way to defend myself.

A picture flashed through my mind, one that I hadn't thought of in years. The picture was an ink drawing I'd seen, of Christ holding a lamb in His arms. I had clung desperately to that picture as a child, afraid of nightmares and monsters. Now, in this living nightmare, surrounded by monstrous enemies, I remembered it. A familiar, loving voice in my memory had said that we were God's people, and the sheep of His pasture.

How could I believe that in a place like this? If Christ held me like He did that little lamb, why had I lost so much, and failed so many times? It couldn't be true. Yet the mere thought of the picture had calmed my fears. I realized my hands had been clenched into fists, and my arms were aching. Even if it held no truth at all, I closed my eyes, picturing that image, and somehow it brought me hope as darkness fell on another lonely night.

The shrill shriek still made me think of tortured souls, and caused me to press my back against the wall behind me. I was so terrified I could hardly move. I could see the tall outline of the young sailor, still hunched from his whipping the previous night. He took slow methodic steps toward me. Sailors would do anything. James had warned me about them when we lived in London. They were filthy and vile and would do whatever suited them. My breathing sped up until I was gulping in air. He was towering right above me.

In one swift movement, he dropped to one knee beside me and clamped his calloused right hand over my mouth before I could cry out. I struggled against him, terrified. He could hold me down with one hand. I abandoned any plan of fighting back and decided to resort to begging as soon as he took his hand from my mouth. He leaned his face close until I could feel his short, ragged breaths on my cheek. "I need two things from you," he whispered in the darkness. "I need you to keep quiet, and I need you to trust me."

I tensed at the very thought. There was no way on earth I

would ever…

With his left hand, he drew something out of a pouch on his belt. Even in the darkness I could see the key. When he removed his hand from my mouth, I forgot to scream. He reached for my wrist, and I watched in amazement as he unlocked the horrid metal band. He reached for my other hand and did the same. He was freeing me.

As the chains fell away, I rubbed my wrists. "Why…" But his hand was instantly back over my mouth. I nodded. I understood his message.

Handing me the key, he motioned for me to unlock the shackles at my feet. Every time I made the slightest noise, he would scowl at me again. When the shackles were removed, and I was on my feet, I followed him to the door of the hold. It shrieked as usual, but I was leaving the tortured door behind, hoping to never see it again. When it closed behind us, we ascended the stairs. He moved cautiously onto the deck above. Glancing around, he motioned for me to follow. On the deck above the hold, there were rows of black cannon gleaming in the moonlight. I stopped to stare at them for a moment, then realized I was falling behind Jackson. He was halfway up the second set of stairs, and I hurried after him, finding myself on another gun deck. Jackson walked to the base of a ladder that led to a hatch in the ceiling. Before climbing, he turned to glare at me. "If you make a sound on the deck above us, it's going to be your last."

I stared at him, wondering if that was a threat or a warning as he scaled the ladder, and opened the hatch noiselessly. I followed him up, and understood his warning. We were in the officers' quarters. My breath caught in my throat as I climbed out of the hatch and he replaced the hatch door. Leading me through a maze of bulging hammocks that lolled back and forth, he moved slower on this deck than the previous two. I was wary of every creaking board and snoring ship mate.

When he reached the door at the end of the deck, he

turned to check on my progress. I wasn't far behind. When I reached the door, he pushed it open.

The first breath of fresh air I'd felt in days caressed my face, and I could have cried. I stepped out into the clear moonlight, and I looked up at the stars, when Jackson gripped my arm and yanked me into the shadows.

He peeked up over a stack of crates and grimaced when he looked back down. "Brice is on watch."

I glanced over the crates and saw the man who'd caught us on the riverbank.

With one more look at the raised forecastle on the other side of the ship Jackson took a deep breath. "Stay in the shadows, and don't fall behind." He ducked from shadow to shadow. I was already falling behind. I tried to be silent, constantly glancing from the deck in front of me to the man standing on the forecastle. He hadn't seen us yet. While keeping my eyes on him, I plowed into Jackson, who was crouched in the shadow of the ship's railing. He managed to catch himself without a sound, but didn't spare any venom in his gaze at me as we pressed our backs against the railing.

The moon was nearly full, casting its light on the deck.

"Jump."

Jackson's voice startled me. I turned to him. "What?"

"Jump." He jerked his head toward the railing.

I could only stare at him, hoping I had misunderstood.

"How else do you think we're going to get to shore?" he asked.

"I thought you were going to take control of the ship." Out loud the plan sounded much more ridiculous than it had in my head.

He rolled his eyes at me. "You really are thick, aren't you? Now jump."

I dared a glance behind me, peeking over the railing. We were anchored at least half a mile off shore. I could never swim that far. I would drown before Jackson even hit the water, but maybe that was his plan. What if I was being duped and this was really his plan to be rid of me? What if…

"Jackson," I whispered. "Brice is gone."

He glanced at the forecastle. "We have to go." He stood and I followed his lead, hoping he had thought of a different plan. Instead he turned and gripped my shoulders, moving as if to push me backward over the railing.

"Wait! What are you doing?" I cried, forgetting to whisper. I dug my fingernails into the side of the railing, sure now that this was his plan to murder me. I strained against him with all my might. Then his grip relaxed, and I dared to look at him. His eyes had softened, and they searched mine. He might have even looked handsome if he hadn't been trying to kill me. "Don't you trust me?" he asked in a carefree tone I hadn't heard before.

"Not really."

He smiled at me, an honest, understanding smile, and I removed my fingernails from the railing. He wasn't going to throw me over, and at this realization, the tension in me released, and I stopped fighting him.

A mischievous crooked grin spread over his face as he gripped my shoulder tighter than before. By the time I realized his trick, it was too late. He shoved me backward. My feet lost their grip on the slimy deck. In a last attempt, I buried my fingernails into his arms, but with one shake he dislodged them, and I went hurtling down toward the water.

CHAPTER 9

My screams could probably be heard all the way to shore. I braced myself for the plunge into the icy water. Instead I crashed onto something hard. I was sure that every one of my bones had snapped. It felt as though someone had punched the air out of my lungs as I lay staring up at the stars. My back was bruised and stinging as I struggled for a breath. Finally air found its way into my lungs. I was in a longboat, suspended by two ropes, one on either side. There were three bench-like seats in the skiff.

Jackson was right. I *was* thick. I glanced up to see him, grinning. I could hear him laughing.

"I hate you," I moaned, sitting up.

"You should have jumped," he called back.

That was the cruelest trick anyone had ever played on me. I'd let my guard down just long enough for him to throw me over. If I ever got my hands on him…

"Jackson!" I screamed too late. Brice was behind him and threw an arm around his throat, pulling him back out of view. The longboat swayed back and forth on its ropes as I stood listening helplessly to the shouts and cursing from above. Amid the shouting an agonized shriek pierced the air. My heart stopped. Everything was silent. Glancing up, I saw a dark silhouette look over the railing. A moment later, the dark figure leapt over the side, and landed right in front of me in the longboat, making it lurch back and forth.

He wobbled, trying to catch his balance. "We have to move."

I was relieved to hear Jackson's voice. Moving to the opposite side of the boat, he turned to me. "Catch!" he called, tossing a glinting object toward me. I tried to catch it, but the object slipped through my fingers and clattered into the hull of the small skiff. I looked up at Jackson, who was rolling his eyes at me. Again.

Snatching up the object I saw that it was knife.

"On three, cut the rope and brace yourself." He positioned himself at the other rope. On his count we would go plunging down toward the water. I prepared myself for another hard, painful landing.

I gripped the splintered rope in my left hand and positioned my knife just above it. I wouldn't fail this time.

"One, two, thr—" The boat swung violently to the left, knocking me off balance. Dropping my knife, I grasped the rope, making the mistake of looking down into the roiling black water. I glanced behind me to see that Brice had jumped from the deck above, landing between us. Jackson didn't see me and was sawing at the rope, trying to cut it before Brice could find his footing, and must have thought I was doing the same.

My knife had slid somewhere down in the hull of the boat, but before I could warn him the rope snapped, and one side of the boat dropped. We were hanging vertically. I gripped a seat in the back of boat to keep from falling. Even if I had kept my knife, it would have been useless. The rope was out of my reach. My fingers ached as I held onto the seat with all I had.

"Cut it!" I heard Jackson shout from under me. Glancing down again, I saw Brice hanging onto the middle seat, and Jackson beneath him, hanging onto the very edge. Brice, who hadn't been caught off guard by the sudden drop, had a tight hold on the seat, and was swinging back and forth in an effort to kick Jackson into the water below.

I saw my knife, right next to Brice's hand.

Bringing one foot up, I planted it on the seat, right next to the knife. He was getting closer to Jackson. Supporting my weight on the seat, I reached my right hand down to retrieve the knife, terrified that I would lose my balance at any moment and plunge toward the water. I knew I couldn't cut the rope before he sent Jackson tumbling into the waves beneath us. Then, an idea occurred to me. Gritting my teeth, I slashed the knife across Brice's hand. He roared. The unexpected shock of pain made him lose his hold on the boat. Jackson barely dodged the sailor as he plummeted down, and splashed into the waves. I turned my attention back to the lone rope above me. I placed the knife handle in my mouth, biting down on it, and stretched until I had a hold on the boat's frame.

As I had learned on the cliff's edge, the strength in my arms and shoulders was nothing to depend on, but with my foot planted on the seat, I pushed myself upward toward the rope until I was hardly a finger's breadth from it. I stretched with all my might, slashing clumsily at the chord, coming nearer and nearer with every swipe. The knife suddenly caught, biting into the rope, but not cutting it. I slashed again and again, trying to saw the thick chord. It frayed. It weakened.

It snapped.

We plunged down toward the waves and landed with a force that rocked the skiff and nearly threw me into the water. I never loosened my grip on the boat, but when the rocking ceased, I turned to look at Jackson. He was gone. He'd lost his hold.

"Jackson!" I shrieked, scrambling to the other side of the boat. His head broke the surface of the water, and he threw up a hand for me to pull him. It was no easy task, and I was wary every moment that Brice was lurking under the water and would pull him back down, but after helping him into the boat, I began to think we'd lost our enemy after all.

"The oars are gone," he said, still catching his breath as he sat in the bottom of the boat.

My heart sank.

I noticed wood floating not far from us. "I see them," I said, motioning toward them.

He nodded, shivering. We scooped handfuls of freezing water out of the way, trying to move the boat closer to the oars. Since they were closer to my side, I already knew I would be expected to lean out of the boat and pull them toward me, and my stomach was already churning at the idea. Keeping one hand firmly on the boat, I leaned out farther than I cared to, my fingertips brushing one of the oars. I was so close. I let myself lean farther over the dark water, and caught hold of the oar. I was so excited I nearly lost my balance. Setting the oar in the bottom of the boat, I leaned out again, less afraid than before. I caught the edge of the oar, and turned back to smile in triumph at Jackson when the oar jerked me down toward the water. Before I could let go, Brice's hands crawled up the oar and clamped down on my wrist. He shook me violently, trying to drag me under. I screamed, fighting to hold on to the boat. My fingers were losing their grip. A sharp click echoed over the water, and the sailor froze.

"Let go, Brice." Jackson's voice shook.

His arms were rigid, his pistol leveled at the belligerent sailor.

"Where are you going to run?" Brice challenged as blood trickled down the side of his face. "He'll find you."

"I said, let go."

Brice obeyed, cursing under his breath. I lurched back into the boat, my heart nearly pounding out of my chest.

Without taking his gaze or his aim off of the man in the water, Jackson spoke evenly to me. "Head for the harbor."

I fumbled for the oars, knowing that it would take us months to get to shore if I was the one rowing. I placed them in the water, and Jackson kept the pistol aimed at Brice until we were a safe distance away. When we'd lost sight of him, Jackson turned back to me, his hands shaking violently, and pointed the gun down. A stream of water dribbled from the barrel as he dropped the useless weapon into the bottom of the boat. "It wasn't even loaded," he groaned, resting his face in his hands.

I didn't know whether to laugh or cry. I was free. We had escaped.

Jackson looked up and motioned for me to give him the oars. "We need to hurry," he said, switching places with me.

"Will Brice alert the rest of the crew once he gets back on board?"

"Why would he? You already did." The familiar scowl made me feel ashamed. He was right. My screams had probably awakened the captain and crew.

I bit my tongue, knowing what I had to say, and also knowing how sour these words were going to taste coming out of my mouth. "I suppose I should thank you for that."

His head snapped up. "Don't you dare!" The creases in his forehead deepened. "This wasn't my idea. If it were up to me, you'd still be back on that ship, headed for the gallows for trying to shoot me. This is all that little girl's scheme."

I was speechless. The gallows? The knot in my throat choked me as I tried to comprehend his words. "What does this have to do with Emily?"

"She wouldn't leave." His short words clipped together. "Connors was going to help her escape, but she wouldn't leave without you. I had to promise to take you to her."

I fought back tears. Sweet, wonderful, Emily.

"You can thank her all you want," Jackson muttered. "But leave me out of it."

A thick damp fog settled over the inlet, blocking the

buildings from view. The familiar rife stench of rotting fish told me we must be nearing the harbor.

We rowed in next to a dock, the dark waves lapping softly against the raised platform. The high tide had brought us within reach of the dock. Jackson gently placed the oars in the boat, and hoisted himself onto the dock. As he did, I noticed the dark stains glistening through his shirt. His wounds were bleeding. I followed his lead planting my hands on the weather-worn dock and pushing myself onto the platform. When I got to my feet, he was staring down the winding dark river at the shadowy outline of The Defiance.

"What's wrong?" I asked.

He didn't remove his gaze. It was as if he was waiting for something. "He's not following me."

"That's good, isn't it?"

He appeared lost, then shook himself. "We should go."

Jackson didn't keep to the shadows, or sneak around as I had expected, but walked in the broad moonlight.

"Where are we?" I whispered hoarsely.

"South End in Prittlewell." He didn't whisper at all.

Just half a day's ride East of London. My home was not far away, and I began to think of ways I could get back. I had no money, but I was so desperate to reach home. The thought of living a comfortable life, working in the Seven Stars tavern, and having a roof over my head made me want to cry. Why had I ever complained? As soon as I got back to London, I would stay there for the rest of my life. I would never leave the city, even if that meant living the same day over and over. Monotony would be a welcome thing after this nightmare.

As we walked I noticed that the buildings were fewer as we walked. Soon there was only the occasional farmhouse, and I realized with a sinking feeling that we were not headed toward London. We were traveling north. I wanted to start running west. I pictured myself flying over the moonlit hills, not stopping until I reached home, but James' words echoed in my mind. *Get her to safety. Then you get home.* His words haunted me, but it was more than that. I needed to see her. I needed to hold her in my lap and know she was all right. Then I would go back to London, no matter how far it was. I would get back home.

We climbed a hill overlooking the harbor. At the top of the hill, I glanced back, and was surprised by the warm feeling that bubbled up in me. I could see the entire harbor coated in silvery moonlight and allowed myself just a moment of happiness. I could taste the fresh air and see the moonlit landscape once more, and they gave me hope. In the hull of that ship I had forgotten how beautiful the world could be. Turning back, I saw that I had fallen behind Jackson's hurried pace.

"Where are we going?" I asked, wishing he wouldn't choose to take the wide moonlit road where we could be seen by anyone coming or going.

"North."

That wasn't helpful in the least and I bit back a spiteful response. "Is that where we'll meet Emily?"

He didn't answer, and since he was ahead of me, I couldn't tell whether he'd nodded.

"Will Cephas take care of her now?"

Jackson glanced over his shoulder at me. "What do you mean?"

"With her parents gone, I assume someone will have to care for her."

He halted in the road, turning to face me. His hardened expression gave way to fear for a brief moment. "What did you just say?"

I stared at him in confusion. "Someone will have to…"

"Not that. Emily's parents. What did you just say?"

"They…" I hesitated. "They died in an accident. Their carriage was driven over a cliff. Emily was the only one who survived."

The stricken look I'd first seen in his eyes when Emily was brought on board the ship returned. His jaw clenched, the muscles in his neck strained as he stared up at the sky. "It wasn't an accident, was it?" His husky voice shook.

I couldn't answer.

"Was it?" he shouted.

"No," I said. "No, I don't think so."

A bitter smile played on his face and he shook his head. "It never is." He turned and continued walking.

I didn't know what else to say, but continued babbling nervously, unable to bear the silence. "That's when I found the note with my name on it, saying to take Emily to Barrow-Haven. Then, when I tried, I ended up on the ship and I didn't know what else to do."

He didn't slow down as I talked. He was always a few steps ahead of me no matter how hard I tried to keep up. "A note?"

"Yes."

"From Cephas?" he glanced back.

I nodded, breathlessly.

"To you?"

"Yes." It sounded more like a question.

He stopped again, and I found myself standing right next to him. Staring up at him.

"Let me see if I understand. You've never met actually met Cephas."

I shook my head.

"You're just here because you found a note."

I bristled at his comment.

"Perfect." He muttered, continuing down the road. "You really don't understand what's going on. You don't know who Cephas is. You don't even know who Emily is!"

I couldn't stand it any longer and raced to keep up with his stride. "I may not understand why so many people would be out to hurt a child, but don't tell me I don't know who she is. I know I'm not the 'Kate' Cephas was trying to reach with that note, but I am the one who found it."

He glanced sideways at me, as if sizing me up, then faced forward again. "None of that matters if you don't know what they're fighting for."

I was tired of being treated like the idiot he thought I was. I stopped in the road. "They're Puritans."

He stopped up ahead, and looked back at me.

"They're fighting for their freedom."

"In all the wrong ways." He shook his head. "They seek to purify a land that must be purged."

His words stunned me. They were not the words of a sailor, but a scholar.

He stared at me, once again as if to size me up. "Did Emily tell you who they were?"

"No," I answered, hoping he wouldn't ask how I knew.

He nodded, satisfied with my answer, then turned and continued walking. "Are you going to continue with her?"

"She's with Cephas, isn't she?" I asked, attempting to catch up.

"Cephas moves around quite a bit. It's hard to keep track of him. She may have found him in time, or he may have moved on, in which case you'll have to catch up with him."

I felt my stomach twist inside of me. How much more of this could I take?

"So," he said, his dark eyes studying me. "Are you going to take her?"

At that moment, I wanted to run screaming in the opposite direction. I couldn't answer his question, but then, a perfect way to avoid it came to mind. "Why don't you?"

"Me?" He looked from side to side, as if wondering who I had spoken to.

"You two are family, aren't you?"

His brow furrowed as he halted again. "Who told you that?"

I had overheard it from his conversation with Captain Scot. "I...no one. You just look alike. That's all." It had been a cover up, but once I said it, I realized that it was true. Emily's hair was blond with tints of red in it. Jackson's hair was darker, but still had the same bronze hints of color. They also had the same, dark, flashing eyes. The only difference was that Emily's eyes shined and sparkled, while Jackson's glinted like cold iron. "How are you related?"

"Her mother was my cousin," he said, clearing his throat.

"I'm sorry," I said sincerely, thinking of my own cousin.

He shrugged it away, and continued walking. "I can't take Emily. Because as soon as I leave you with her, I'm headed back."

I stared at him, my mouth hanging open. "To the harbor?"

"No. To the Defiance."

CHAPTER 10

"You're going back?" I hurried my steps to catch up with him, trying to read his expression.

He only nodded.

"But he'll kill you."

He shrugged. "He can try. I'm not afraid of Scot, and he needs to know that. If he kills me, it's not going to be a shot in the back. I'm going to make him do it one lash at a time."

His stubborn stupidity made me want to scream.

"Besides," he continued, watching me out of the corner of his eye. "Just because you're completely inadequate for this job, doesn't mean you can push it off on me."

I felt my temper spark. "Inadequate?"

"Yes."

"And just what makes me inadequate?"

"You have a jumpy trigger finger. You scream too much. And you nearly got Emily killed." He hadn't even paused to think. "Those are my top three. Do you need more?"

I could finish the list myself.

"This is all a mistake," he muttered. "Emily would be better off in the hands of someone else. Anyone else."

I felt my temper ignite, and blaze through me. "I was the only one who saw that accident. I'm the one who listened to her cry herself to sleep the night her parents died, and I'm the one who brought her this far. So I apologize if I don't meet all your qualifications, but I care about what happens to her!" My words astonished me, and I was amazed to find that they were true.

He laughed at me.

It was infuriating that my fiery reaction hadn't upset him in the slightest. I took a deep breath. "I promised I would help her in any way I could."

He was smugly satisfied. "You should have considered what you were up against before you promised her something like that. Besides, what does it matter? She's just a little girl. She won't remember what you promised her." He glanced at me again, out of the corner of his eye, watching my reaction, probably hoping I would explode again so he could laugh at me.

I looked up at him. "If you believed that, you wouldn't be taking me to her."

"What I believe," he said, staring straight ahead. "Is none of your business."

We continued following the dusty path for several hours. My feet were heavy, my head was throbbing. Jackson's quick pace had slowed considerably. He never stopped moving, but I began to notice that he was stumbling more often. Perhaps it was the light, but he seemed pale. Beads of sweat trickled down his forehead, despite the cool night air. His eyes were unnaturally bright as he focused on the road ahead. Before long, he was trembling from head to foot. I recognized his behavior, and had to swallow back the fear. We needed to stop before the fever caused him to collapse.

"Should we stop and rest?" I ventured.

He scowled at me, his teeth chattering as if it was the middle of winter rather than spring. "Why? Are you tired?"

"Yes." The truth was I could have kept going, but we needed to stop for his sake.

He shook his head. "We're not stopping. I want to reach

Emily before dawn."

I couldn't take orders from him any longer. I stepped in front of him, and he halted. "Listen to me! I don't know where we're going, but I know that I can't get there by myself. You are just as tired as I am, and if you drop dead on the road I'll be stuck out here all alone. So sit down!" I pointed a shaking finger at a patch of grass next to the path. He was so much taller than me that if I hadn't been so frightened, it might have been comical.

He stared at me, his eyes wide. He looked so weak, I knew I could physically force him if it came to that. He gaped at me for another moment, then swallowed. "Yes, sir."

I couldn't tell if his answer stemmed from habit or humor, but I couldn't take a joke at the moment. We both sat down to rest. The right side of the road was guarded by trees, the left overlooked a stream that swished along the bank. The water looked so calm and harmless in the moonlight. One never would have guessed the terrible beast it could be. It was just like so many people. Calm, and even beautiful at a glance, but vicious at heart.

When I'd caught my breath, I turned to Jackson to say something. He was curled up on the hard ground, asleep. I bit my lip to keep from smiling, glad we had stopped.

Why had he done it? Why had he brought me this far? I thought of the tender way he had held Emily. I knew his love for her was greater than he would ever admit. He didn't have to help me. He could have left me on the Defiance, and by his own admission he would have. Yet here I was. But if his love for her was so deep, why would he abandon her to go back to the Defiance?

I realized I was still staring at him, and turned away. It didn't matter why he did what he did. There was no reason to concern myself. He was spiteful and arrogant and it was a mercy our time together was ending.

I glanced at him again. What was it like to have a father

cruel enough to beat you to death? I had lost my parents, but I had never doubted their love. Jackson was a fool, but I understood the cold glint of fear in his dark eyes. I had known that hunted feeling as a child and seen it in the eyes of my cousin the night we ran.

She had beaten James until he was almost senseless. I waited until she fell asleep, the bottle still tucked under her arm, and found my cousin. He was curled up, sobbing on the dirt floor. We had endured many such nights, but this would be the last. I scooped water from a bucket, jostling it in my clumsy, seven-year-old hands. Kneeling beside him, I held it to his lips, telling him that he was brave and that he'd saved me. Anything to make him stop crying. He shoved my hands away, the thirsty soil drinking up the few drops I hadn't already spilled.

"You've got to get out of here, Katy," he gasped.

"We will," I promised. "We will. You'll see."

He shook his head. "I always slow you down. You know I do. You'll never get away with me tagging behind."

I brushed the hair from his tear stained face. I was a fast runner, but I doubted if James could even walk.

"She'll sleep until tomorrow afternoon," I reminded him. "We could be halfway home before she ever notices."

"Katy," he groaned. "There is no home. There's nowhere for us to go. If she catches us again…" His lower lip trembled. "I can't…I can't do it anymore."

"You won't have to ever again," I promised, taking his clammy hand in mine.

I sprung to my feet, unwilling to waste a minute.

"What are you doing?" he asked.

"Looking for the keys."

"Around her neck."

I glanced at the bag, and shuddered at the thought of drawing that close to her. At any moment, her snoring would stop, her eyes would open, and she'd knock me to the ground before I could run. She had been so nice the day we'd first met her. When we'd been taken to the fishing cabin in the woods I'd hoped to call it home, but it had become a prison. Fortune Cole had the kind of smile that stretched placidly across her face. There was nothing real about it. Everything about her was red. Her mane of frizzy hair, her swollen hands, and her face when she was angry. She had been so warm and kind that first day. Then that had all ended. She drank from her bottle and screamed and shouted, punishing us for the slightest misstep or for nothing at all. For a year we had endured it. I needed those keys.

I held my breath until my chest was about to burst. I leaned forward, pushing back the fear. I reached out a tiny hand and stretched open the drawstring bag around her neck. She stirred and I jumped back, dropping the bag and gulping down a scream. When she resettled, I poked my hand forward again. The bag was empty. My knees nearly buckled. I turned to James and shook my head.

A crash made us both jump. I couldn't keep back my scream this time. She didn't rouse from her stupor. The crash came again, but it was quieter this time. James and I exchanged a knowing look. The door. The wind was catching and slamming the door. It wasn't locked.

"We have to go," I whispered breathlessly.

"Katy, I can't!" Huge tears fell down his bony cheeks.

"I'll help you. You have to come with me, James. I can't go alone." Without giving him time to argue, I slung his arm over my shoulders and helped him to his feet.

"What about the dog?" he asked, his voice shaking.

My heart pounded. I hadn't thought about the dog. He always sounded the alarm, and even tried to hunt us down before. "We'll just try not to wake him."

"It won't work."

I didn't listen. I couldn't think about the dog. The front door crashed again. She snorted, and I was sure that at any moment she would start up and snatch something to throw at us. She, rolled over, and continued snoring. When I felt at liberty to breathe again, I moved through the inky darkness, and gently pushed the door open. It groaned on its rusted hinges.

The night wind caught a handful of rain and flung toward us. James coughed and sputtered as the drops flew at our faces, but for me, that rain was my first taste of freedom.

Yet, it proved to be a weapon formed against us. I glanced around the darkened yard, and noticed the dog. He was stretched out on his side in the rain, perfectly still. I bit my lip, moving forward, never taking my eyes off of the animal. As we hobbled across the yard, he never moved. I thought it was odd that he would stay out in the rain like that.

As we staggered in the dark, the rain blinded us, and deepened the muddy roads. Our progress was slow, and I shuddered at the moaning of the wind. It sounded like a howling beast chasing us, but every time I looked back, the path was empty.

James pleaded with me to stop, begged me to slow down, even though we were hardly moving as it was. He said he couldn't go farther, but I didn't listen, knowing that he was afraid of running away. If he convinced me to stop, I knew he would try to convince me to go back, and I knew it would work. Then James' cough began. It rattled in my ears. Between coughs, he continued to plead. I was about to relent when he went limp at my side. His weight dragged me down, driving my face into the mud. I sat up, wiping the grime from my face. "We'll stop!" I shouted over the pounding rain, thinking this was a show of dramatics.

He didn't answer. He didn't move.

My eye filled with fearful tears, and my heart began to pound so hard I thought it would burst. "James?" I leaned over him. I brushed the soaked mop of black hair from his eyes.

He didn't respond.

I started to panic. "I'm sorry!" I shrieked. "We can rest. It's all right. James. Please don't die. I'm sorry! We never should have run. You were right. I'm sorry!"

A sound from behind made me jump. Lightning flashed in the distance, and I saw a dark figure on the road. She was coming. She was coming after us. With all the strength I had left, I threw my cousin's limp arm over my shoulder and tried to drag him. Though only a year older, James was so much bigger than me that it was impossible to drag him. Thunder pounded in the distance, causing me to lose whatever common sense I had left. Every step was a frantic instinct. Every breath was drawn in terror until I couldn't take another step. My limbs quivered all over, and I dropped into the warm, soft mud. I closed my eyes, unsure of whether I would ever open them again.

I awoke several days later in the home of a minister and his sister. It was never clear how we had arrived there. Reverend Durham said he'd found us on the steps of his back porch, and when I told them of our experience on the road, his sister Miss Durham said the angels must have carried us the rest of the way. The Durhams became our family. At last we had a home. At last, we were happy.

I paused in my memories, remembering what it had been like to enjoy the peace and safety of people who loved me. James had healed, though he always walked with a slight limp. It was constant reminder that he had protected me when no one else had. When everyone had failed me, he had been there. I had never been truly alone. Emily had. I wanted to believe that there were others who would take my place. Perhaps the real Kate, the one who had been meant to receive the note would step forward and take over. She would do a much better job than I had. But what if she never appeared?

I glared at Jackson. This should have been his responsibility. After all, they were family. He should have been the one to step up, instead of running like the fool that he was, all the way back to the Defiance to be killed by his own father. I could feel my face begin to burn with anger. *He* thought *I* was the idiot.

Get her to safety. Then you get home. He'd said to take her to safety. If she was safe, my job was finished, regardless of where her grandfather was. That was as far as my responsibility went.

Do you remember what it was like to be no one's responsibility?

Fear twisted my stomach. All of my worst fears had followed Emily's arrival, the water, the darkness, the loneliness had been more real and more terrible than in my nightmares.

I had sounded so brave when arguing with Jackson. In truth I couldn't wait to get back to the tavern, curl up in my room, and cry. I would never leave London. I would never leave that tavern. I would stay in that room for the rest of my life.

Yet, that thought didn't comfort me. In fact, it terrified me. The idea of living in fear, too scared even to step outside made me feel empty. I didn't want a life like that, but James had. If I had listened to him, if I had only been content he would still be here.

I heard a stirring behind me and groaned, not ready for the battle to begin again.

Jackson was furious with me for letting him sleep. He'd wanted to reach Emily by dawn. Didn't I realize the sun would be up in the next hour? Didn't I see that we were trying to hurry?

I knew I had done the right thing. Angry as he was, Jackson now had the strength to argue which, though irritating, was an improvement.

Even when his ranting had stopped he stormed several paces ahead of me and I struggled to keep up. "Why do you even care?" he grumbled.

"What?"

"You're not family. You're not even supposed to be here. So why do you care? Why do you even want to help?"

"Because it's the right thing to do." I couldn't keep the sarcastic edge out of my voice, hoping I had made it clear enough that his choice was the wrong one.

When I looked up, Jackson was glaring at me once again. "Save your preaching."

I bit back my response, but couldn't resist the chance to irritate him. I knew he'd hate me for asking, but it wasn't likely he could hate me anymore than he did at present. "Why on earth did they call you Reverend Jack?"

He turned away, his jaw tight. "It's just a name." He reached into his belt, and withdrew the same pistol he'd used to fool Brice. He held it up for me to see. "Do you know how to load one of these?"

I stared at him, dumbfounded. "I can fire it."

"I know *that*." His voice was as heavy as his footfalls on the path as he stomped along. "Can you load and clean one?"

I shook my head struggling to keep up with his pace.

"You'll have to learn. If you're going to help Emily, you'll need some protection."

The thought made me feel sick.

"You'll need powder, wadding, and a lead ball to fire it. They should have everything you need where Emily is staying."

His long, capable fingers slipped up and down the gun as he ran through the steps. He demonstrated with imaginary ammunition how to pour in the right amount of powder, stuff the barrel with wadding and the lead ball, how to keep the hammer forward while loading and cock it back before firing. Then how to clean the gun and start all over. He ran through the instructions so fast, I knew I would forget the steps before we reached Emily, but I wasn't about to admit it.

I shivered. "I hope I never have to use that."

"I hope you don't either."

I looked up at him, wondering if I had just heard his first non-insulting comment.

"You're a terrible shot."

Why did I even dare to hope?

Just as the sun peaked over the horizon, we crested a hill. Beneath us was an empty valley with a river running through it. As we drew closer, I noticed a smattering of tiny houses. If we hadn't been searching for them, I'd never have seen them. They were so secluded, and silent. At first, I assumed the quiet was because of the early hour, but as we walked through the village I noticed the darkened windows. Where was everyone?

One house at the end of the street was lighted. I started to head for the door, but Jackson restrained my arm. "There's one more thing you should know." He reached into his shirt, slipping something from around his neck and dropping it into my hand.

In the early light, I saw the signet ring and chain. "Where did you—"

"Keep that away from Scot no matter what happens. It's not Emily he wants. He's after the ring, and he knows she has it."

"But it's just a ring."

"It's also a key."

My curiosity was piqued. "A key to what?"

He glanced from side to side as if about to confide a secret. "I don't know."

I tilted my head to one side, incredulous. "Then why should I believe you?"

Jackson's hands were shaking again, whether from fever or fear I couldn't tell. "Because it's all Scot talks about and he'd kill me if he knew I had it and gave it to you."

"He's going to kill you anyway," I reminded him.

"Whatever happens, no matter what he promises you, no matter what he threatens to do, keep the ring hidden."

The urgency in his voice struck terror in me, and I shuddered involuntarily. "I will."

I knocked on the door of the cottage, noticing that Jackson chose to hide in the shadows. "Coward," I mumbled.

"I can hear you," he whispered.

"I know full well you can…"

The door swung open and light spilled into the street. A woman stared up at me, her gray hair pulled back into a tight knot, her plump frame taking up the whole doorway. "Yes?"

I was lost for words. I suddenly couldn't think of what to say. My mind was completely blank. I glanced at Jackson in the shadows, and he nodded, urging me on. "I…I was wondering," I stumbled, my tired voice unable to form words. "I'm looking for…"

"Kate?"

I looked down and saw a little golden head, peeking around the woman's skirts. "Emily!" I dropped to my knees as she ran into my arms. Stroking her hair, I couldn't control the sobs that shook my body. She was safe. It was all worth it if she was safe. She pulled back and wiped the tears from my cheeks, then fell back into my arms. "You're all right," I whispered. "Thank God you're all right."

The plump woman watched us for a moment then ran back into the house, saying she'd left breakfast on the stove.

I held Emily at arms' length, taking in the sight of her sweet, freckled little face. I leaned forward and kissed her forehead. "I'm so sorry."

She smiled back at me, then her gaze traveled upward to something behind me. "Jack?"

I turned and saw Jackson's tall frame just a few steps behind me. Giggling, Emily ran from my arms and right into his. I was stunned. He bent, catching her up in his arms as if she was nothing. He was laughing, his grin as bright and merry as hers. I couldn't help but smile as I stood to my feet, watching both of them. I'd never heard Emily laugh before.

He set her down, and she threw her arms around his neck.

"Thank you," she said, kissing his pale, hollow cheek.

The bitter, hard-hearted sailor melted away as he stroked her hair. I noticed the tears standing in his eyes.

Perhaps I had misjudged him.

She pulled back, and took his hand in both of hers as he stood. "Come inside!"

I crossed my arms defiantly, daring him to deny her.

He slipped his hand from hers and her big brown eyes, searched his. "What's wrong?"

"I can't stay, Em."

Her lower lip trembled. "But—"

He knelt down, putting a finger over her lips. "I've got a job to do."

Two tears slid down her cheeks.

I hated Jackson. He was the most heartless, selfish person I had ever met.

"Are you coming back this time?" she asked, her lower lip trembling.

He glanced up at me, warning me not to spill his secret. As if I wanted to be the one to break the news to Emily that her beloved Jack was going to get himself killed because of his stubborn pride. I could only glare at him. He looked back to Emily.

"I'll be back," he promised.

Everything in me wanted to march forward, rip Emily away, and slam the door behind us.

She looked at the ground.

"Hey." He cupped her chin in his hand. "Look at me. I kept my last promise, didn't I?"

She turned and looked at me, and I tried to disguise my anger until she looked back at Jackson.

"You can trust me," he promised.

The innocent girl nodded.

I could have strangled him.

"Oh, and just between us," he leaned forward, and whispered something in her ear, his eyes shining with mischief. When he finished she nodded. He kissed the top of her head and stood. "You go inside."

She ran past me into the house. He watched her fondly, then his eyes met mine and the cold, sarcastic sailor reappeared. "What was I supposed to say?" He shrugged, reaching for the pistol.

I was too livid to reply. I held out my hand for the pistol, but he hesitated. He brought it nearly to my hand, then pulled it back in indecision. I didn't know what this new game was, but I was already furious with him. "What's wrong? Don't you trust me?" I cried.

He smirked.

I hadn't realized the humor of it until the words left my mouth.

He laid the pistol in my upturned palm. "Not in the least."

He tried to release it, but I closed my hand around the pistol, pinning his fingers down. I wasn't finished. "Just so you know, when you break your promise to that little girl, you will break her heart again. But what does it matter? You certainly won't be here to see it, and someone else will have to clean up your mess."

His lip curled in anger, and he ripped his hand away. Without a word, he turned on his heel and walked up the road. I was so angry I could have screamed. He'd be dead in less than three days. If not by his father's hand, then from the whipping. I didn't care. It served him right.

So why did my blood run cold at the thought?

CHAPTER 11

I listened, but something was missing. Something was wrong. What was it? Waves. Where was the sound of the waves slapping against the ship? I rolled over and felt a soft mattress. I opened my eyes. Where was I?

I sat up, the ropes beneath the mattress creaking as I did so. In the darkness, I reached around me, searching for a hint as to where I was. My fingers brushed against my sleeve. It wasn't the ragged black dress I'd been wearing for ages. It was soft wool or linen perhaps.

I fell back onto the pillow. I was finally clean and warm and safe. I would never take a full night's sleep in a warm bed for granted ever again. I never wanted to leave here.

I noticed that light was seeping in under the door, and in the windowless room, I couldn't tell what time of day it was. I slipped out of bed, feeling around for my dress. When I found it I couldn't believe it was mine. I felt stitching in the places that had torn. The sharp scent of lye soap tickled my nose, as I pulled the garment over my head. Once I was dressed, I cracked the door open. It was not sunlight, as I had suspected, but lamplight. The room was quiet and still, lit by a single lamp on the table.

"Good morning, dear."

I jumped at the sound of the woman's voice, and turned to

see her full form coming from the kitchen. The chair under her creaked as she seated herself by the fire and resumed her mending.

Her greeting confused me. "Is it still morning?"

She gave a little laugh. "Oh, no. You slept away all of yesterday and last night. It's not morning still. It's morning again."

I sat down in a second chair by the fire, still rubbing the sleep from my eyes. I had slept for so long. I wondered if Jackson had made it back to the Defiance. Had he made it that far? Had Scot found him already? I took a deep breath reminding myself that it didn't matter.

"You must have had quite the walk," the woman said without looking up from her mending.

I nodded.

"You're welcome to stay here as long as you like."

It took me several moments to realize why I was fighting back tears at her words. They were the first kind words I'd heard in days.

She noticed my tears, and I brushed them away, laughing at myself.

She only smiled at me. "I'd ask for your name, but Emily hasn't stopped talking about her 'Kate' since you arrived here. It was a struggle just to keep her out of your room so she wouldn't wake you."

"I'm Katherine Elyot."

"Amelia Lawrence," she said, without even a slight pause in her mending.

"This is a quiet town," I observed, surprised at how comfortable and safe I felt, sitting down by this woman's hearth and talking with her.

"It's an empty town."

"Where is everyone?"

Her needle halted for the first time, and her hands fell limp in her lap. She gazed into the fire. "I will smite the

Shepherd, and the sheep of the flock shall be scattered."

The verse made my stomach twist. I knew it well. I had witnessed it first hand, and here it was again. She offered no other answer.

"What keeps you here?" I asked.

She shrugged. "Sentimental old widow like me can't just drop everything and leave." I saw the twisted expression of worry and pain before she looked back at her mending. "Most of my loved ones aren't in this world anyway. It doesn't matter much where I settle." She turned back to her needlework. "I don't blame the others for leaving, of course. Cephas our shepherd was taken, like our Lord, in the middle of the night nearly a week ago. It took all but a few days before this village was empty." She sniffed, brushing her cheek with the back of her hand. "That little girl has been a light in this house since she came here three days ago. Tragic, what happened to her parents."

I nodded. "What family does she have?"

"Cephas is her grandfather. He's all she has left."

I felt my temper spark. He wasn't *all* she had left. If Jackson wasn't such a stubborn fool she might have had a chance at a decent family.

"I'll aid you in any way I can," she offered. "But Emily needs to see her grandfather." She waited for me to respond. "You are taking her to Cephas, aren't you?"

I sighed. "I don't know yet."

• • •

All that rainy day I wandered around the house, wondering what to do. I tried to make myself useful, but Mistress Lawrence claimed that there was nothing to be done around the house. She bore the load of housework and cooking, saying it was her pleasure.

When Emily awoke, she seemed to be avoiding me. It

didn't make sense. The widow had described her as eager to see me, but perhaps she had said that to pamper my vanity.

At noon, I saw Emily sitting by the dead, empty fireplace, staring into it, lost in thought.

I settled myself next to her, unsure of what to say, or how to begin. I cleared my throat uncomfortably. "You're quiet today."

She nodded.

"Do you miss your grandfather?"

I waited for a word, a look, a tear, but she only gave a slight nod.

I felt my stomach turn as I continued. "We could keep looking for him if you like."

She shook her head, without hesitation. "I don't want to go anywhere."

"All right then." I was surprised, but not displeased. She didn't want to continue and that made two of us. She was here with Widow Lawrence. She was safe. She was no longer my responsibility.

Suddenly feeling the need for fresh air, I stood and walked to the door, stepping out into the drizzling afternoon. The sky was dark and moody. I would leave tomorrow, head back to London, and leave this nightmare behind. I stared down at the puddles, unable to stop the memories of many such afternoons when James had jumped in puddle after puddle as a little boy, splashing, laughing, living. The ache in my heart took my breath away every time.

Beside one of the puddles was an indent in the earth. I stepped out from under the eaves, into the rain, hardly noticing the drizzle, as I bent over what had to be a footprint. It was too large to belong to anyone in the house. It appeared to be from a man's boot, and it looked fresh. Catching my breath, I glanced all around me, wondering if something would jump out. Slowly, I backed into the house. As I closed the door, all of my perfect plans began to melt away, like the footprint in the rain.

• • •

That evening I found myself staring into nothing, lost in my own thoughts. The events of the past few days continued to run through my mind. It was as if an explosion had gone off, and I was still staggering from the shock of it, unsure of which direction to run.

"Miss Elyot." Widow Lawrence was staring at me, fearing for my sanity no doubt. I couldn't count how many times she'd caught me staring at nothing. "My eyes are troubling me this evening," she said, rubbing her temples. "Would you read a Scripture to us?" She passed me a Bible.

"Of…course," I fumbled, unsure of what else to say. I stared at the worn, brown leather cover, and did not see the safe, legal name of King James, or the year 1603. I noticed my hands were shaking. I knew full well why it had a blank cover. I opened the front cover and silently read the title page.

The Bible
And Holy Scriptures
Contained in the Old and New Testament

Beneath that, there was printed a picture of the Israelites, huddled by the Red Sea, and Pharaoh and his armies, descending the hills to enslave them. Framing the ink picture were the ever-familiar words.

Fear ye not, Stand still and behold
The salvation of the Lord, which He will shew you this day.
For the Egyptians whom ye have seen this day,
Ye shall never see them again.
Exodus 14:13

I fought back tears and memories as my gaze fell on the words at the bottom of the page.

"The Lord shall fight for you,
Therefore hold you, your peace."
Exodus 14:14

At Geneva Printed by Rovland Hall
M D L X

The empty town, the secret signet, Emily's family, and now this. How much more could I endure? James had been right. I wasn't ready for this. The memories were still too fresh, too painful. I knew the color must have drained from my face. I couldn't betray myself. I couldn't let my secret slip.

"Is there anything you would like to hear?" I asked, breathlessly.

Widow Lawrence glanced upward, considering. "Perhaps the forty-third chapter in Isaiah."

Oh, why had I asked? Couldn't she have picked something else? Anything else? I knew the passage by heart, but flipped the pages in the weathered volume, knowing that recitation would give my secret away. Tears made it nearly impossible for my eyes to focus on the tiny black lettering.

"But now thus saith the Lord that created thee, O Jacob, and he that formed thee, O Israel, Fear not." I stopped, unable to continue. *Fear not.*

"Why, what on earth is the matter?"

I glanced up at the widow and felt the tears sliding down my cheeks. I tried to brush them away. "I'm sorry," I apologized. *"Fear not: for I have redeemed thee, I have called thee by thy name; thou art mine."*

I looked up, thankful to be finished, but Widow Lawrence motioned for me to continue reading.

"When thou passest through the waters, I will be with

thee; and through the rivers, they shall not overflow thee..." I hastily dried my cheeks with the back of my hand, knowing I was making a fool of myself. It was a battle to keep my voice calm and steady. I simply had to get through this. "*When thou walkest through the fire, thou shalt not be burned; neither shall the flame kindle upon thee.*" On the verge of sobs, I slammed the Bible closed. Standing I passed it to the widow. "Please forgive me. I'm tired this evening."

She watched me, a knowing look on her round, upturned face. "It's quite all right. I hope I haven't upset you."

"No," I answered, and with that, I turned and left the room.

I closed the door gently behind me, pressing my back against it, unable to stop the flood of tears. Slipping down the door, I sat, hugging my knees and trying to quiet my sobs by muffling them in my skirt.

That Bible. That verse. The memories stabbed me with excruciating force. Feelings I thought I had learned to suppress welled up inside of me.

Guilt.

Fury.

Fear.

Grief.

What was I doing here? Why had I gotten mixed up in all of this? I burned with hatred, and sobbed with remorse as the memories came in unrelenting succession.

• • •

"What are you doing?"

I jumped at the sound of James' voice. I hadn't heard him enter the study.

"Looking for something," I answered, without turning to the doorway to face him. Why on earth was I so flustered?

"What are you looking for?" James' newly deepened

voice had finally stopped cracking like a disgruntled bullfrog's. It was booming, and even frightening at times.

"The Bible."

"It's right there on the desk."

I glanced down at it out of the corner of my eye. "Oh, there it is." I made no move to fetch it, hoping James would leave.

Instead he entered the study, picked up the thick leather-bound book, and held it out to me. "Why do you need it?"

"I—" My face burned. I was no good at lying, but he simply would never understand the truth. "I need to look something up." I reached for it, but he pulled it out of my grasp, an amused grin spreading over his features.

"You?"

"Give it to me!" I shouted.

"Kate, you practically have the whole thing memorized," he laughed, holding it beyond my reach. "What could you possibly have to look up?"

"None of your business! Give it back!"

"Children!"

We both turned to see Miss Durham in the doorway. She would call us children until we were as gray as she was. "Andrew is writing. Please be civil to one another."

James handed me the Bible as she left.

"Thank you," I said primly.

"What do you need it for anyway?"

"I told you. I need to look something up." I leafed through the pages, pretending to search.

"What do you need to look up?"

I slammed the Volume closed. "If you *must* know, Master Lindon asked me a question that I couldn't answer."

"Lindon?" His voice had a certain bite to it that told me I had guided this conversation in the wrong direction. "When were you talking to him?"

"A few days ago. We saw each other in town."

James snatched the Bible from my hand.

"What are you doing? Give that back."

"You don't need this." He held it behind his back. "You don't need to answer any questions of his. You can let Reverend Durham do that. It's his job, isn't it?"

"What is wrong with you?" I asked, trying to dodge around him. It was no use. He blocked my every attempt.

"I don't trust him," he replied.

I laughed. "Why ever not?"

James shrugged, leaning back on the desk, folding his arms across his chest. "None of the other men in town trust him either."

It irritated me that James used the word *other* as if he were already one of the townsmen. He was only fifteen, and hardly a year older than me.

"The men in this town don't trust anyone," I shot back.

"And you know exactly why."

I couldn't answer. I did know why. "Tell me something James, did Jesus command us to love our neighbor?"

"He did," James conceded. "He also said to watch out for wolves that dress like sheep."

"That's not what Master Lindon is."

"How do you know? He could be a wolf. He grins just like one."

"He does not!"

"Children!" Miss Durham stood in the doorway, a warning eye on both of us.

James gave a disgusted sigh, tossed the Bible down on the desk with a loud thump, and pushed past her, leaving the room.

"What was that about?" She asked, as the slam of the front door echoed through the small cottage.

"He's simply being stubborn again."

When she was gone, I brushed my hands over the leather cover of the Bible. There was something so comforting about its smooth, well-worn front. I opened it to the title page, looking at the familiar ink picture of the children of Israel huddled at the edge of the Red Sea.

"The LORD will fight for you,
Therefore hold you, your peace."
Exodus 14:14

I froze, feeling suddenly riddled with guilt. What I was about to do was wrong. I didn't even know why, but I knew this wasn't the way things should go. Sneaking and lying wasn't the answer to anything. Then I thought of James. I had to prove that I was right and he was wrong, and I could only think of one way to do that. Tucking the Bible under my arm, I slipped out the door.

"I have something for you."

Charles Lindon couldn't ever stop looking handsome. Even now, as he rested under a tree eating his noon meal, I had to focus in order to keep my tongue from getting twisted. "Do you now?" he asked, winking at me. Whenever he winked, my heart galloped along like a runaway horse. True, he was nearly ten years my senior, but I was quite sure that I was mature for my age.

I set the Bible in front of him. "This is for you."

He grinned at me. "There must be some mistake, Miss Elyot. I already have a Bible."

"This one's different," I said simply. "When we spoke the other day you told me that sometimes you worried about the accuracy of your translation by King James. I thought you could take this one and compare the two."

"That was very thoughtful of you, but I didn't mean to sound doubtful. I'm sure there can't be a better translation."

"Oh, but there is!" I insisted, opening the front cover. "Do you see all these passages between the verses? They explain what the chapter means."

"What are these?" he asked, motioning to the hand-written notes scrawled in the margin.

"Oh, those are Reverend Durham's notes. I hope they don't get in your way."

"Of course not," he answered. He smiled, and I had to push back the panic as I remembered James' words. His smile did have a certain, frightening glint to it. "Thank you for all your help, Miss Elyot. Maybe I'll enjoy living here, after all." He winked at me again, and stood, walking away with the Bible under his arm. He didn't grin like a wolf at all. What had I worried about? James was stubborn and blind. He just didn't understand Charles Lindon the way I did.

• • •

I woke while it was still dark, and was surprised to find myself, still huddled on the floor. My cheeks were wet from crying in my sleep. I rose, stretching all the aches in my neck and back, then headed for the front room to light a fire. I had no idea when the sun would rise, but I knew I wasn't going to fall back to sleep.

After stoking the fire, I sat back in the hard kitchen chair, watching the flames lick around the kindling. I noticed the Geneva Bible on the hearth and picked it up, holding it in my hands. The comfort it used to bring me by its soft, worn, leather touch was now replaced by a dead ache. I turned to the previous night's passage and stared at it unseeing. I knew the verses all too well.

"*When thou passest through the waters, I will be with thee; and through the rivers, they shall not overflow thee.*" Reverend Durham's voice had been soft and gentle, just as he was. His little flock had loved him dearly, as had I.

The verse had been his answer every time I had asked if he was afraid. He had good reason to fear. There were men who would have liked to kill him. He was more than just a

Puritan minister. Reverend Durham was a writer. He wrote anonymous pamphlets that were printed in our little village, then taken by messenger throughout the country. Everywhere they went, they brought hope and truth to the people. They spoke out against the Church of England and encouraged the brothers and sisters in our faith, and for that, Reverend Durham could be killed. Yet every time I voiced my worries, he would reply with that verse, until one day I asked him where it was.

When he told me, I went to look it up, having safely received the Bible back from Master Lindon some weeks before. No one had even noticed it was missing. It's wonderful pages crinkled and turned as I flipped to Isaiah, but the forty-third chapter was missing. It simply wasn't there, and my heart began to quicken. I ran my finger through the crease in the middle, and felt the jagged edge. It had been ripped out. Panic began to overwhelm me, as I shut the book. I would be found out for sure. I couldn't lie. I was terrible at it, and I knew it was wrong. If anyone, especially Reverend Durham, found the missing page and asked me directly, I knew my secret would be over. I had to find Master Lindon. I had to ask him what had happened.

"Why does the Bible make you cry?"

Emily's voice startled me. I realized tears had slipped down my cheeks and onto the pages. I searched for an answer. "It reminds me of people I love, and I know I'll never see them again. You understand that, don't you?"

She nodded, solemnly. "I like it here," she said.

I had begun to adjust to her rapid change of subject. "Do you?"

She nodded. "I'm glad I live here now. I don't want to leave."

"Why not?" I asked.

She didn't answer for several moments and I began to wonder if she'd heard me. "I don't want to get lost again." Her voice was nothing more than a whisper. I saw a tear fall from her dark, glimmering eye.

"Emily, I won't lose you again."

She looked up at me, her gaze seeing right through me. "Promise?"

I couldn't speak. I couldn't promise. She was right. I had no way of knowing what would happen. Cephas was the only family Emily had, at least the only family she had that was worth depending on. There was no way of knowing where he was. He could be imprisoned or even executed before we ever reached him. I took a deep breath.

Emily saw my hesitation and took that as an answer. "I just want to stay here."

"I'm sure your grandfather misses you."

She only shrugged.

• • •

"When are you leaving?"

I turned from the window, my heart drumming at the widow's words like the pounding rain that beat against the window. Her tone was not weary, but warning.

"I don't understand," I said, only wishing that that was the truth.

She stood from her chair. "I don't think that's what troubles you. I think you understand more than you care to."

I began to shrink back. I had suspected that this conversation was coming, but I dreaded it all the same. "We can't leave. Emily doesn't want to go. Besides, I have no idea where to look, or how I would ever find Cephas," I babbled as she walked toward me.

"You're being watched," she whispered.

I closed my eyes, and nodded, remembering the footprint in the mud. I had known it then, but I had wanted to ignore it.

"It's not safe here anymore. You must move on."

I hung my head, knowing that I couldn't fight this any longer. "What do you want me to do?"

"It's not what I want that matters," she said placing a piece of parchment in my hand.

My breath grew quick and shallow as I saw my name printed on the folded letter. I looked up at the widow.

Her voice was soft and timid. "He gave that to me, just before they took him. He knew what was coming. He said to give it to you, and only you."

Guilt spread through me like a chilling wind. It couldn't be me. This letter had been written for another Kate, a braver, smarter, more trustworthy Kate. I slipped into my bedroom once again, lighting a candle to read by in the dim, windowless room. Before I opened it, I noticed an inscription on the back. Hoping it was an address, I peered at the lines.

> *Disturb us, Lord when,*
> *We are too pleased with ourselves,*
> *When our dreams have come true,*
> *Because we dreamed too little,*
> *When we arrived safely,*
> *Because we sailed too close to the shore.*
> *~Sir Francis Drake*

A poem? Why, with all that was happening would he choose to write poetry? Why not something more helpful? I broke the seal, still feeling as though I was eavesdropping on someone else's conversation.

Dear Kate,

You need to trust me, and do exactly as I say, because I know you. I know you forward and backward. I know you're cautious. I know you're loyal, but I know you better still. You're terrified. You're afraid of so many things that you've lost count. But one fear screams above all the others. You're afraid that you'll fail this time. Why not? You failed before. I understand, Kate. I've spent years terrified that if I did what God has called me to do I would only endanger everyone around me.

What I'm asking you to do is crazy. You should be afraid. You should be petrified. But don't let that fear drive you. God hasn't given us a spirit of fear. Don't let it be the deciding factor. Don't let it stop you.

They're coming for me, Kate, and there's nowhere to run. I haven't got much time. I know you still don't understand. I know you must think I'm a ghost or a phantom or a madman, but I'm begging you. Please hold on to my little girl. She needs you. Don't let her, or anyone else tell you otherwise. Don't think that you're replaceable, Katherine. I didn't choose just anyone. I chose you. I need you to do this for me, because no one else can. God is with you, Kate, whether you still believe that or not. He has laid His hand on you from the day you were born. Don't listen to your fear.

I can hear them coming. I can't ignore it any longer. I know where they'll take me. You know it too. You've been there before on your darkest night. You went to visit someone else, but I was there. I was watching.

Sometimes God asks us to do wild things, insane things, that we would never have the courage to do on our own. Rely on His strength. If you don't, you will fail. But, if you trust Him, no weapon formed against you can prosper. Put your trust in Him, Kate, and be prepared to meet me, where your darkest night found both of us.

Simon Cephas

CHAPTER 12

Don't think. Move. The same fearful words that had forced me to row that skiff propelled me now. Deep inside, I knew that this was the right decision, but that didn't stop my hands from trembling or my stomach from tightening. The rain had poured all night. After she had drawn me a map directing me to a home where we could rest, I had decided that the best time to leave would be an hour or so before dawn.

"The Rowtons are good people," she assured me now. "They'll take care of you as long as you need. Follow the map, or they'll be impossible to find, all tucked away in the woods."

"Thank you again for everything," I said, mechanically.

She waved me away as if she'd done nothing at all for us. "I'll go fetch the girl."

Again my stomach knotted. She was the last piece to fall into place. Emily didn't know we were leaving. We'd made all the plans after she'd gone to sleep, and if she refused to come with me, all of our plans would be for naught. I silently prayed that the widow would explain it in a way that would make her understand, without frightening her.

To my surprise, Emily appeared a short time later, tired, but dressed and ready to leave. She didn't say a word, her lips drawn into a thin, pale line. I stared at the widow in amazement, wondering how on earth she'd done it, but afraid to ask, as if it would break the spell.

"Are you ready?" I asked Emily.

She gave a groggy nod.

"All right, then." I picked up the leather satchel the widow had given me. Inside was the letter from Cephas, and Jackson's pistol. As the front door opened to a dark, rainy morning, I took Emily's hand in mine. A line from the letter came back to me. *God hasn't given us a spirit of fear.* I finished the verse in my mind. *But of power and of love and of a sound mind.* I couldn't let fear drive me this time.

We made our way, up out of the rainy valley as the sky began to lighten. We were both cold, wet, and miserable by the time we reached the road, despite the warm clothes the widow had provided for us.

I withdrew the map from the satchel, careful to shield the ink drawing from the rain.

"When are we going back?" Emily asked, teeth chattering.

Her words confused me. "We're not."

She slipped her hand out of mine, and stood still on the path.

"Emily, what's wrong?"

"We need to go back." I could hear the edge of terror in her voice.

"Don't be silly. We're going to a different house. Then, we're going to find your grandfather."

She looked so stunned, that I thought she might not ever move from her spot. Then, without warning, she turned and raced toward the valley.

"Emily!" I shouted, running after her. I overtook her in moments, and caught her by the shoulders, trying to catch her eye. "Emily, what are you doing?"

She looked up at me, frightened tears streaming down her face. "I want to go back." She fought against me. I had never seen her like this.

"We can't go back it's not safe!" I fell to my knees on the

muddy ground, gripping both of her arms and forcing her to face me.

She looked at me, not angry or defiant, but terrified.

"What's wrong?" I asked.

Her lower lip trembled. "You lied to me."

"I didn't!"

"She said that we were just going for a walk."

The Widow Lawrence hadn't told her everything. That was why she had agreed to come. "Emily, you have to believe me. I didn't know. I thought she told you."

"No!" she yelled, trying to pry my fingers off of her shoulders without success. When she realized it was hopeless, she sank to the ground, sobbing.

This was no conjured performance. She was terrified. I leaned over her, wondering what to do.

"Why can't you just go home?" Her words were like a splash of cold water to my face.

"What?"

"Just go home. You don't want me. So just go home!"

I felt the same dull, sickening pain I'd experienced when I landed in the longboat. The air had been punched from my lungs, and I could hardly move. The walls I had put up now sought to crush me. She had seen right through me. "Emily…I–"

A sound made me stop.

Horses. One of them whinnied in the distance.

Voices. Men's voices called over the rain.

In a panic, I lifted Emily to her feet, gripping her hand and leading her toward the woods on the side of the road. I ducked behind the trunk of an enormous tree, just before the group of men came around the bend in the road. I knew we weren't far enough away from the path, but I was afraid to move, afraid to make a sound. I pulled Emily into my lap and held her tightly, afraid she wouldn't cooperate. She fought against my grip until I realized I was holding her too tightly. I loosened my arms around her. As the men came around the corner we could hear their voices drifting over the drizzling rain.

"And you're sure they're still there?" asked an eerily familiar voice.

"Brice, would I have walked all night in this storm if I wasn't?"

They halted, just on the other side of the tree, and the sailor pointed the way.

"Down in the valley. Last house on the left."

"Anyone else there?"

"Just a little old widow."

"Perfect. This should be easy."

"Haven't seen a sign of Connors or Jack."

"All in good time." Brice gave a chuckle. "Scot can find anyone he wants. They'll be dead in less than a fortnight. I can promise you that."

I clapped my hand over Emily's mouth. She couldn't make a sound. Not now.

Brice's friend laughed and they continued down the road, toward the widow's house. I shuddered to think of what they might do, but something in me made me feel that the widow could handle herself.

I released Emily, expecting her to dart out of my lap, but she didn't move. I glanced down at the map in my hand, and decided to consult it before we went any farther. Ink poured off of the parchment as it disintegrated in the rain. The map was useless.

· · ·

We staggered through the forest, hopelessly lost. I could hear Emily's teeth chattering.

"My hands are prickly," she shouted, stumbling over a tree root beside me.

"They're just cold," I mumbled. My hands weren't

tingling. I couldn't feel them any longer.

"Can we stop?" she asked, for what must have been the ninetieth time.

I finally relented. We were going in circles. All the trees looked the same. James had always said I had no sense of direction. He had been absolutely right. He would have known where to go.

I sat down in the soggy earth, leaning against a tree. Emily did the same, resting against the tree, opposite me. I had stopped believing an hour ago that the Rowtons even existed, but I still couldn't find my way to the road.

I glanced down at the crumpled wad of disintegrating parchment in my hand, and tossed it as far as I could, silently punishing myself once again for letting it get wet. I leaned my head against the tree trunk behind me and closed my eyes. I was *not* going to cry. It wouldn't help anything, and once I started, I knew I would never stop. We would just be here until dark, and then freeze to death overnight. I just needed to rest a few minutes. Just a few minutes of silence.

"What's that?" Emily's voice grated in my ears.

"What?" I asked sharply, without opening my eyes.

"That."

I opened them reluctantly, and saw her pointing to the tree trunk above me. Glancing up, I didn't see anything out of the ordinary. "I don't know." I closed my eyes again, hoping she would drop the subject and let me think.

"It's a hand print."

I didn't bother to open my eyes again. "No it's not. It's just a tree."

"Yes, it is."

I heard rustling and glanced up to see her, standing right over me, studying the tree bark. "Emily, it's nothing," I sighed, twisting around to get a better view of where she was pointing. I could only see a dark blot on the trunk. I stood, and leaned closer. It *was* a hand print. It had run somewhat in the rain, but it was unmistakable, staining the bark a dark muddy red color. It was blood.

I gasped, pulling Emily a step back, as if the hand would reach out and grab her. The rainy silence was eerie. I glanced down. Emily was staring at me as though I had just lost my mind. She hadn't noticed, or didn't care that something was wrong. Relief coursed through me, as logic resumed its reign. I was overreacting. A hunter must have been out here and skinned an animal.

"What was that?" I jumped, hearing a rustling nearby. I motioned for Emily to be completely silent, listening for the sound again. My gaze wandered over the endless landscape of trees, searching for any sign of life. I was being ridiculous. It was probably just an animal, a harmless, innocent animal.

Emily jerked her hand away from mine, and I realized I must have been crushing it in my fear.

I froze. I had seen something move in the greenery. I let my eyes sweep the section of forest in front of me again, slower this time. I saw it again, in the midst of thick trees, huge green eyes were staring at us. I gripped Emily's hand again. The green eyes met mine. How had I missed the face that was watching us through the branches? The face was frightened and wary, like a doe, ready to bolt at any moment.

"Please," I said gently. "We're lost. We're looking for the home of Thomas Rowton. Is it nearby?"

The trees rustled and a girl as thin as a spring sapling emerged from them. She must have been twelve or thirteen. Her eyes were the color of the spring leaves that clustered around her, her hair curled into ringlets around her face, the tan color of tree bark. No wonder I hadn't seen her. I had never believed in dryads, elves, or fairies in the woods, but at that moment, it wouldn't have been hard to convince me of their existence.

"Why are you seeking them?" she asked, a slight brogue to her airy voice.

I was speechless, trying to remember why we were seeking them. "Widow Lawrence sent us."

She nodded, and turned as if to leave. Afraid she would vanish, I followed after her. She moved noiselessly. I couldn't understand how she was finding her way. Then, as if she had conjured it into existence, a cabin came into view, overrun with vines and shrubbery. It was so well hidden I would never have found it.

"Thank you," I breathed.

She nodded, speaking in a hushed voice. "Thomas Rowton is my father."

I looked down at Emily. She was as enamored with this elfin stranger as I was. The girl's bare feet padded up the wooden stairs, onto the porch of the cabin. She pushed open the door. "Mama?"

I followed after her, standing behind her, as Emily and I stepped into the darkened room. Steam filled the little cottage as a woman inside hung blankets to dry beside a fire, pulling them from a tub of steaming water. She turned at the girl's voice.

"Janey, what on earth?"

"The widow sent them, Mama."

The woman was tall and thin, and must have looked exactly like the girl when she was younger. "Come in out of the rain, then," she said, her gentle voice matching her graceful movement as she hung the last blanket, and walked toward us.

"Emily?" The woman's gaze drifted from the little girl to me. "And who's this?"

"Katherine Elyot," I stammered. "I'm…I'm a friend."

The woman nodded, and looked back to Emily, dropping to her knees, and put her arms on the Emily's shoulders. "How you've grown. Such a beautiful young lady."

Emily gave a chattering smile.

"And soaked to the skin, too." The woman rubbed her

hands together, and stood leading us toward the fire. "I suppose my blankets will just have to make room." She slid them to either side of the makeshift laundry line that was tied to the low-hanging rafters of the cabin's ceiling. "I suppose we'll be making them stretch before the day is out. There's not much else to offer you, I'm afraid."

I glanced over my shoulder to thank her as we settled by the fire, when I noticed two tawny heads peeking from a doorway that must have led to a second room. They were identical except that one was smaller than the other.

"It's all right, boys," their mother called. "Look who the Good Lord has brought us."

They stepped shyly into the room, watching us.

"Henry, Jacob, do you remember Emily Blake?"

The taller boy nodded. The younger one shook his head.

"And this is Miss Elyot."

Just then, the front door creaked open and a towering, broad-shouldered figure filled the doorway. The shy boys both broke into grins and flew toward the man. He laughed, putting a hand on each of their heads, and leading them into the house. "Did you catch something, Papa?"

The man had a deep, rumbling laugh. "Not this time."

I caught a glimpse of their mother who was not smiling. As the door closed behind the man, she looked fretful. Janey wore the same face. As soon as the boys had stopped their jumping and their father had sent them into the next room, he turned to his wife.

"Where is he?" she asked her husband.

His face broke into a grin. "He's headed home."

She put a hand to her heart. "Praise God."

The only one who looked disappointed was Janey. The girl stared at the floor.

"Who's this, then?" he asked turning to us. It was easy to see where Janey had picked up her brogue.

"You remember little Emily."

He nodded. "Indeed I do. You've grown up since I saw you last."

Emily beamed.

Mistress Rowton motioned to me. "And this is Miss Elyot."

"How do you do?" he greeted, removing his dripping hat. "And what is it that brings you so far from the world?"

I opened my mouth to reply.

"No." His wife cut me short. "We'll talk about all of that over a nice hot meal, but for now, I want all you men to go into the next room and shut the door. We've got to get these girls out of the soaking wet clothes and into something more comfortable before they catch their death. Janey, fetch your other dress, the one you outgrew, and see if my old working dress is in any condition to be worn. They'll need to put on something while their clothes dry out."

The woman of the house had us warm and dry before another hour had passed. I wondered if this was what it felt like to have a family, a mother to fuss over you, brothers and sisters running about. I glanced at Emily and had the feeling she was wondering the same thing.

• • •

As the fire crackled in the hearth, the sound of the rain had finally relented. The Rowton family gathered around the fire with their supper in steaming bowls.

"So tell us where you've come from," Thomas Rowton invited.

My stomach tightened. I stared at the ground. "It's quite a long story." I wasn't even sure if I remembered where it started or how long ago it was. It felt like years. I glanced up seeing five expectant faces, and realized, that living out here as they did, these people probably lived for long stories. The two youngest, Henry and Jacob had their eyes wide with expectation as they inched closer.

Where to begin?

I cleared my throat. "We met many miles north of here. Emily had been in an accident, and she had been thrown from a carriage and fallen from a cliff."

The littlest boy's mouth dropped open, showing off the gap where his two front teeth undoubtedly belonged.

"Emily's mother and father were killed in the accident. Their carriage went over the cliff, and Emily fell onto a ledge below."

The adults exchanged grief-stricken looks, and I was reminded that I was the only one who knew about the death of Emily's parents, and that wherever I went, I would be the bearer of this news.

"Did you really fall off of a cliff?" The older boy hunched forward, gazing at Emily in awe.

She drew back, frightened by the attention.

"Henry, don't interrupt," his mother chided, her voice tight with emotion.

I continued with the chronicle of our journey, and was amazed at how much the Rowtons, especially the boys, were captured by the story. It certainly hadn't been enjoyable to live through. I left out many of the details. Losing James was one of them. I didn't trust myself to tell it without crying.

When I reached the part about the ship, it was too much for two little boys to hear sitting down. They jumped to their feet and assaulted both of us with countless questions about ships, oceans, and sailors.

By the time their parents had seated them again, the two boys fidgeted helplessly, desperate for a happy ending. I told them of my escape with the help of a sailor, and how the man in the water had tried to drown me by holding onto the oars.

When I ended the tale at the widow's house, the two boys were disappointed. I could tell they had hoped one of us would shoot something, or fall off one more cliff for good measure.

Their parents, however, were exchanging looks that I couldn't understand. At one point in my story, Mistress Rowton had sent a questioning glance to her husband, to which he had nodded. I couldn't begin to understand what the silent signals meant, but Janey did. Her green eyes were wide as she read her parents' faces.

"Were you really on a ship?" The older boy directed his question at shy little Emily.

She nodded timidly.

"And you escaped?" The youngest one had the sweetest little lisp.

She nodded again.

"*You* wouldn't have." The older one said to his little brother, putting an arm around his neck and wrestling him to the ground.

"Henry, Jacob, Enough." The boys halted at their father's deep, echoing voice.

"We might go on a ship one day." The little one's toothless grin had officially stolen my heart. "Papa says if—"

"Jacob," his father interjected. "Fetch the Bible, won't you?"

Jacob did as his father instructed, completely oblivious to the tension that had arisen like an unexpected storm. His brother, who must have been Henry, probably didn't understand it either, but was obviously enjoying an opportunity to glare condescendingly at Jacob and elbow him in the ribs when he sat down again.

"Boys," their father warned, before he began again. "It'll be short since we've already had such a story from Miss Elyot, but what she said reminded me of something. He flipped the fluttering pages with skill and ease, finding the page within moments. "Do you remember what we read last night?"

The boys glanced at one another guiltily. "It…tt said my name," Jacob offered timidly.

"That it did." Master Rowton smiled affectionately at his

son. "Do you remember what it said about the waters?"

Janey nodded. The boys shook their heads.

"Janey, what did it say?"

"They wouldn't flow over us."

I somehow managed to keep my jaw from dropping. Those words had found me, even here.

Master Rowton found his place in the Bible. "Jacob, stop your fidgeting. Hold still and listen. *'When thou passest through the waters, I will be with thee; and through the rivers, they shall not overflow thee.'* God protected Miss Elyot and Miss Emily in the waters and the rivers, didn't He?"

They all nodded, even Emily.

"And so He will protect all of us, and bring us safely home."

CHAPTER 13

I stirred from a long, peaceful sleep, not knowing or caring what time of day it was. Pulling the blankets up under my chin, I opened my eyes and waited for the light to make sense of my surroundings. I was alone in the cabin, hearing the sounds of laughter and joyful shrieks outside. Warm, late sunlight streamed through the window. I wondered if it was just my exhaustion or if these truly were the softest blankets I had even encountered. I glanced down at them, then sat up with a start. The morning sun revealed what I had not been able to see in the dark of the previous night. The sheets, though washed and thoroughly cleaned, were streaked with muddy red stains. All of the secretive glances and wordless conversations of the previous day that had led me to believe I was not the only guest the Rowtons had received in the last week. My heart began to pound as I wondered what on earth had happened to the last guest and why their bedding was stained with blood.

The front door clicked shut, and I looked up to see Mistress Rowton, her long hair down, her feet bare, a bundle of plants in her arms. "Up with the sun, are we?"

My heart slowed to its normal rate again, and I was ashamed at the worries that had flown through my mind. I apologized for sleeping late, but Mistress Rowton dismissed my comment. I considered asking after the stains, but caught myself. It was not my place to ask. These were not wealthy people, yet they had showed us every kindness. I would not have criticized their hospitality for all the world.

Heading outside, I sat on the steps watching Emily running and laughing with the Rowton children. I'd never seen her this happy.

"Janey, you can be Miss Kate. Emily can be herself. Jacob will be the captain, and I'll be the sailor!" Henry ordered.

"I want to be the sailor!" Jacob moaned.

"Well you can't!" Henry's diplomacy was breathtaking.

"Jacob," his sister soothed. "You can be the sailor next time."

He pouted, and I stifled a smile.

They acted out the story, starting with the cliff, but just when Janey was reaching for Emily's hand, the older girl noticed me, and her cheeks turned a dark shade of pink. I only smiled, hoping she would continue, but the spell had broken. She dismissed herself from the game, coming instead to sit next to me, and watch the children play. With the loss of Janey, Henry told Jacob he could play me instead of the captain. Jacob declined in disgust.

"Do you often play with your brothers?" I asked the girl beside me.

She straightened. "I occupy them to keep them out of Mama's way, but their games are usually silly."

I bit my lower lip, trying to keep back my smile. I had seen the utter enjoyment on her face. "That's very sacrificial of you."

She beamed. "Thank you."

I watched them play in the morning sunlight for what must have been an hour. Janey soon grew tired of watching and went inside, but as I enjoyed their theatrics there grew a vague, sick feeling inside me. I couldn't quite place where it had come from.

"They'll be playing that until the sun goes down."

I started and glanced up to see Thomas Rowton standing behind me, watching the children play. I hadn't heard him come out.

He laughed, watching Jacob tackle his brother to the ground while Emily watched, astonished at such brutish behavior. "It was hard getting them to sleep last night. They went on and on about your thrilling story. You're quite the hero."

"Please don't." I felt the tears forming, blurring the sun-dappled stage on which the children performed. "I am many things, Master Rowton," I managed in a husky voice. "But a hero has never been one of them." One tear slid down my cheek, and I hoped he wouldn't notice.

"I didn't mean to upset you," he apologized.

"No, it's not you." I tried in vain to keep my tears back. "I'm sorry."

He waited as I brushed them away, embarrassed.

"Something bothering you, then?"

I nodded, unable to speak around the lump in my throat.

"Care to ease your mind?"

I glanced up at him as he leaned against the door frame. Master Rowton was a busy man. He had a house to tend, a family to feed. Why was he taking the time to talk to me?

I gazed into the endless sea of trees. "I'm not who you think I am. I'm not who Emily thinks I am. It's all a lie, a pretense, a joke."

I heard the floor boards creaking and turned to see him seating himself on the top step. "And just who are you?"

Plenty of words came to mind. *Orphan. Idiot. Traitor.* "I'm a fool."

"And why is that?"

I gazed at the little girl dancing back and forth in the shade with her playmates. "I couldn't protect her."

"Protecting her isn't your job. It's God's."

"Then why didn't He?" I couldn't stop the words from flying out of my mouth. "Why did He let her parents die? Why did He let me find her? I shouldn't have. That note wasn't really to me, and now Cephas is sending more of them, telling me that it's only going to get harder, and that I have to keep going. But I can't! I can't go any farther. I feel like such a liar for pretending that I belong here, and that I know what I'm doing." I buried my face in my hands.

He said nothing. I didn't blame him. How could I expect him to have all the answers I was searching for?

"Do you still have one of the letters?" he asked.

I reached inside the satchel the widow had given me and retrieved the letter, handing it to him, hoping he could make some sense of it.

He examined it for some time. "This isn't to you?" he asked finally.

I shook my head.

"You're not Katherine?"

"I'm not *that* Katherine."

"How do you know?"

I bit my lower lip, trying to restrain my tears. "Because that letter is written to someone who's brave and loyal and irreplaceable."

"And?"

"I am foolishly, hopelessly, laughably replaceable. Besides, it's impossible."

"Why?"

Again, I struggled, searching for an answer. "Because, I've never met the man. The odds are too great."

"Odds don't usually apply to God. Or to Cephas, for that matter."

I turned away. "I can't continue. It wouldn't be fair to Emily."

"And you don't need to."

I glanced up in hopeful expectation. Those were the

sweetest words I'd heard in weeks.

He nodded, slowly. "You've been through a lifetime of sorrows in only a few days, if I understood your story."

"I hope I will never experience anything like it again."

"Then take a time of rest and relief, but don't forget sometimes God takes us out to sea, because we'll never find Him in the harbor."

I watched him, trying to comprehend his meaning.

"He has to push us, disturb us, take us where we would never go on our own."

"My life hasn't just been disturbed," I couldn't soften the bitterness of my voice. "It's been tossed and rolled and wrecked."

"But without that tossing and rolling, we'd never cry out. If we weren't about to wreck, we'd never start searching for God."

"I did," I said, thinking of all the years I'd spent with the Durhams, studying, listening, learning. "I was quite the militant Bible student before my life was tossed."

"Jesus doesn't want a Bible student, Miss Elyot. He wants a child, a follower. He wants you to seek Him on the good days, and trust Him on the hard ones."

I shrugged, wishing I could believe him. "It's like trusting a stranger."

He didn't look shocked or disapproving. He just smiled back at me. "I've seen the way that little girl leans on you. You were a stranger to her, weren't you?"

"But she doesn't trust me. She knows I'd rather be anywhere else. She would rather I left her here than try to help her anymore, and she has every reason to feel that way."

"I wouldn't go that far."

I thought about how furious I'd been with Jackson for the false promises he'd made to her. "I can't keep lying to her. I'm not who she thinks I am."

"God knows who you are."

The comment brought a sickening fear to my stomach. "Maybe that's why He's punishing me."

"He's not punishing you." His firmness surprised me.

"You don't know what I've done."

"It doesn't matter." He gazed at the children playing in the leaf-covered earth. "If Jacob or Henry or Janey ran away from home, they would be cold and hungry and frightened, but not because I was punishing them. That's just what happens when you run away from home. If we run from God we're going to find ourselves lonely, depressed, and terrified. That doesn't mean God is punishing us. That's just what happens when you run away from your Heavenly Father. Now, if I'm looking for my lost children, am I going to threaten them with their coming punishments?" His eyes shone with a father's love as he shook his head. "I'll call them by name, and when I find them, I'll pick them up and carry them back home."

"I wish it were that simple. God's voice is just too hard to hear. I don't know what He wants from me."

"He wants you to run from your hiding place and into His arms. You know something, Miss Elyot? There is still so much I don't understand about God, but I know He loves us. It's all I can be sure of in this life." He stood to his feet. "And I know something else." He placed the letter in my hand, and pointed to the word *Kate*. "He's calling you by name. I don't know how much clearer you want Him to be."

• • •

He's not punishing you. I considered Thomas Rowton's words and wondered if he would have said that if he'd known who I was and what I'd done. He'd said it didn't matter. I'd tried so hard to convince myself that it wasn't my fault, but there was no way around it.

Charles Lindon never gave me anything more than a smile, and in return, I'd handed over my home, my life, and everyone I loved. He'd been in town for a year, but I was never able to tell if he saw me as anything more than a little girl. He asked me so many questions about our church, our way, and he was especially interested in our Bible. I had asked him about the missing page, and he claimed to know nothing about it. I told myself that it had always been missing. Reverend Durham surely would have known why it was gone if I'd asked him, but I never did, just in case. Master Lindon never approached me, never promised me anything, never let me believe we were more than friends, but that didn't matter. I still gave him the Bible. I still showed him the print shop. I still told him the town was wary and suspicious for a reason, even if I didn't tell him what that reason was.

It happened on a cold, raw day in November. James had left the village to visit his sweetheart in the next town. I was nearly sixteen years old, and thought myself quite the young lady. It had been a hard year. Disease had taken Miss Durham home to be with Jesus, and though I believed that with all my heart, there had still been many hard days when my faith was weaker than my grief.

I knew something was wrong the moment I turned onto the main road through town. A wagon and horses I didn't recognize stood right in front of the print shop, where all of the Puritan pamphlets were hidden. I'd had nightmares about a day like this. I ran down the street and turned into the print shop. Strange men had lifted the floor boards, exposing the tracts and pamphlets beneath. The workmen didn't even see me as they tore up the floor. Years of labor and concealment were all destroyed in a matter of minutes. I begged them to stop. There was a mistake. They didn't understand. Finally one of them grabbed me by my shoulders and shook me.

"Where's the Reverend?"

"I—I don't know!" I stuttered.

"Yes you do, you little whelp! Where is he?"

"I don't know!" I shrieked, tears pouring down my face.

"Campbell," someone called from the doorway. "Davys found him."

"No!" I cried as the man released his grip on me. "No!"

I fled from the print shop. They would brand the cheek of anyone involved with pamphlets, but when they found out that Reverend Durham was the writer they would hang him. I ran down the street, frantically searching for anyone who would help, but the people were all frightened of being identified with the crime.

I ran to Master Lindon's home, my feet hardly touching the ground. I pounded on the door, begging him for his help, but he wasn't home. There was nowhere else to run.

Just then I heard the sound of cart wheels and turned to see the unfamiliar carriage making its way down the street with a guarded escort. In the back of the cart sat Reverend Durham. I instinctively ran toward the cart, but stopped in the middle of the street. Sitting next to the driver, riding proudly through town was Charles Lindon, escorting his catch, his prize, his prisoner.

I couldn't move. Everything I had believed about him. It was all a lie.

He saw me and glanced down, his wicked grin never wavering. Reaching a hand up, he tipped his hat and winked at me, thanking me for all my help.

I had done this.

I couldn't cry. When I looked up, I was standing in the print shop with no memory of having walked there. Destruction was everywhere. The printing press had been hacked to pieces. Black ink stained what was left of the splintered floor boards. I stood in the middle of the mess I'd made, unable to move in the damp, dark hole we'd used to hide the precious pamphlets. I sank down in the dirt, too afraid to move or to speak or to cry.

• • •

The Rowton children went inside with Emily, but I sat on those steps for most of the day. The rain returned, and I watched the trees from under the eaves.

I looked down at my name etched in ink on the parchment. This journey was going to break my heart. I might never finish it. It would pull me to my limits and through my greatest fears. It had already. I knew if I was on my own, I would go insane before I could be of any use to Emily. My fear would drive me to madness, but Master Rowton's words came so strongly. *He's calling you by name.* Could that be? Were those letters God's way of calling me? I shoved the idea aside. There was no chance of that. God knew the traitor I was, that I couldn't be trusted. He understood that I was completely incapable even if the writer of these letters obviously did not.

Looking down at my side, I jumped when I noticed Emily sitting beside me. She had been so silent that I hadn't noticed her. She said nothing. Her chatter had irritated me when we first set out. Now I wondered what I could do to get it back.

"The Rowtons are kind people," I said cautiously.

"I don't want to leave. I want to stay here."

I rubbed my eyes in frustration. "Emily."

"I could stay here," she interrupted. "I could stay and you could go home."

I covered my weary eyes with one hand.

"I know that's what you want." Her thin, airy voice had tears in it.

"I just want you to be safe."

"I am," she said, quickly. "I just need to wait."

I looked at her, but she wouldn't meet my eye. "Emily." I felt my throat constrict. "He's not coming back."

A tear spilled down her cheek. She didn't answer.

"You can't continue to wait for him. He's gone. He's probably out on the ocean by now." *Or at the bottom of it.* I thought with a shiver.

"He said he would come and he will," she murmured.

I couldn't take this anymore. I stood to my feet, tromped down the steps, and began pacing in front of them. "I have done all I can to help you. I've done things I never dreamed of doing, gone places I pray I'll never go again. All that sailor did was abandon you, and make promises that were impossible to keep. And yet you would wait a hundred years for him to come back, but you wouldn't trust me to take you on a walk. Why?" I turned to see her wide dark eyes, staring at me as if I'd lost my mind. Perhaps I had. I knew I couldn't expect an answer. She probably didn't even know what I was talking about. I turned to leave. I needed to think. I needed to be alone.

"Jack smiles."

I spun around, confused by her words. "He what?"

She shrugged. "He smiles."

I could feel the angry heat rush to my face. A hundred, biting replies coming to mind, but I stopped myself. That was really all she wanted. Something so simple, yet impossible. I was too tired, too frustrated, too frightened to even attempt a decent smile.

Emily drew her knees up to her chest hugging them as she stared straight ahead. "He'll come back. I know he will! He loves me, and he never…"

I climbed the stairs slowly, sitting next to her. "He never what?"

She didn't answer.

"Emily," I placed a gentle hand under her chin. "Don't be afraid. You can tell me."

She met my eyes, and I got the uncanny feeling that I wasn't staring into the eyes of a six-year-old, but one who had suffered enough for a whole lifetime. "He never lost me."

"Oh, Emily," I scooped her up into my lap and let her sob, as I held her. "I know. I know I lost you. I'm so sorry, but *I* love you. I love you, and I'm not going to leave you here, or anywhere else. I'm going to get you home, and if I can't do that, then you and I will find a place to live, and I'll take care of you. I love you, Emily." And I was astonished to find that I meant every word. No. I had promised myself. I had vowed never to fall into that trap again. For reasons I could never understand, I endangered and hurt everyone I loved. I couldn't let it happen again. I needed to push her away before she got hurt, but something deeper prevented me. It was the love I had so feared. I loved this child with such an intensity that I knew I would do anything to keep her safe. I knew I would never let anything touch her. Was this how mothers felt about their children? Where had this feeling come from? It was wonderful and powerful and it terrified me.

CHAPTER 14

Thomas Rowton's long strides made him quickly visible in the forest brush. I knew I had to speak with him, but was afraid of what he might tell me.

"Master Rowton."

He didn't hear me, or even see me. As he reached the front door I saw that his face was ashen. Wondering what was wrong, I followed him inside.

His wife was facing the window when he entered, but must have heard his heavy footfalls. "Did you fetch me that flour from the widow?" She turned and her smile vanished at the sight of her husband. A silence fell over the little house. Even the boys stopped their fidgeting, and stared at their Papa.

"What's wrong?" Mistress Rowton asked.

"She's gone."

I grew sick thinking of Brice and the other sailor riding toward her house the day before.

Mistress Rowton placed a hand over her mouth as tears filled her eyes. "God help us," she whispered.

"Why would they take her?" I asked.

"No one said she's been taken anywhere. She could have finally made up her mind to leave like everyone else." Thomas Rowton's voice brought a steadiness back to my thoughts.

"But she'd be all alone," Janey said.

Her father nodded. "I'm going to find her."

Mistress Rowton appeared worried and about to protest when she caught his eye.

"Orphans and Widows in their trouble," he said simply.

She closed her eyes, nodding in agreement.

I glanced at Emily, standing beside Janey. She was my responsibility as the widow was the Rowtons'.

"Do you know where they're keeping Cephas?" I asked.

They all turned to me as if they'd forgotten I was there, and I realized the question was completely out of place.

"They'll have taken him to London. Newgate Prison." Thomas Rowton answered.

My stomach churned and my knees felt weak. *Not there. Anywhere, but there.* How could they expect me to take a little girl to that terrible place? Then, my own memories of Newgate Prison ran through my mind. It had been the darkest night of my life, but I wouldn't have traded it for anything. Cephas needed to see Emily. It could very possibly be the last time they would ever see one another. Every day that he remained in that prison his life remained uncertain.

"We need to go." The sound of my own voice startled me. I glanced at Emily, expecting resistance, but she nodded and came to my side, entwining her hand in mine.

Master Rowton nodded. "You're right. He'll want to see Emily, and he'll no doubt have special instructions for you."

The term *special instructions* sent a jolt of fear through me, but I remembered my promise to Emily, and it gave me the smallest measure of courage.

• • •

Leaving the Rowtons was a difficult parting. Each of the boys stared at the ground, and were the quietest I'd ever seen them. Henry told Emily she wasn't a bad playmate for a girl, and

Jacob graciously bestowed upon her his favorite rock and a handsome toad, which he'd been keeping in his shirt. Emily accepted both gifts with no less grace than if they had been flowers and sonnets.

Janey brushed away tears as she hugged Emily goodbye. Mistress Rowton said again what a charming young lady she was growing up to be, and Master Rowton lifted her into his arms reminding her to behave herself and say her prayers every night. She promised to do both, and was set back down on the ground.

For a brief moment, I wondered if I was doing the right thing. She was so happy here, and these people loved her. My doubts raged inside me as I said goodbye to each of the Rowtons, youngest to oldest. Mistress Rowton gave me my satchel, having packed it with "all the necessaries." I peeked in the top, and saw enough food for several days. Just as indecision threatened to drown my resolve, Master Rowton looked right at me. "You're doing a good thing, Kate Elyot. Don't let the Devil tell you otherwise."

I was choking back tears as I thanked him. He was right. I couldn't turn back. I had a job to do.

As I was turning to leave, Master Rowton cleared his throat. "When you see Cephas, would you give him a message for me?"

"Of course." I said, attempting to read his expression.

"Tell him that Timothy is on his way home." A grin tugged at the corners of his mouth. He glanced at his wife. She was also smiling, as if they two shared a secret. "And if the two of you should meet up, give Timothy our regards. If you hurry, you just might catch him in London. He'll be headed to Newgate as well."

As we walked down the road I dropped the signet ring into the satchel. It was far too heavy and awkward to fit on my hand, but I was nervous about letting it out of my sight for even a moment. I waited for Emily as she released her gifted toad into a nearby puddle. I watched her, curious as to why she had come so willingly without so much as a moment's hesitation this morning. When I asked her, she took a long time to answer.

"Jack told me to listen to you," she said at last.

For the first time, I doubted Emily's honesty. "When did he tell you that?" I was unable to keep the edge out of my voice. I hadn't heard him say that or anything else that had been the slightest bit helpful.

"He whispered it to me when he brought you to the widow's house."

A vague memory flashed in my mind. I had been too furious to even notice at the time, but now I remembered his smug grin as he whispered in her ear, saying something about it being just between the two of them. "He said that?"

She nodded. "He said that you were very brave and very smart, and that I should listen to you."

My mind raced. Why would he say something like that? After all of the slights and insults he'd dealt me why would he sing my praises to Emily? Was he just that desperate to shirk his responsibility? Perhaps it had been his way of making up for calling me inadequate. But what if he had been sincere? The thought made my cheeks burn.

That was impossible. I reminded myself that there was nothing sincere about him. He had lied to Emily, abandoned her, and if she ever found out why it would break her heart. Yet my heart still drummed as I wondered if his father had found him.

The clouds and chilly air abated somewhat as we neared London. I remembered how I had despised the noise, the stench, the crowded streets, but now I could see buildings in the distance as we crested a hill, and the familiar sight made me feel safe. If I closed my eyes I could imagine that none of this was real, that if I went to the Seven Stars Tavern, I would walk right to our room and James would be there, and this nightmare would all be reversed.

"Kate, are you ever afraid?"

Her question caught me by surprise. I didn't know whether to laugh or cry. "Everyone is afraid sometimes."

She looked at me. "I mean, really afraid."

I understood her question and knew it was not something to make light of, but even as I formed an answer, the pit of my stomach twisted. "Yes, Emily. I have been."

"What do you do to stop being afraid?"

Her questions were taking all my strength to answer. I knew I ought to say something carefree. I ought to tell her that I simply faced my fears, but that wasn't true. I stuffed them in the back of my mind, and used all of my strength to keep them there, afraid that if I let them out, I would go mad. "I don't know," I bit back my tears, feeling helpless.

"Whenever we were afraid, my mother would teach me a verse from the Bible. And once I'd learned it, I wasn't as scared as before."

"What verses did she teach you?" I asked, seeing a chance to distract us both.

She shook her head. "I don't remember them all."

"What do you remember?"

A wistful smile crossed her face. "I remember the one about the Shepherd and the field and the waters."

"Sounds like a Psalm."

She nodded. "But I don't remember how it starts."

I choked back the knot in my throat. "*The Lord is my Shepherd.*"

"I shall not want." She paused, trying to remember.

"He maketh me to lie down in green pastures."

"And leads me next to the still waters." Once again, she paused, puzzled.

"He restoreth my soul," I said, my voice low.

"And leadeth me in the paths of…right…rich…"

"Righteousness," I finished. "For His Name's sake."

I felt her grip my hand a little tighter. "The next part always makes me sad."

Both of our voices grew hushed as I recited the next section, Emily joining in whenever she could remember. "Yea, though I should walk through the valley of the shadow of death, I will fear no evil. For Thou art with me. Thy rod and thy staff, they comfort me." Emily was quiet as though she didn't know any more, but I couldn't halt the words. They had never been so real to me. "Thou doest prepare a table before me, in the sight of mine adversaries: Thou doest anoint my head with oil and my cup runneth over. Doubtless, kindness and mercy shall follow me all the days of my life, and I shall remain a long season…"

Emily's breathy voice joined mine. "In the house of the Lord." Her voice was hardly a whisper. "I like that one."

I nodded. "So do I."

"Did your mother teach you to say that, too?"

I gave her hand a gentle squeeze. "No, Love. A very, very dear friend taught me to say it."

"I have a question."

I looked down at her, hoping that it was easier than all of her previous questions.

"If God is a Shepherd, does that make us sheep?"

I nodded. "I suppose it does. I think there's another verse that says we're His people and the sheep in His pasture."

"What else does it say?" She moved closer to me as she walked.

I stopped, turned to her, and picked up, carrying her close. "It says He carries the lambs in His arms."

With a deep breath, I glanced down at Emily, who was staring at me, a look of awe on her face.

"What's wrong?" I asked her.

She glanced down at the ground, embarrassed that I had noticed her.

"It's all right. You can tell me."

She laid her head on my shoulder. "I like it when you smile."

I leaned my head on hers, overcome with the dangerous love I had struggled against. "I do too."

"Do you know any other verses?"

I nodded. "A few."

"Could you teach me some? I like to say them. They help me fall asleep at night."

I scoured my brain. "All right, then." What could I teach her? "Try this one. 'I will give thanks, unto the Lord.'"

"'I will give thanks unto the Lord.'"

"'His praise shall be in my mouth continually.'"

As I taught her the Thirty-Fourth Psalm, we walked down the hill along the river bank, toward the city. It wasn't until we were very near London that I noticed how calm I was. I couldn't think of when that had happened. I couldn't remember a decisive moment when my mind had stopped spinning, but it had as we walked through green pastures, beside the still waters.

Crashing and clanging and shouting could be heard, even from a distance. Stopping to rest in the early afternoon, we found a spot under a tree with the river rushing by, and though we said very little, something between us had been restored. When we finished eating some of the provisions Mistress Rowton had given us, I stood, wanting to reach Newgate Prison before dark. I knew I would probably have to bribe my way in if we arrived after sunset. Emily didn't get up.

"We've got to head for the city," I said, trying to coax her into moving, but she was staring at something in the trees. "Emily?"

She stood up, and thinking she had finally heard me, I slung the satchel over my shoulder. When I turned around, however, she was walking deeper into the trees, not toward the city.

"Emily, where are you going?"

She pointed straight ahead, and I strained my eyes to see what she was looking at. It was a little house, by the river.

Taking her by the hand, I took several cautious steps toward the structure. Nothing moved. It looked completely abandoned. When we reached the doorway, I bent low to glance into the little hovel. It was a one-room cabin. The pitiful space inside could hardly be called a room. There were a few logs and long forgotten ashes in a makeshift fireplace, a bucket by the door, and a threadbare mattress in the corner. It was peaceful, the sound of the river drowning out the noisy city, but something about its loneliness sent a chill down my spine.

• • •

We continued toward the city, but as the buildings grew closer, and more people passed us, I thought I should look at the letter once more. Finding a place that was hidden from the busy road, we stepped aside. Reminding her to stay close, I told Emily she could play by herself for a few minutes while I studied the letter. Reaching in the satchel, I was confused when my hand brushed against a pocket within the bag. Inside was a weighty leather pouch. I pulled it out and studied it. Opening the drawstring, I caught my breath. It was ammunition. A powder horn, lead balls, paper wadding. Mistress Rowton had sent more of *the necessaries* than I'd expected. Slipping the pouch back in its place in the satchel, I dug until I found the letter. Thomas Rowton had said Cephas would be at Newgate Prison, and so would Timothy whoever that was, but I was curious about the clue from the letter.

I know where they'll take me. You know it too. You've been there before, on your darkest night. You went to visit someone else, but I was there. I was watching.

On your darkest night. I wondered what that could mean when the memory hit me so hard, I could barely breathe. My darkest night had been at Newgate Prison.

. . .

"Kate!" The first human voice I'd heard in two days echoed through the bones of the print shop. It couldn't be. I was finally losing my mind. I was sure of it.

"Kate!" The voice cried my name in such desperation.

I wanted so much to call back, but the words were locked inside. The waves of fear pulled me under. They dragged me down as I tried to fight to the surface. I knew the air in my lungs would only last so long. I knew that this would be my last chance. I knew that I had to fight, but the fear was too strong. If he found out what I'd done, would he leave me here?

"Kate, please answer me!"

I opened my mouth, but no sound came out.

A fierce cry erupted in the street. He thought I was dead or that I'd been dragged away or that I'd abandoned the town like all the others. What could I do? I was too weak to rise, too weak to even call out to him. The first warm tear slid down my cheek, followed by flood. I continued to sob, desperate to get his attention. The crying outside stopped.

"Kate?" The cracked door swung open and he saw me in the midst of the rubble. Bending down over me, he brushed the tears from my face. At the warmth of another person's touch, something in me melted, and the words came as he threw his arms around me. "James, they're all gone."

"I know. I know," He comforted. "But you're safe."

He settled next to me. We didn't say a word. What was there to say? Just like that night on the road, we were all that we had left.

I buried my face in my hands. "It was all my fault. You

were right. I should never have trusted him."

"Enough!" he shouted. "It's not your fault. It's Lindon's, and he's the one who'll pay for what happened here."

James could justify all he wanted, but as we journeyed to London, I knew where the blame lay.

Newgate Prison was a dark, massive building, created to contain evil. James and I were permitted to see Reverend Durham in a separate room, just the three of us, with guards posted outside. I told him everything.

"Oh, Katy, my sweet Katy," he soothed, taking my cold hands in his trembling gasp. "You're forgiven, but why did you not come to me and tell me your troubles?"

I couldn't answer, but sobbed as he held me as only a father could. He leaned forward and whispered in my ear. *"When thou passest through the waters, I will be with thee; and through the rivers, they shall not overflow thee."*

That was the last time we saw him. He was executed for the writing of Puritan pamphlets just three days later. He was dying, while wicked men like the ones who'd murdered my parents lived on. Where was the just God I'd heard so much about?

• • •

I stared at the letter through my tears, and finally believed that it was meant for me. It's author knew what had happened, knew who I was, knew what I had done. Yet, he still chose me. Tears brimmed in my eyes at this realization. I had felt guilty for so long, but he had seen me on my darkest night, and still he chose to trust me. I was resolved then to do whatever I could for him. I would take Emily to Newgate to see him, and I would do whatever he'd asked of me. No matter the cost. No one had ever believed in me like this.

"Miss Elyot?"

The voice stirred me from my thoughts, and I looked

around me. Emily was still sitting by herself, making a little village out of pebbles. I could see no one else. I turned around, and saw a young man standing a few steps behind me.

I glanced from side to side, wondering who he was. "Yes?"

He cleared his throat, as if unsure of what to say. "Cephas sent me. He's been waiting for you in Newgate Prison."

I thought of Master Rowton's message. He'd told me that if we hurried I might catch up to the young man headed home. "Timothy?"

He took a step forward, his face brightening. "Did Cephas mention me?"

I smiled, pleased with myself for guessing correctly. "No. It was Thomas Rowton. He said we might meet up. I hear you're headed home."

He laughed. "News travels quickly. It's a pleasure to meet you. Could we talk for a moment? Alone?" He glanced at Emily, and fear gripped me as I wondered what news he'd brought that he didn't want her to hear.

"Of course," I stepped aside with him, telling Emily to wait where she was. I turned to him able to keep an eye on Emily, playing behind him as we talked.

He was smiling at me, an odd, awestruck smile, that made my heart speed up.

"Did you have something you wanted to tell me?" I asked.

"Oh, of course, I'm just..." He blushed slightly, scratching the back of his neck. "I guess I'm a bit overwhelmed. I don't really know how to tell you this."

"Has something happened to Cephas?"

He held up both hands. "No. No, nothing like that. He sent me here to tell you..." he stopped, mulling over his thoughts. "To tell you that there's been a mistake."

I tilted my head to one side. "What sort of mistake?"

He paced around me, searching for the right words. I turned around to watch him.

"Have you been receiving messages from Cephas?"

I nodded, hesitantly.

"You see, those messages weren't meant for you."

My heart dropped. I had only believed in their authenticity for mere moments, yet I was at a loss for words.

"Cephas left them for another of his friends. Katherine is only a code name. He never dreamed that a Katherine would really find the letter. He was positively sick about it when he heard, and sends his apologies. I can't imagine what you must have suffered for his mistake."

I couldn't answer. All of it had been for nothing. It was all pointless. I looked up searching for words, and saw a compassionate smile on his face.

"If you don't mind my saying so, Miss Elyot, you're an amazing young woman."

I shook my head, feeling sick.

"But you are. All of this for a complete stranger. I'm in awe."

I wished he would look away. His *awe* was making me uncomfortable.

"I'll escort the girl to Cephas from here," he went on. "We can't ask you to continue, under the circumstances."

"Oh, no, it's all right. I'd like to take her to her grandfather. I promised her I would."

He set a calloused hand on my shoulder. "I'm sorry, Miss Elyot. I can't allow that. London is a very busy city, and the mission we're called to is a very dangerous one. I'm afraid three people would simply be too many to maneuver through the streets. It would attract too much attention. Besides, I don't know that they would even let you in to see Cephas, since you're no friend or relation."

I was speechless. No friend. No relation. I was a mistake.

"Please try to understand. I just want to help you."

I didn't understand. I couldn't. This wasn't right.

"Your hesitation amazes me." He smiled.

"What do you mean?"

"Most people would jump at this chance. After all, she's not your responsibility."

He was right. All I had done since the whole ordeal began was complain and try to find a way out, and now I had my chance. Why was I so upset? The answer, of course was seven years old, with golden hair, and a smile that could light up an entire room.

I loved Emily, and I wanted what was best for her. I thought of how I had failed her on the river, on the Defiance, when we left the widow's. No matter how much I wanted it to be true, she didn't really need me. She would have a better chance at safety and happiness if I simply stepped away. Maybe it wasn't my love for her that made me hesitate as much as it was my longing to be needed, to be chosen.

"I'll say goodbye then." I started to turn, but he stopped me, putting a gentle hand on my arm.

"Miss Elyot, if I am to go to Cephas, I'll need more than the girl. I'll need the key."

I stared at him blankly for several moments, before I grasped what he was saying. I reached in the satchel for the signet ring. "Does he want the letter back?" I struggled against my tears.

"If you don't mind."

For one brief moment, my life had had meaning. I'd had a purpose, but as I folded the letter neatly and placed the ring on top, it was all disappearing like mist on a cold morning.

He reached out to take it, and my heart stopped. On his wrist was the word *Ferox*. I stepped back in fear, clutching both the ring and the letter, the words coming breathlessly to my mouth. "You—you're a fake."

His mouth dropped open in surprise as if that had been the last thing he'd expected me to say. Then, the look of shock melted away, and an arrogant smile showed through. "And you're a fool."

I whirled around, not daring to breathe.
Emily was gone.

CHAPTER 15

Why had I turned my back? I felt light headed. Not again. I couldn't lose her again. I'd promised to keep her safe. I needed to think. Turning back around, I saw that the young man was sauntering back toward the city. I waited for the icy fear to seize my heart, but instead something else overtook me. It was anger. It was rage. It was a love for Emily that was so great, I couldn't contain it. I reached into my satchel.

"Don't take another step," I warned. "I don't want to kill you."

He halted and turned. A brief look of surprise or perhaps fear, broke his smile for a moment.

My hands were shaking and sweating as I tried to grip the pistol.

His cocky smile returned. "Should I flee for my life?"

I met his gaze. "You can try."

"You don't have what it takes."

"Were you there the day I tried to kill your captain's son?" I took a step forward.

He shook his head. "A lucky shot."

"Lucky for him."

He leaned his head to one side, daring me to shoot. "How do I know it's loaded?"

I cocked the hammer. "Why don't you try to run, and

we'll find out."

He shook his head. "What do you want?"

"I want Emily. I don't know what you did with her, but I want her back." I swallowed the lump in my throat. "Now."

He shrugged. "That's out of my control. You'd have to talk with Captain Scot."

"Then take me to him."

He chuckled. "He wouldn't give you moment of his time."

"Let that be my concern."

"Devil's Tavern isn't exactly what you'd call a suitable establishment."

"I don't care. Show me the way."

He grinned. "I'll take my chances." With that, he turned and ran toward the city, knowing that I couldn't shoot him, even if the gun had been loaded.

· · ·

I shoved my way through the busy streets, knowing I couldn't miss a moment. Having lived in London for some time, I knew exactly where Devil's Tavern was. I also knew exactly *what* it was. As I stood breathless on the street corner, staring at the building my stomach churned, and I feared I might be sick. The stench, the shouting, and the cursing brought back horrible memories of the Defiance.

I will be with you.

The voice was so strong. It rang through my thoughts.

"Show me what to do," I whispered tremulously.

My knees quivered as I ascended the steps and pushed open the door. The smoke and smell of liquor were so thick that I fought to keep from choking. I could hardly see in the dark cavern. When someone touched my shoulder, I jumped back in alarm.

"You're in the wrong place." A paunchy man who must have worked in the tavern swayed back and forth, unsteadily.

He leaned back looking me up and down. "That is, unless you're looking for a job."

The anger that sparked in me at that moment made me forget my fear. I scanned the room, spotting a private table in the back, where the captain sat alone. "I'm here on business. I need to speak to that gentleman."

He followed my gaze to the back table, then laughed. "Get out of here."

He turned, heading back to his counter, assuming I would simply turn to leave. I wanted nothing more than to do just that, but I took a deep breath of the hot rife air and made my way to the table.

I stood right in front of him. "Captain Scot?" I sounded like a mouse in a den of wolves.

He didn't look up from his nearly empty glass.

"Captain Scot," I said a bit louder.

He took another drink, draining the glass.

"Captain Scot!" I shouted above the din.

He turned and motioned for someone to fill his glass again.

He heard me. He knew I was there, and he knew why. Yet he refused to notice me. I burned with rage as a nervous boy tried to refill his glass. This was exactly the way it had felt on the Defiance. It was like I didn't exist.

With shaking hands, the boy tried to give the captain his glass, but before he could take it, I snatched it from the boy's hand and hurled across the room. The glass shattered against the wall, the ale dripping down toward the floor. "You will acknowledge me, sir."

The room grew suddenly very quiet. No one moved. Any hope I had of slipping in and slipping out unnoticed was gone. I felt the heat rising on the back of my neck. Every eye in that room was on me, but Captain Scot's attention was all that mattered, and I had it.

"How dare you!" The tavern worker, who'd tried to

discourage me earlier ran up behind me. "I'm so sorry, Captain Scot. Jim, get him a new glass. I'll see her out, personally," he growled through gritted teeth. He took me by the arm and began to yank me toward he door. I had lost my chance. I had ruined any hope of an audience with Captain Scot.

"Hold on, Stevens." His rough, gravelly voice made me hold my breath.

The man trying to drag me out halted and turned around.

"It was a misunderstanding. She's correct. She had some business to conduct with me, and it slipped my mind. Hope you don't mind the mess."

Stevens looked as baffled as I was. He stared, gaping at the captain. "No, of course not, sir, but…"

"Bring the girl over here."

Stevens didn't move.

"I said bring her here!" the captain erupted.

Stevens obeyed, and once again I was standing in front of Captain Scot. He looked up at me, and for the first time he spoke to me. "Tell me, Miss. How do you take your spirits?"

Several of the men in the tavern laughed as he motioned to the chair across from him.

I sat down in the offered chair. I wasn't used to this side of the captain. When the men had returned their attention to their drinks, the deadly captain I knew showed through the mask of cordiality. He leaned over the table. "What do you want?"

I met his gaze, remembering how it had terrified me that day on the ship. It was still piercing as though he could see my every weakness, but this time that didn't bother me. "I want Emily," I said evenly.

He leaned back in his chair and smiled. "I'm afraid I can't do that. You see, Emily's family to me, and I feel I have a right to spend time with her."

"She doesn't have what you want."

He shrugged innocently, as if he didn't understand what I was saying.

"I'll offer you a deal," I said, amazed at the calm in my voice.

He laughed, and leaned forward, as if to whisper something confidential. "I don't deal with lunatics. Trade Secret."

"Neither do I." Reaching into the satchel in my lap, I found the ring without ever glancing down. "I suppose we have nothing more to say. Good day." I slipped the ring on my finger, and stood up.

"Leaving so soon? I haven't even bought you a drink yet."

I tried to hide my smile. When I sat back down he folded his arms across his chest. To my amazement, I was getting under his skin.

"What do you want?" he demanded.

"I told you what I want."

A smile crossed his face. "Do you know Cephas is in prison?"

"I do," I answered, wondering what that had to do with the conversation.

"Can't tell you how long I've wanted to see that happen. You see, the only problem is, I don't have any evidence, and I can't get a confession out of him. It makes little difference to me whether I have the ring or the little girl. One would close the deal, and the other would make him talk, so tell me why I should trade one solution for another?"

I glanced down at the signet ring in my hand, and Jackson's words came back to me. *It's also a key.* I gazed up at Scot, trying to sound confident. "I know you want this more."

He laughed. "It is tempting, but I don't know if I'm willing to trade my own flesh and blood for it." Reaching into his pocket, he withdrew a sheet of parchment. "One of my men intercepted this day before last. It's from Cephas, though it isn't signed by him, written to a Kate. You wouldn't happen to know who it's for, would you?"

I resisted the urge to reach out and snatch it. With a deep breath, I managed a sweet smile. "Oh, did he write me a letter? What does it say?"

Scot laughed. "You'd love to know, I'm sure. What about this? I'll trade the letter for the ring."

Without breaking my smile, I shook my head. We were getting nowhere, neither of us would budge. Then I saw Scot's face as he looked at the letter, and it suddenly occurred to me what a genius Simon Cephas was.

"Why would you hold onto something that's useless to you?" I asked.

My question caught him off guard. "This? It's actually full of useful information."

"That you can't understand. It's driving you mad. I can see it. You can't interpret the letter. There's only one person who can."

"Rather confident, aren't we?"

"Cephas wrote those letters to me. I'm the only one who can understand them. I'm here to get Emily. I will trade you the ring for her life."

"And I throw the letter in for free, because I'm a good person?"

"I don't think you're understanding my meaning, Captain. I care about that little girl, but I'm not with them. I'm not one of them. This isn't my fight. I'd be ready and willing to share any information you need once I get my hands on it."

"Let me be sure I understand. You wish to trade information you don't yet have for the letter. That sounds like a rather risky investment on my part."

I leaned forward. "Once I deliver that little girl to him, Cephas will tell me anything I want to know. So tell me, Captain Scot, what is it you want to know?"

Scot grinned. "The location of the lock."

"Done." I stood to leave.

"You're forgetting something."

"What's that?"

"I trade for a living. It's customary to make a deal, then exchange the items of trade."

"Certainly. When you deliver Emily safely to me, I will hand over the key."

He stood, his chair scraping against the floor. I flinched involuntarily. "You're not in any position to make that decision."

I took a step forward, feeling a rush of anger. "Yes, I am. I know how badly you want this key, Captain Scot. You'd probably just kill me for it, but you can't do that because you need me. You need the information that only I can provide." I couldn't believe the blatant coolness of my voice. "You will deliver that girl to me safely at the bridge as soon as possible. Or we don't have deal." I turned around, and headed for the door.

"Don't do anything you might regret." His words made me halt. "Betray me and I *will* kill you."

I mustered my strength for one last glance over my shoulder. "Will you?"

A smile crept across his face. "Jackson enjoyed testing me as well. Make his mistake, and you'll die as he did."

. . .

I stumbled through the darkening city, staring straight ahead. What I had just done was madness. I had made a deal with Captain Scot. What if he didn't follow through? What had I done? I looked up and saw that I had reached the notorious London Bridge. Why on earth had I said to meet here? This was the most disturbing place in the whole city. Guarding the bridge was a tower, where criminals were executed. Their heads were placed on spikes across the bridge.

My knees finally gave out, and I collapsed with my back against the bridge's cold stone wall. The sun had set by now, and I was thankful no one could see me as I curled up, exhausted. For the first time, I questioned the rightness of my decision to trade the ring for Emily. It was all the evidence Scot needed to condemn Cephas, Emily's only family. Jackson had warned me not to give it up, for anything.

Jackson.

Scot's threat had not fallen deaf ears. He had killed his own son. Jackson was dead.

I leaned my head back against the wall and felt a single tear slip down my cheek for the young man whose love for Emily had saved my life. Whatever I'd had against him was no longer important. He was gone, and I'd never been so sick at heart to be proven right.

I pulled his pistol from my satchel and gazed at it in the dim light cast by the lamp above me. I had never noticed the carvings that ran all the way up and down the wooden handle and barrel. Designs were whittled all over it, and I wondered if he'd carved them in his spare time.

I stared at the pistol in my hand, wondering if I could even remember how to load and clean it, the way he'd shown me. Reaching in my bag I retrieved the ammunition the Rowtons had given me before we left. I would not be caught off guard again.

• • •

"She didn't come for you." Brice's whining voice drifted over the foggy night air.

I gripped my knees and stood up, knowing he wouldn't see me until I stepped into the light of the street lamp. I could see them through the misty darkness. Brice dragged Emily, along by the hand, moving much faster than she could. The fiery feelings that gripped me at that moment were almost

149

more than I could bear. I had never felt that much in my life. I caught myself in time. Brice would use my love against me in any way he could. I desperately tried to make myself remember that I was in control. Scot wanted this ring even more than I wanted Emily's life. Or at least, that's what Brice had to believe.

"Keep up, you little rat." He stumbled forward. Was this man ever sober?

Emily whimpered as he drug her behind him, too tired to resist.

"Enough of your blubbering." He lifted his hand to strike her.

"Brice!"

He spun around.

I held the ring over the side of the bridge. "I have a deal with Scot. If you harm her, you break that deal."

He stared at the ring like a starving animal. His eyes drifted down to me, and the starving animal salivated. "Well, well, well. Looks like we came to collect. Bold, aren't we?"

"Give me the girl," I said, not removing the ring from its position over the rushing black river.

"Fine then. Take her." He shoved her toward me, and I noticed her hands were bound in front of her. She tripped and couldn't catch herself.

She looked unhurt and, I fought my urge to run to her and pick her up. I held the ring toward him, desperate to make my hand stop shaking.

He took it from me, and turned to go.

"You're forgetting something."

He swerved around. "Am I?"

"The letter."

"Of course." He reach into his pocket. "Why do you want it?" He turned it sideways. "It's all a bunch of gibberish," he slurred.

I held out my hand. "That's my business."

"You know…" He shoved the parchment back inside his jacket taking several swaggering steps toward me. "No one ever remembers the messenger. You get the little girl. Scot gets the ring. What do I get?"

His eyes glinted as he leaned over me. *Show me what to do.* I pleaded silently. "That's between you and your captain."

I tried to turn away, but he gripped my left arm pulling me toward him. His breath was so foul, I could have vomited. "I'd rather it was between you and me," he whispered in my ear.

I reached my free hand in my satchel, and cocked the loaded pistol.

"I have some influence in Newgate Prison," he said with a sly grin. "If there's anyone you'd like to see, anyone you'd like to have released, maybe I could work something out for you."

His jacket hung open revealing the letter inside. In order to reach for the parchment, I'd have to drop the pistol. I had to keep my eyes on him, to keep him distracted. I managed a nervous smile. "You'd do that for me?" As I released my grip on the pistol, I fought to keep my hands from shaking.

His grin was sickening as he leaned even closer, his breath hot against my cheek. "For a special price."

I slipped my hand inside his jacket, my fingers finding the letter.

"Brice!" a voice called from a distance.

He turned away, just as I had a hold on the letter. It slipped out of his coat, without his notice, as he sent an irritated glance toward the man running up the bridge. "What do you want?"

Another sailor hurried into the light, catching his breath. He leaned over to Brice, whispering something I couldn't make out. When he'd finished his message, Brice turned a deep shade of red and looked at me, eyes blazing. "You little witch! You planned it all out didn't you?" He cursed, kicking at nothing. "How much time do we have?"

"Less than an hour."

"Idiot," he cursed himself, then glanced up at me. "You thought you could outsmart me didn't you?"

I stared at him, having no idea what he was talking about.

Brice and his friend pounded down the bridge, disappearing into the darkness. I had the letter and little girl, and that was what mattered. Remembering this, I turned around to see Emily, still frozen with fear in the pool of light. I got down on my hands and knees, untying the ropes that bound her little hands. They had left red raw marks. "Oh, Emily. I'm so sorry. I had no idea. I just turned my back for a second."

I expected her to shy away from me as she had before. Instead, her knees buckled, and she fell into my arms, sobbing. Her little arms gripped my neck so hard, I thought she would never let go. "It's all right." I scooped her up, and held her close until her cries quieted. I started to set her down.

"No! No! Please. Please don't put me down," she begged.

"I won't. I've got you. Don't be afraid. I've got you." I was overcome once again with how inadequate I was for this job, but if the deal Brice had offered was any indication, Cephas was suffering. There was only so long he could hold on in that prison, and we had to get to him before his time ran out.

"Where are we going?" she asked as we maneuvered the dark streets.

"We're going to see your grandfather." I didn't care if it was nearly midnight. I would wait at the prison until morning if I had to, but nothing was stopping me this time.

· · ·

Emily was so heavy in my arms, I feared I might drop her by the time we reached Newgate Prison. There were lamps burning inside, so I assumed that at least one prison guard

152

would be on duty. I considered waiting outside, but there were sounds of stumbling and scraping coming from the alleyway beside the prison. I thought we would be safer inside, but when the doors closed behind me, I thought again.

Instead of one prison guard, there was a crowd of men, all shouting, and jeering. It was as if I'd walked into a tavern, not a prison. They were gathered around a fight of some sort, but the crowd was so thick and the light so scarce, I couldn't even see the men fighting.

I spotted a door on the other side of the room. No one had noticed us, and I knew I could slip around the fight and through the door toward the cells without ever being seen. I pressed my back against the wall, no longer able to feel my hands after carrying Emily so far. I crept along the edge of the room, as noiselessly as possible. The men shouted and cursed, screaming with excitement. I was terrified one of them would notice us. Then, suddenly one cry rose above over the others. "Do you hear that?"

The men stopped their shouting.

I froze.

"It's midnight," one of them said.

I listened, and heard the church bells chiming.

"He'll kill us! We need to go!"

Before the fifth strike of the bell, the entire had crowd rushed out the front door. Within moments, the place was absolutely still, and we were alone. I shook my head in confusion. What had just happened?

A sound caught my attention. Glancing down, I saw someone stretched out on the ground. I took this man to be the loser of the fight. I continued toward the door, keeping my eyes on him. He pushed himself up from the ground, but was unable to stand. I stopped, watching as he began to drag himself away from the front door. Why wasn't he following the other men?

The seventh bell struck. He was crawling in a panic,

scraping and stumbling along the ground as if his life depended on it. He was heading in my direction, toward the door to the cells.

I knew he would see me. When he reached the door, he pulled himself up by the handle and leaned all his weight against the frame.

The bell echoed a tenth time. He still didn't noticed me as he withdrew a set of keys and unlocked the door. He must have been the jailer. As he pushed the door open, a blast of cold air filled the room. Emily shivered in my arms. Just when I thought he would slip through the door without seeing us, she spoke.

"I'm cold," she whispered, as the eleventh strike rang out.

The jailer halted and looked at us. In the dim, torchlight, I could hardly see his bruised, swollen face. He didn't move. The cold air from the corridor chilled me, as I clutched Emily, unsure of what to say, or how to explain.

"Get in," he said suddenly.

I stared at him, confused.

He reached for my hand, and jerked me toward the open door. "Get in!"

The edge of panic in his voice, made me take a cautious step toward the doorway, holding Emily tighter.

"Now!" he yelled, shoving me into the corridor.

The bells struck midnight.

I stumbled, flying forward, dropping Emily, and landing right beside her. I looked up in time to see the jailer slam the door shut.

A deafening roar thundered through the room, shaking the prison at its foundation. There was a blinding light from behind the door. I knew I was screaming, but I couldn't hear myself. I could feel the searing heat, see the light, hear the thunder. Then all was darkness and silence.

CHAPTER 16

I could hear crying. *Emily.* I tried to move, and coughed up ashes and soot. "Emily?"

She didn't answer, but her cries continued. I pushed aside several chunks of wood and debris. Every candle and lamp had gone out, the only way to see was by the light of the burning embers scattered over the ground. I sat up, and tried to make sense of the dull, ashy air. "Emily?" I spotted her, not two steps away from me, on her knees, in the midst of the rubble. I crawled toward her, trying to avoid the still smoldering wood that was strewn all over the ground. She was staring at the rubble in front of her, sobbing uncontrollably. "Emily, are you hurt?"

She didn't answer.

I followed her gaze. It was the jailer who had pushed us into the corridor. The explosion had buried him under the remains of the door, exposing only his burned and bruised face. He lay perfectly still. "Emily, don't," I said, hoping she would spare herself from the dreadful sight.

She didn't remove her gaze.

"Emily!" I took her chin in my hand, turning her face toward me.

Tears spilled from her brown eyes as they met mine. "It's Jack."

My heart thudded, dully. Jack? That was impossible. Jack was already dead. I glanced at the body in the rubble. Through the burns and bruises, I recognized the face. Scot had lied to me, but now I wished he'd been telling the truth. If he had killed Jack, at least Emily wouldn't have known, wouldn't have had to witness it. I pulled her into my lap and held her as she cried. "I'm so sorry, Emily."

"You were right," she gasped between sobs. "You were right. He's not coming back."

"Listen to me," I said, fighting back tears, as I gripped her tighter. "I was wrong. I told you that he didn't care about you, that he was selfish, and I was wrong. He did this to protect you, to keep you safe because he loved you."

She cried all the harder, and I cried with her, telling her I was sorry again and again. I was sorry for the things I'd said to Jackson, sorry for the way I'd portrayed him to Emily. I was sorry for bringing her here tonight.

Emily stopped crying suddenly.

"What's wrong?"

She crawled out of my lap, and toward Jack's body.

"Emily." Why was she doing this to herself?

She acted as if she didn't hear me, and continued to stare.

"Emily!"

The dead man coughed.

Emily's eyes lit up, and she leaned forward.

His breathing was ragged at first, but he began to move. His hand stirred the debris as he slowly raised it to his face. Emily caught it in both of hers, and held it against her cheek. His eyes opened.

"Em?" his voice cracked above a whisper.

I heard voices and shoes scraping against the debris in the next room as people came to view the damage. We were in the darkened corridor, but they would search it eventually. This was our chance to exit unnoticed.

"Emily, we have to go."

She looked up at me in shock, and stood to her feet. "What about—"

"I'm sorry. We have to leave him."

She sat back down defiantly. "No."

"Emily. We don't have time for this." If we were found, we could be questioned, and even blamed for what had just happened. Lawful justice wasn't something to be depended on. We had to get out of here.

"We can't leave him." Her whisper was harsh.

"They'll find him. He'll be all right. I promise."

She glanced down at the coughing, beaten, half-conscious man, then back up at me, unimpressed. It wasn't my best argument. I didn't care. "Say goodbye, then we need to go."

She folded her arms in front of her, refusing to move.

I leaned closer, right beside her ear. "If I have to drag you out of here, I'll do it."

"What happened here?" came a slurred voice from the other room. I knew that voice. So did Jackson. I could see him tense at the sound.

"Brice," he muttered.

I stared at him for a long moment. Leaving him here to be found and rescued was one thing. Leaving him here to be murdered by Brice was another.

I crawled toward him. "Can you stand up?"

He was beginning to shake, as he nodded.

"I suppose we'll find out," I groaned. Digging in the rubble, I found his hand and leaned over to him. "Don't make a sound," I hissed through gritted teeth.

I attempted to lift him to his feet as the rubble covering him slid to the floor. Though not as quiet as I'd hoped, the sound didn't attract the attention of anyone in the next room. It took all my strength to put his arm across my shoulders. My knees trembled under the extra weight, and I had no idea how I would walk this way for any distance. "Is there a back entrance?" I asked.

He gave another shaky nod, and we began to make our way down the darkened hall. Emily held onto my skirt, staying as close as she could. When we'd arrived at the prison, I hadn't thought that anything could be worse than carrying Emily one more mile. Carrying Jackson was so much worse. He stumbled along beside me, making our progress painfully slow. As we moved through the hallway, past several cells men and women were shouting over each other. Some were screaming from fright, others crying that there had been a prison break. In the darkness, I couldn't tell if they were shouting at me or at one another, and I didn't care.

"Did he get out?" Jackson asked in a whisper.

"Who?" I managed between gasps.

He didn't answer.

I saw the back door. It was swinging on its hinges open and unlocked.

I scoured my brain, trying to think of anywhere we could hide. I glanced down at Emily. I knew the perfect place.

We were out on the street headed for the woods, when he asked the question again. "Did he get out?"

"I don't know who you're talking about," I grumbled, wishing he would just keep quiet until we were out of the city.

I moved as quickly as I could in the shadows my knees nearly giving out from the weight and the fear and the fatigue. When we reached the outskirts of the city, I forced myself forward, knowing we were nearly there. It felt like hours until the hovel by the river appeared in front of us, a shadow in the dark woods. I stumbled through the doorway, knowing that I had to move quickly. I laid Jackson on the cot in the corner. My shaking hands dug through the satchel, finding a flint.

"Did he get out?"

"Would you stop asking me that? I don't know!" I struck the flint into the fireplace, once, twice. On the third try it caught, and I bent to blow on the little fire. It smoldered, then grew, lighting up the dark little cabin. I turned around to look at the work ahead of me, and wanted to cry. How was I supposed to do this? I had worked alongside Mistress Durham for those ten years, learning to tend the sick and the wounded, but now I felt helpless. Moving toward the cot, I bent beneath the low ceiling.

Jackson's eyes were wide and dark as he stared into vacant space. His face was the color of old parchment where it wasn't dark with bruises or singed with burns, and he gasped for breath. I knelt down, nearly tripping over Emily, who was staring at him, fear written on her face.

Show me what to do, I prayed.

"Can I help?" Emily asked, and I looked at her, knowing how much Jackson meant to her. If I couldn't save him…

Reaching out, I set a hand on her sweet golden curls, now dusty with ashes. "Pray," I breathed. It was all I could say.

She nodded, folding her little hands in front of her, resting her head against them.

I reached for Jackson's hand. It was cold and moist.

"Did he get out?"

I had to calm him down. "He got out just fine," I said, hoping that was the right answer.

He relaxed slightly.

"You're going to be all right." I felt a stab of guilt, and wondered if I was lying.

I could practically hear Miss Durham's voice. *Ask him questions.* Normally, I would have asked someone in this state about their home, or their family. The homeless sailor, with a father who had tried to kill him wasn't exactly a candidate for such questions.

"What were you doing in Newgate?" I saw that the debris had burnt through his left sleeve as well.

He shook his head. "I—I don't know."

"What do you remember?" I asked gently. His arm had suffered the most severe burns, and I braced my stomach at the sight, searching for anything to be used as a bandage.

"Connors," Jackson said in a shallow gasp.

"First Mate Connors?"

He nodded.

"Were you with him?"

He nodded again.

"And how is he?"

"Nervous. He's nervous, but it will all work out."

"Of course it will." I continued to ask questions. The answers he gave made no sense, and some were almost laughable. I shredded the hem of the white petticoat the widow Lawrence had given me, and used it for bandages.

Emily never left her spot. She was kneeling by the cot, her hands folded, one over the other, her head drooping as she fought to stay awake.

"When I die tell Cephas—" That was as far as the sailor got before I tightened the bandage on his arm. He cried out in pain, his eyes wide.

I turned to Emily. Her eyes were wide as well.

Waiting until she turned to her folded hands, I looked at Jackson who was staring back at me as if he'd just remembered that I was the girl who'd tried to shoot him. I leaned close, not wanting Emily to hear me.

"I'll be brief," I said. "I don't know what's going to happen. I honestly don't know what I'm doing, but that little girl has been on her knees for you since the moment we arrived. So don't you dare talk about death, and if you're going to head for glory tonight, please do me a favor and wait until we're gone."

His stared at me blankly.

I let out a tense breath. It wasn't fair of me to take out my anger out on him. "Now is there something you want me to tell Cephas?"

"Tell him..." He gasped for air. "Tell him I was on my way home."

My hands halted in their work. Thomas Rowton's words

were pounding in my mind like thunder.

Tell him that Timothy is on his way home.

I looked down, the realization with such force that my breath caught in my throat.

I had caught up to Timothy. He was on his way home. He was in Newgate Prison. I couldn't answer. Tears stifled any response I could have managed.

"And tell him I didn't run. He needs to know."

I swallowed the lump in my throat. "I will."

I felt him relax.

I lost track of time as my hands worked, and my mind raced. If he was Timothy that meant that he knew the Rowtons. He'd been there. I was sure of it by the way they'd spoken of him. He'd stayed there, perhaps even left the same day we had arrived. We'd just missed each other. He was headed home. What did that mean? Had he been trying to find Cephas, as well? Was that why he'd been in the prison? It was too much to take in.

I remembered after some time that I hadn't kept him talking, but he was still awake, and appeared more aware than before. Fetching water from the creek, I sprinkled some on his dry, cracked lips and turned to move the bucket out of my way.

"Thank you," he whispered in the firelight.

I looked up, not quite believing what I'd just heard. "Don't you dare thank me," I quoted in a husky voice. "If it were up to me, you'd still be back in that prison. This is all that little girl's scheme." I motioned toward Emily.

He reached over, covering my cold, trembling hand with his, worn, calloused one. He looked up at me earnestly, his dark eyes searching mine. "Thank you."

My reply caught in my throat, and I looked away as the tears formed in my eyes. My heart convulsed with the same terrifying emotion that overwhelmed me when I held Emily. He had to live. There was so much I didn't know about this young man, so much I'd never thanked him for. I stared upward, willing my tears not to fall. When I turned back I saw that he had fallen asleep, his breathing steady and even. I had done all I could do.

I ran my fingers through the dark hair that had tints of red so like Emily's, and took a deep breath. "Please don't die."

• • •

I curled up in the opposite corner exhausted, only to find that I couldn't close my eyes. I couldn't take them off Emily. Why had I looked away?

I had been tricked and flattered and talked right out of my resolve, yet again. My life had revolved around my failures. Just when I thought I was doing something right, I was fooled and hurt everyone around me. All I wanted was to live alone in the back room of the Seven Stars where I couldn't love, couldn't hurt, couldn't fail anyone. That was all I wanted. If I'd had any assurance that Jackson would survive the night I would have been tempted to head to London, leaving them to take care of one another. He would do a far better job than I had.

How could I have let myself be so easily tricked? I considered my conversation with Scot's spy. When he had told me that my involvement was a mistake my heart had dropped. I'd felt so lost, and confused, but he'd been wrong. Those letters were written to me. No one could take that away now. Cephas, whoever he was, believed in me, and trusted me like no one ever had. That was why I wanted to finish this. I had to find out why anyone with as many friends as Simon Cephas would choose someone like me, so out of place, so weak..

I sat straight up, remembering that I had the next letter. Digging in the satchel I'd discarded on the ground, I found the paper. The seal had been torn, and the page was wrinkled and smudged, but it was my next clue.

> *Dear Kate,*
>
> *Living for Christ is not an easy thing to do. Submitting your life and your carefully laid plans to Him is even harder. Weeks ago I wrote you a letter, feeling completely in control, believing that I was finally going to pay back the debt I owed you. Now I write you another letter, one that I can only pray will reach you if you arrive too late. I have written in the past asking for your help. I've even begged you. I've asked you to face some of your worst fears, and some of mine. I know you feel inadequate and you want nothing more than to run, but God has a purpose for our dark days. He understands those fears that grip you and I. He knows, Child. He knows. He has a plan for us both though I can't see what it is, from this dark place. Don't settle for the plan that brings you the least pain, Katherine. Trust Him, and He will bless your belief.*
>
> *I dread telling you what you must do, what I swore I would never ask of you. I know you promised yourself...*

The letter stopped. I was at the end of the page. There was no more to read. I searched the back of the parchment. It was blank. I searched the bag for a second page. There was nothing. My stomach was in knots. Deep inside, I knew what he had been about to ask of me.

No. It couldn't be. He would never ask it of me. I had to speak with him, had to hear my fears contradicted. I looked outside to see that the sky was lightening. It was nearly dawn. I didn't know how I would do this. How could I be who Cephas and Emily needed me to be? I gazed back down at the letter, my eyes falling on the words, *Trust Him.*

It had been so long I'd forgotten how. Leaning back against the wall, I stared up at the low ceiling, with no strength left. "God," I whispered. "I don't know why, but I believe that You've chosen me for this, even though I've failed. I feel so lost. I don't know what to do. I don't know how I can go on like this, but I want to trust You. I want to know that I didn't give up, that my fear didn't stop me, but I need Your help."

At the end of my prayer, I felt no different. My stomach was still tight, my tears still on the verge of spilling over. Then, a thought came to my mind, so strong that I knew it couldn't have come from me. It was one of the verses from the Thirty-Fourth Psalm I'd taught Emily the day before. I said it out loud. "*I sought the Lord, and He heard me.*" Three times in the last day, I had prayed the same, simple prayer. *Show me what to do.* And every time, God had answered. Every time, He had guided me. Today would be no different. Despite all that had happened, He had not abandoned me, and He never would.

I pushed myself to my feet as the sun peeked up over the river and shone through the little doorway, filling the cabin with a glossy golden light. I knelt next to Emily, rubbing her back gently. She yawned and lifted her head. "It's time to go," I whispered.

"Jack," she gasped, her eyes opening wide.

"He's all right." I motioned to him, sleeping peacefully.

She threw her arms around my neck. "I asked God."

"And He heard you." I hugged her tightly, reminded of why I had started out on this journey to begin with.

Emily and I each ate a little, and I felt I had the strength to get to the city, thankful I wasn't carrying anyone this time. Leaving some food next to the bucket of water, I took one last look at the sailor, still so mystified by his sudden appearance. Emily was confident in his recovery, and I hoped that her prayers would fill in where my skill had failed.

CHAPTER 17

"No prisoner by that name." The man scratched his chin, and swallowed whatever it was he'd been chewing.

"Are you sure?"

"Missy, I patrol this prison dawn to dusk, and there hasn't been anyone by the name of Blake here in years."

I had refrained from using the name Simon Cephas. I knew it to be only a code name, but I was growing desperate.

Assuming his business with me was finished, the man leaned his girth against the wall a second more, then dusted the ash off of his jacket and returned to work. I followed him around to the front of the prison holding Emily by the hand. The entire front wall had caved in, allowing anyone on the street to see its blackened interior. I could see all the way to the doorway at the back of the room, where Jackson had pushed us into the corridor. Surveying the black shriveled remains of the front room, I shuddered to think what might have happened if he hadn't. "Jackson," I said to myself, amazed I hadn't thought of it before. Emily was not the only one related to Cephas.

I wasn't surprised when the prison guard rolled his eyes at me, as I tried to get his attention.

"Do you have a prisoner by the name of Jackson?" I asked, hoping that this family connection would be the right one.

His face changed from one of annoyance to one of suspicion. "Not anymore." He turned his back to me and entered the crumbling burnt building.

"What does that mean?" I asked aloud in frustration, but he had disappeared into the dark building. I simply stood in the middle of the street, watching people walk back and forth, some assisting the prison guards in the cleanup, others on their way to and from the market. Unlike us, all of them had a place to go. My knees were shaking again. I had to sit down. Every setback was heartbreaking. Every delay felt impossible to overcome. I was weary and dazed and Emily didn't look much better.

The buildings cast a shadow across one side of the busy street. We took shelter in the alleyway, sitting on the side of the street like beggars. I pulled out the letter, reading the last few lines again.

I know you promised yourself...

"I won't go back."

Emily jerked at my side, and I realized she had dozed off and the sound of my voice had wakened her. She laid her head back down on my lap and was asleep in moments.

I'd promised myself I wouldn't go back. I didn't need the rest of the letter to know what was being asked of me, but this time Cephas was asking too much. Besides, what I was supposed to do there was a mystery. What if I got all the way there, only to find out that I'd made a mistake, and gone all that way for nothing?

I roused Emily. I had to get out of this city before I lost my mind. I would have looked for an inn, but we had no money. I would have found a Puritan's home, but I didn't even know where I would begin to search. I would have gone back to the little hovel in the woods, but if something had happened to Jackson, I didn't want Emily to see it. The heat, the noise, the people all made it impossible to think straight. It was an all too familiar feeling. It was exactly why I'd hated living here.

I sat bolt upright. Why had it taken me so long to remember?

. . .

The Seven Stars Tavern hadn't changed a bit. Of course, I hadn't been gone for more than two months, even though it felt like years. The owner, Master Hogan, though disappointed not to see my cousin's brawny, hardworking frame was pleased enough to see me and offered me a night's stay in return for a day's work. I couldn't imagine standing on my feet for another moment, but I decided to give it what little strength I had left. I washed my face in a back room, knowing I would have to be somewhat presentable if I was to be serving people their meals. Finding a blanket, I set Emily in the corner of the dining room where I could watch her while I worked. She fell asleep before I could even apologize for the situation.

At the end of the day, I could hardly see straight. Master Hogan showed us to the back room. I had thought of it so often since we'd left, and was surprised when tears pricked my eyes as I walked through the door. Emily climbed in the bed without a word, and was asleep, in moments.

I tried to wipe away the tears, but as soon as I would control myself enough to wash them away, a fresh wave of them would catch me by surprise. I knew why I was crying. It was James. He wasn't here. I didn't know why I was so heartbroken by that. It wasn't as if I'd expected to walk in and see him standing by the window. It was the same disappointment I had felt up North, only deeper. James wasn't here, any more than my parents were there. At the very least, I had hoped to walk into this room and feel as though I had come home. Instead, I felt as much a stranger here as I had on the Defiance. Not only that, but as I looked around, I was reminded of every reason why I had begged James to come North with me. I hated this place. It was filthy, perched right on the dusty street. The open window with no glass hadn't bothered me when James had been here, but I suddenly felt vulnerable with it now. I tried desperately to get ahold of my emotions, and crawled in bed beside Emily. The aching in my back, my arms and my feet reminded me of something else. I hated this job. I didn't even blow out the lamp before sleep overtook me.

• • •

"Are you ever afraid?" The gray day made Emily look pale, as I wandered through the woods, carrying her in my arms. Where were we going?

I glanced down, at her wondering why she was asking me again. "Well," I started. "Like I said before..." My words were cut short. Just behind us, the shrieking howl of a wolf pierced the air, making my blood run cold. My skin prickled at the sound. I began running, heart thrashing, feet pounding. They were getting closer, following our scent. I stumbled. She gripped me, terrified. They were coming. I couldn't stop them. I got to my feet again, and pounded forward, breaking through the trees, into an open field.

"Kate?"

I spun around searching for the voice that called to me.

"Kate."

There he was up on the hill. I had to follow him. I had to get to him.

I turned to check my pursuers. I turned too late.

"Kate. Kate!"

I opened my eyes. I was in the tavern room. The lamp was still burning in the dark. Emily was right next to me, looking concerned. "Did you have a nightmare?"

I felt my heart thrashing in my chest, and nodded.

Emily laid down next to me again. I put my arm around her and she curled up beside me. "Sometimes I have nightmares too."

"I know," I said, trying to keep my voice level. "You cry in your sleep."

I could feel her nod. "So do you."

I closed my eyes, starting to drift off when I started awake. The dream had begun again, as soon as I started to doze. I tried to clear my head of the images that had been so real. I tried again to relax and close my eyes, but in seconds, I sat back up, thinking I'd heard Emily screaming. She lay next to me, sleeping peacefully. It didn't matter how many times I attempted to sleep. I would wake moments later in a cold sweat.

What if I looked away again, and something happened? What if I closed my eyes, and she disappeared again? I couldn't lose her. I was her only protection. I couldn't sleep, couldn't close my eyes, couldn't stop watching her.

• • •

We couldn't stay in the Tavern. That was the one thing I had learned from my sleepless night. I could not live the rest of my life in this place, and I wasn't about to ask that of Emily. I had to follow the letter's instructions. It was my last hope. This wasn't Emily's home, and after a night here, I was reminded that it wasn't mine either. There was a gaping hole in my life, one that I'd tried to ignore. I didn't have a home. It didn't matter where I went. I would never have a home. My plan had been to safely deliver Emily, then come back here. That's what James had instructed me to do, but I couldn't do it. I couldn't live here. There was nowhere for me to go.

I planned to leave early, but couldn't bear to wake Emily,

and she slept for several hours past sunrise. It was well earned. I watched her enviously, wishing I could sleep for nearly an entire day. The scant hours I'd had had been stolen away by nightmares.

I knew which direction we were headed in, and knew it would take several days to get there. We ate at the tavern, saving what little food remained in the satchel for the journey ahead. It was nearly midday by the time we stepped out on the street, heading West toward the edge of town. When we had finally waded through the crowded streets and reached the outskirts, the sun was low on the horizon.

I built a fire, neither of us speaking much as we ate the last of the food given to us by Mistress Rowton.

Emily curled up beside me, but I knew she wasn't asleep yet. I didn't want to upset her, but I'd been keeping back my questions for nearly two days now.

"Emily, what did they do to you?"

She didn't answer for a long time, and I wondered if she had heard me. "Someone grabbed me when you were talking. I tried to scream, but his hand was on my mouth. They locked me in a dark room, all day, and at night we walked so far."

I felt her tears soak through my skirt.

"I thought they were going to throw me in that river."

I stroked her glossy little head. "Emily, I wasn't watching you. It's my fault they took you again." I had given up fighting my tears. "I'm so sorry. I know I promised. It was my fault."

She didn't answer.

"I don't blame you if you're angry at me."

She still didn't answer. I glanced down at her. She was asleep. I leaned over and kissed her cheek, knowing I was forgiven.

There was no way I was going to sleep, exhausted as I was. I didn't even want to try. Instead, I decided to practice the only means I had of defending myself. Setting Emily beside me, I reached for the pistol and ammunition in the satchel. If I had been prepared, they wouldn't have stolen Emily. If I had been prepared, Brice would have been at my mercy, not the other way around.

My fingers shook with fatigue as I poured in the correct amount of powder from the horn, stuffed the barrel with wadding, dropped in the lead ball, checked to see if the hammer was still forward. I then imagined cocking it back, firing, then using the rod to clean the barrel, and start all over. I went through the steps over and over again. I wanted to be ready at any moment.

• • •

The sound made me sit bolt upright. I had started to fall asleep, pistol in hand. I had to stay awake. The sound came again, louder this time. Something was in the woods. My heart pounded in fear. Gripping the pistol, I wondered if I would have the courage and wisdom to fire it.

I stood up, and turned around. The trees were dark, and still. I took a few steps forward. A twig snapped to my right, and I swung around, aiming the pistol at a shadowy silhouette in the trees. The figure raised its hands in surrender.

"Step into the light." I ordered.

The figure obeyed, taking cautious steps forward. "It's me," said the tall, lank sailor as the light fell on his face.

"Jackson." I didn't lower the pistol. "Or is it Timothy?"

He looked confused. "Timothy Jackson, actually."

"You look terrible." It was the first thing that came to mind. He was still scarred and bruised and slightly hunched over from his injuries. I wondered how he'd even made it this far.

His eyes were still on the pistol in my hand. "You can put that down now."

I glanced down at the weapon leveled at him, fighting to

keep my hands from trembling. "What are you worried about? I thought I was a terrible shot."

His eyes widened. "Did I say that? If—if I said that I must have been joking. I've seen what a good shot you are. Actually I still have splinters in the side of my head from…"

I cocked the hammer. "What do you want, Timothy Jackson?"

"At the moment, I just want you to put that down."

I couldn't put it down. It was all I had for protection, my last shred of control. I would have aimed that pistol at Simon Cephas himself if he had snuck up on me like that. I shook my head. "What's the matter? Don't you trust me?"

"No."

"Then, at least we agree on something." For a moment, my vision blurred, and it was all I could do to stay standing.

He looked at me earnestly. "I just want to help you."

"The last person who told me that kidnapped Emily." Instinctively, I glanced back at the fire to make sure she was still there.

"Well, that makes perfect sense. I'm here to kidnap my own cousin."

Neither of us moved. The weight of the pistol made my arms ache. I couldn't stop their shaking. It was only getting worse every second.

He took a cautious step toward me as if seeing through my defenses. "I know you're scared. I just want to help you," he repeated.

"Prove it," I said, blinking hard to keep the world in focus.

Keeping one hand up, he reached into his jacket.

I kept my finger on the trigger.

Cautiously, he withdrew a piece of parchment, and held it up in the light. "For you."

Lowering the pistol, I noticing the way his shoulders sagged in relief. I reached out to take the parchment, but suddenly everything began to spin. My head felt light, and my hand couldn't reach the extra two inches to take the paper from him. It dropped to my side. I heard the pistol land with a thud in the dirt, and was amazed it didn't go off. I couldn't keep going any longer. I couldn't take another step, or say another word. He stared at me in confusion, and asked me a question, but his words were lost in the pounding of my heart and the sound of my own breathing. My vision began to close in from all sides, dark blotches staining my sight. I staggered forward, grasping out in front of me for anything to hold onto, as the ground rushed up and the darkness swallowed me.

CHAPTER 18

My eyes opened to the sunlight, sifting through the trees. In front of me, the remains of last night's fire lay in a crumbling pile of dust. I rolled over, shivering in dawn's chill. Three days and nights of constant fear had taken their toll. My limbs were heavy as I sat up. Emily lay next to me.

I shuddered, remembering my display the night before. What had I been thinking? That was just it. I hadn't been thinking for days. I had only been acting. It was all I could do. I glanced behind me, seeing Jackson seated several yards away, leaned against a tree, watching the eastern sky. I stood up slowly, embarrassed, hoping he wouldn't notice.

He turned to me, and to my surprise gave an easy smile. In the sunlight, I could clearly see the burns down the left side of his face.

I let my gaze slip to the ground as I took a few steps forward, my cheeks burning. "I need to apologize for last night. I was being a fool, and I'm sorry."

He nodded, and turned back to the rising sun, shaking his head. "It's all right. I've been such an idiot."

I made my way forward until I was standing beside him, and seated myself on the damp ground not far from him. I choked back tears. "I can't thank you enough for what you did that night in the prison."

He turned to look at me, his expression blank. "What are you talking about?"

I looked away, realizing he didn't remember. "I'm sorry. I didn't know…"

"It's all just bits and pieces."

There was a long moment, as both of us tried to think of something to say.

"How much do you remember?" I asked, feeling my gut wrench as I wondered if he would recollect that I had tried to leave him there in the rubble.

He turned to me, giving a shrug. "Enough."

I glanced at him for a moment, then looked back at my hands folded in my lap.

"What were you doing there?" We both asked at the same time, then turned away, embarrassed.

"I was taking Emily to visit her grandfather." I waited for his answer.

"I was trying to set him free." He cleared his throat and continued. "Connors and I and a few others had planned to get Cephas out of prison. My job was to take the position of a jailer, then, on my midnight watch release him."

"What happened?"

He shook his head. "Brice and all the others were waiting for me."

"Did they start the explosion?"

"No. It was Connors. It was all part of the plan, a distraction, I suppose."

"Those distractions don't always go the way you plan. Do they?" I couldn't hide my smile at the recollection of the day I'd nearly shot Jackson.

"No. They don't. When Brice got a hold of me, I couldn't get word to Connors or tell him wait on the gun powder. Then, they all bolted."

I nodded. "They had a ship to catch."

He looked away, troubled. "After that, I don't remember

much."

"You didn't miss much."

"What happened?"

"Nothing, really." I couldn't keep the grin from spreading over my face. "But you have this uncanny habit of not dying when any decent person would."

He laughed, shaking his head. "Runs in the family."

"Yes. Well, it's very irritating."

"I'll remember that."

It felt good to smile, but I felt my throat constrict with the words that were coming. "You shielded us from that explosion." I was surprised at how fast the tears welled up. "If you hadn't been there …" I choked back the emotion, hoping I was making sense. "I don't remember much of what I said last night, but I want you to know, I didn't mean a word of it. Emily and I aren't doing very well on our own, and we're grateful for your help."

"Well I'm just returning the favor I guess."

We looked out at the sky for a long time, before he dug in his jacket pocket, retrieving a piece of paper. "You never did look at this." He held out the scrap to me, and I reached out, taking it from him.

Unfolding the sheet, I stared for a weary moment at the contents, then folded the paper again, without reading the rest. I felt sick. I couldn't read it just yet.

"Brice had it. I thought it might be important."

I turned away. "It's the second half of Cephas' letter."

"Like I said, it looked important."

"Thank you." I nodded, trying to regain control. "You should wake up Emily," I said, still turned away from him.

"That's all right. I'm sure she'd rather see you."

I stared at him in amazement. "Why?"

He shrugged. "You're the one who's taken care of her all this time."

"You're the one she won't stop talking about."

"You saved her from Scot."

"You came back from the dead!"

He struggled to his feet, as if to go wake her up, but paused. "I hated you."

I glanced up at him, my tone dry as dusty streets of London. "This may come as a surprise, but I actually caught on to that."

He cringed. "I know. It's just that I couldn't help it. You were…you were everything I should have been to her."

I stared in amazement at his confession. Was I truly hearing this?

"You were a complete stranger, and yet you did more for her than I ever have."

"And I'm making a wonderful mess of things," I interjected.

"Oh would you just stop it?" he cried. "Stop talking about what a mess you've made. Can't you see it?"

I stared blankly at him. "See what?"

"You! You've been dragged to the bottom of a river, held prisoner, almost killed. Yet you're bold enough, or maybe just stupid enough to keep going. Anyone in their right mind would quit. So stop telling me what a failure you are!"

It was the harshest compliment I'd ever received. I looked away. "You're the one who told me I wasn't fit for this job."

"How else was I supposed to get you to keep going? All you would do is argue with me. I thought maybe if I could put you down enough, you'd convince yourself to keep going."

I stared up at him, incredulous. "That's a twisted way to look at things."

His cock-eyed grin appeared. "But it worked, didn't it?"

I felt the smile tug at the corners of my mouth and wondered why my cheeks were burning. "Well lucky for both of us, Emily is very forgiving. She only remembers what you did right."

He shook his head. "And what was that?"

"You smiled."

He stared at me in confusion.

"Don't you trust me?" I asked.

"I haven't decided yet," he called over his shoulder as he turned to go wake her up.

I glanced over my shoulder, wanting to watch this.

With some difficulty, he knelt down next to her. As he set his hand on her arm, she seemed to dwarf in size, looking so tiny beside him. "Em," he whispered, stroking her golden hair.

She stirred, slightly. "Jack?"

His face reflected the love that I knew was on Emily's face. Before he could move, she had leapt up, and thrown her arms around his neck. Tears stood in his eyes, as he glanced at me.

I gave him a little nod, just to let him know I'd told him so. I understood the joy in his eyes, the joy of being forgiven by one you loved.

"Don't leave again," Emily said softly, laying her head on his shoulder. "We need you."

He stood up, still holding her tight. "I need you too."

$$\bullet \quad \bullet \quad \bullet$$

I was alone, in the stillness of the woods. Jackson had taken Emily into the city. Having received a few days wages as a prison guard, he had enough money for provisions for the journey ahead of us. Emily had refused to leave his side. I had argued that someone might recognize him. He had replied that it would be impossible for anyone to recognize him, considering he was dead. I disagreed with this logic. He didn't seem to care.

With the two of them in the city, I knew it was time for me to open the second page of the letter, no matter how much I dreaded it. Fishing in my satchel for the first page, I read the end of it, to see if they matched up.

I dread telling you what you must do, what I swore I would never ask of you. I know you promised yourself...

My stomach knotted, as I turned to the second page.

...you would never go back, because you fear the demons that are there, but that's the funny thing about demons. We pray and pray that God will vanquish them, because we believe in His power. We know that He is big enough to simply speak a word, and make our troubles disappear, so we feel forgotten when He doesn't. But He wants so much more for you than to simply pluck you out of your troubles, Kate. He doesn't just want to make your giants disappear. He wants you to know what it's like to slay one. Pray that He will give you enough strength to face them, to fight them, to conquer them. It won't be won in a solitary battle, but it will be won in the end. So fight, Katherine. Fight back your fears. Fight to forgive. Fight for your freedom.

There will be someone waiting for you, just as there was the first time you arrived. They will wait as long as they can, but they cannot wait forever. Time grows short.

Simon Cephas

"I can't," I whimpered to myself. I was too weary, too frightened, too weak. I had no strength left to fight. I couldn't go back. I couldn't face all that I'd left behind. I set the letter in my lap, and glimpsed writing scrawled on the back of the second page. Turning it over, I looked closer.

Disturb us, Lord, when,
With the abundance of things we possess
We have lost our thirst, For the waters of life;
Having fallen in love with life,
We have ceased to dream of eternity,
And in our efforts to build a new earth,
We have allowed our vision,
Of the new Heaven to dim.

~Sir Francis Drake

Thomas Rowton's words came to my mind. *He has to push us, disturb us, take us where we would never go on our own.*

I could hear Jackson and Emily returning through the dense forest. They were talking and laughing. A thought flashed through my mind. I didn't have to let on. They didn't have to know that I understood the letter. Anything was better than going back. My gaze fell on the last words of the letter.

Time grows short.

Reluctantly, I came to my senses. I didn't have to time to be stalled by fear, nor did I want to lie.

"Here we are," Jackson laughed, emerging from the trees, with Emily right on his heels. Both of them were grinning as though they had a wonderful secret. At seeing me, their grins disappeared. "What's wrong?"

I pasted on a smile. "Nothing."

"Where are we headed?"

I stuffed the letter in the satchel. "Riversend."

"Where is that?"

"On the coast. Just a few days east of us."

"Did he say why?"

I shook my head. "I have no idea."

• • •

We left the echoes of London behind without looking back. None of us wanted to remember the things that had happened there. Our morning's progress was slow, due more to Jackson than to Emily. He never once complained, but the beating from the prison had taken its toll, and he walked at a painfully slow pace. I pretended not to notice, adjusting my pace to match his, trying not to make him feel like he was slowing us down.

Honestly, I didn't mind taking our time. The longer it took to get to Riversend the better. I knew this was going to be difficult and painful, but I could see no way to avoid it. I didn't want to talk about it anymore than I wanted to do it, and I knew my short answers weren't enough to keep Jackson's questions away. To avoid the subject, I silently read the poem on the back of the letter over and over as we walked. Reading and walking proved more difficult that I'd expected and I stumbled on the road several times.

"Maybe you should wait to read that until your sitting down," Jackson suggested after I nearly landed face down on the road for the third time, barely catching myself before I fell.

"I can manage," was my short, less than confident reply.

Long after noon we stopped for a much needed break, and for the first time all day I put the letter back in the satchel and rested. After we ate I began to doze off, watching as Jackson and Emily talked and played.

"Miss Elyot?"

I startled awake, seeing both Jackson and Emily grinning at me.

"Should we head out again?"

I glanced at the dipping sun. "Yes," I said, shaking myself. How long had I been sleeping? It could have been moments or hours for all I knew.

As we walked, I dug into the satchel but found no letter. Where was it? Had I lost it? What would I do if it was gone? I started replaying the words in my mind. I knew where we were going, but these letters were filled with little details. If I didn't read them carefully, we could end up completely turned around.

"Lose something?" Without looking, I could hear the crooked grin in Jackson's voice.

"I can't find the letter." I took off the satchel, and set it alongside the road, dumping out its contents. "I know I put it in here."

I heard Emily's giggle and Jackson shushed her playfully. Couldn't they see what a problem this was?

"If we can't find that letter, we could end up going in circles," I reminded them.

"Can't have that, can we?"

"I fail to see what is so funny." I spun around to see Jackson and Emily on the verge of hysterical laughter. Neither of them offered an answer. They just stared at me. "Emily," I said in a stern tone.

She giggled and pointed at Jackson, whose mouth dropped open in feigned innocence. "You little traitor!" he chuckled.

I stepped toward him, holding my hand out for the letter, still not much amused.

"What?" he asked, as if he hadn't the faintest idea of what I wanted.

"The letter."

"What letter?" He winked at Emily, searched himself, then drew the letter from his pocket as if by accident. "Oh, this letter?"

I nodded, willing to put up with his humor.

He started to hold it out, then jerked it back as soon as I reached for it.

"Give that to me," I sighed, reaching for the letter again.

"Oh no you don't." He held the parchment just out of my reach. "You have to tell me the truth first."

"I haven't lied to you."

"You haven't lied to me *yet*."

I crossed my arms in front of my chest. His grin was aggravating. "What does that mean?"

He tapped his fingers on the edge of the letter. "Emily says that you cried when I died at the prison. Is that true?"

I shot a glance at Emily, whose cheeks were pink with excitement. She shrugged sweetly, and I felt tempted to call her a little traitor myself. "You didn't die."

He held up a hand to stop my argument. "That is completely beside the point! No diverting from the question."

I looked from one to the other as they both waited for an answer. I was trapped. "I don't think 'cried' is the right word," I answered, skirting around the question.

"You know you're absolutely right. I think she said 'wailed' or was it 'sobbed,' Em? I can't remember."

As he glanced down at Emily, I saw my opportunity and grasped for the letter while he was turned away. Without even turning to see me, he shot his arm up and the letter was out of reach once again. "No. You did not answer the question."

I stared at him, trying desperately to think of another way out that didn't involve playing into his game. Now was not the time for this. Couldn't he see that? My patience was thin to the point of cracking.

Then I looked down at Emily. She was laughing and giggling. She didn't laugh very often when it was just the two of us. I was taking this too seriously. Emily was right. I needed to smile.

Jackson was still waiting. "Maybe you forgot the question. Would you like me to repeat it?"

"No." I would join in the game for Emily's sake, but that didn't mean I had to lose.

"Well then?"

I leaned forward. "It had been a long day, and you were not the first tragedy to occur." Satisfied with myself, I turned to walk away. I didn't need that letter.

"Then that's a 'Yes.'"

I stopped, feeling the unfamiliar pleasure of a smile that wasn't forced. "Why does it matter?"

He walked up next to me, his cocky grin softening, as he gently set the letter in my hand. "I don't know."

A few hours later we made camp, Emily and I gathering stones and kindling for a fire. Jackson disappeared into the woods for an hour and returned with a brown hare for supper. As he dressed and cooked it over the fire I held Emily in my lap. We'd made a game of tossing pebbles at various surrounding objects. Emily counted her winnings one by one.

Emily asked Jackson to bless the food which he did with surprising ease, and familiarity. As we ate, I glanced up at him. "Did you stop at the Rowtons'?"

He nodded, swallowing a mouthful of food.

"For how long?"

Jackson gave a long, exhale. "To be quite honest, I don't know." He looked up, seeing my obvious confusion. "After I left you and Emily at the widow's, I walked out of the valley. I wasn't thinking straight. I don't know how long I'd walked before I looked down and realized I wasn't on the path anymore. I had no idea where I was. It was like a nightmare. I must have collapsed."

Emily and I stared at him in disbelief.

"They found me. They said the fever should have killed me, but..." He shrugged, looking down at his food. "Like I said it runs in the family."

"You should have stayed at the widow's," I felt my chest tighten with guilt. I had known how sick he was. I'd seen it on the road. I had known he wouldn't make it back to the harbor, but my pride had stopped me from insisting, and it had nearly killed him.

He smiled. "Did they tell you I'd been there?"

"No," I answered. "They did say that Timothy was on his way home, but I didn't know what that meant."

The stained sheets, the secretive glances, even the bloody

hand print that had led us to the house. It made sense at last. The Rowtons, at least the parents, must have known from my story, just who the sailor was that had helped Emily and I, yet they hadn't said a word. "The Rowtons are wonderful people," I said.

He nodded. "I've known them since I was Emily's age. He's one of Cephas' closest friends, even does a bit of the pamphlet writing. That's why they live so far removed from town. The work they do needs to be kept safe."

"Their caution was rewarded," I said, shuddering to think of what would have happened to those children had their father been found out.

"Thomas Rowton has a wisdom that's…well, it's hard to argue with."

"I know what you mean."

"He set me straight on a lot of things."

"What did he say?" I bit my tongue, too late. "I'm sorry. I didn't mean to…that's none of my business."

He shrugged. "He let me ramble, only asking a few questions, making a few comments. I gave him my reasons, my arguments, and every excuse I've stockpiled in the last two years. If he'd tried to argue with me I could have matched him word for word, but he just listened. At the end of my rambling, I realized how pointless it all was. Then, he sent me in the right direction, and wished me well. It meant a lot that he trusted me to make the right decision."

I smiled. That sounded like Thomas Rowton.

Jackson stood, stretching. "We've got a long day of walking tomorrow. How far did you say this place was?"

"It's thirty miles from London."

He groaned slightly. "That sounded shorter when you said it this morning. Have you been there before?"

I nodded, absently. "I grew up there."

"Perfect, then you won't get us lost."

I gave a faint smile at his words.

"Something wrong?"

I shook my head.

"Well goodnight, then." He turned and walked several yards away, settling himself between us and the road.

I glanced at Emily who had settled herself near the fire and I curled up beside her. As I drifted to sleep, I wondered if Jackson remembered what he told me the night of the explosion. He hadn't run. As much as he portrayed himself as a prodigal I knew there was more to his story.

CHAPTER 19

I managed to stall our departure until late morning the next day. I didn't want our time in Riversend to come one moment sooner than it had to. After an hour, I insisted that we stop so we could rest and eat, taking as long as possible to do both. In the late afternoon, I mentioned that we ought to look for a place to stop for the night. We walked along the dusty path, Emily having fallen asleep on Jackson's shoulder.

"You're waiting for something." It was a statement, not a question.

I stared at him, confused. "Am I?"

He nodded. "You're stalling. We could have reached Riversend by this morning, but we've been stopping early and starting late."

I smiled. "Maybe you're just not used to traveling with women and children."

"Maybe." He gave a knowing smile, seeing my mask for what it was.

I bit my lower lip. "I grew up in Riversend. My cousin and I were raised by a Puritan minister and his sister, after my parents were killed." When he said nothing, I rushed on. "It was a wonderful life, and I was happy, and I'm not complaining." Tears began to sting my eyes and I struggled to hold them back

"What happened?"

I hesitated. "A man moved to Riversend. He was kind and unassuming. He'd come searching for the writer of the Puritan pamphlets. He never said so, of course, but everyone could see right through him." I choked back the ache in my throat. "Except me. I gave him the evidence he needed to convict Reverend Durham. I wasn't being careful. I just thought..." I paused, trying to read his calm expression.

He looked up and as our eyes met I turned back to the road ahead.

"It doesn't really matter now." I brushed a few tears away, my fingers icy against my hot cheeks. "I gave him the Reverend's Bible with all his personal notes. They compared the writing in the Bible to the writing of the original pamphlets. The next thing I knew Reverend Durham was put on trial and executed for heresy, and the town scattered. It was my fault. I haven't seen Riversend since, and I hoped I never would."

He was quiet, and I wondered what was going through his mind.

"There are plenty of places I hope I'll never see again," he said at last.

"I know stalling is just a waste of time," I apologized.

"At least we're headed in the right direction, and you're not trying to lead us in circles."

I smiled. "It *did* cross my mind. This is just one more thing I never would have done if not for Emily. This has pushed me so far beyond my limits."

He shrugged. "I suppose that's what love does best."

I stared at him, wondering where on earth those words had come from, but before I could say anything, he hurried forward, trying to catch someone's attention as we neared a village.

"Excuse me."

The old man turned to look at us, his weathered face

softening into a smile at seeing Emily. "What can I do for you?"

"Is there a place we could stay tonight? We don't have much money, but we'll give you what we can."

"There's no inn here."

Jackson nodded. The day's walk had wearied him more than any of us. "Then I guess we'll keep moving."

We started to walk away when the man piped up. "Would you mind sleeping in a barn?"

He led us to a house just small enough for a few people, with a barn beside it. "Hope you don't mind sharing it with the animals." The barn door creaked open.

Jackson shook his head, going inside with Emily.

I stopped beside the farmer. "Thank you so much. We won't be any trouble, and we'll be leaving early in the morning."

He smiled congenially. "There's a work shed as well, if you'd be more comfortable."

I turned into the barn, seeing Jackson as he set down a recently awakened Emily.

"Such a charming family. How old is your daughter?"

The farmer's question made my cheeks burn, as I turned back to him. "Actually—"

"She's seven," Jackson answered before I could explain.

• • •

"What is it like on the other side of the world?"

Jackson looked up from the lantern at Emily's dreamy question.

"You did go there, didn't you?"

He smiled, leaning back to look at her. "It's very, very hot."

She crawled up next to him, leaning against him. He put an arm around her tiny form. "The air is heavy and sweet."

189

"Does it ever rain?" She asked, shivering against the cold shower that pelted the barn door outside.

He nodded. "And the rain sounds like a thousand horses all running at once. And when it stops raining, the air shines, like it had a bath."

She giggled.

"And the fish are all bright colors, and then there are the dolphins."

"What's that?"

His eyes shone with the secret. "Now, if I know your mother, she told you all about the merrows and the selkies and the mermaids."

She nodded.

"Dolphins are just like that, except they're real."

"Are they wicked, or do they grant your wishes?" she asked.

He laughed. "You know, I never did catch one to find out, but a friend of mine caught a monkey."

"Do *they* grant your wishes?"

"No. They follow you around, climb all over you, and get into trouble." He began to poke at her, making her giggle and squeal with delight. "They're a lot like you, you little monkey."

"I am *not* a monkey," Emily said, with the deepest gravity and sincerity.

Jackson and I exchanged amused looks.

She glanced up at him and whispered, "I'm a dolphin."

The laughter that spilled over flickered in the air like firelight. It was easy and warm and comforting.

When it had died down, Emily ventured another question, leaning against Jackson. "What would you have wished for?"

Jackson took several long moments to answer. "That's a good question."

I noticed Emily's blinks becoming longer as he considered his answer.

He laughed at himself. "I would have wished that I could come home to you."

"But I thought…" A yawn broke off her sentence. "I thought you liked it there."

"Yes, well, monkeys aren't very good company. I was lonely without you, Dolphin. All by myself on that big ship, night after night, I would have given anything to be back here with you."

I noticed that Emily didn't even respond. Her eyes were closed, and her breathing steady. "I think you lost your audience," I observed.

Jackson looked up as if he was surprised to see me sitting there. He shrugged. "It wasn't much of a story anyway."

I watched as he laid Emily down beside him and covered her with a cloak. I wondered for the hundredth time just who this man was.

He glanced up and caught my eye. "What?"

I looked away. "Nothing."

"Did I do something?"

"No. No, I just…" I looked right at him. "I'm sorry. I'm just…confused."

He nodded.

"The other side of the world sounds like a lovely place," I said, trying to change the subject.

He shrugged. "I don't know. I never really saw much of it."

"But I thought…"

"There's only so much of the world you can see when you never take a shore leave."

"You never left the ship?"

He shook his head.

"But why?"

"Because when you're half way around the world, all you want is something to cut the pain, and someone to end the loneliness, and all the port cities know it. Everywhere you turn, it can be bought with a couple of coins. I knew once I stepped foot on shore, I'd fall like all the rest."

The gravity of what he was saying made me shiver.

"I suppose most of the men took it to mean that I thought I was better than them. They saw me as the reverend who was always looking down on them. That's where the name comes from."

"It does have a nice ring to it."

He shook his head. "They all thought so, too."

"I don't know how you survived on that ship for two years."

He shrugged. "You just learn to keep your mouth shut and your eyes down."

I nodded. Connors had said something similar. "If Scot is such a tyrant, why do the men stay?"

"Because deserting a trade ship is a capital offense."

"Oh." I felt my throat constrict, realizing once again what he had risked to get me to Emily.

"The only other option is mutiny."

"Did anyone ever attempt that?"

"Only once." He stared into the fire. "Scot always knew if there was insubordination aboard ship. He knew all the signs. Scot has a way of looking at people and seeing right through them. It's a twisted talent he has, knowing your worst fears and your greatest weaknesses. He knew without asking which men had started the mutiny and demanded the paper to prove it."

"What would a paper prove?"

"Most mutinies start with a piece of paper. The men write their names in a circle, so that each one shares the blame equally. Then, it's passed around the ship. Scot demanded the piece of paper, and when he didn't get it, he began to beat the men one at a time. Guilt or innocence didn't matter. He lashed one after another until I couldn't take it anymore. I gave him the document."

"You?"

He nodded. "I hadn't signed it yet, so I couldn't be held responsible. I just wanted it to stop."

"What did he do?"

"Nothing. He lectured the crew, told them that if he would have chosen to prosecute, every name in the circle would have been hung for mutiny. The beatings stopped, and things went on as normal. I was pretty proud of myself."

"He didn't punish the men?"

"Not that I can prove, but not one of those names ever made it to the Indies. They all disappeared through unfortunate, unexplainable accidents."

I shivered at the thought.

Emily stirred, making a soft, gentle sound in her sleep. I felt relieved at the sight of her sleeping peacefully after so many hours of listening to her cries in the night.

"Merrows and selkies and mermaids?" I asked, curiously, unable to hide my smile. "Those don't sound like proper Puritan tales."

His smile returned. "Heathenism, I know."

"Oh, frightfully paganish," I laughed.

"Emily's grandmother, Cephas' wife, was from Ireland. She said those stories were her only connection with home. When she died, Clara, Emily's mother, told them to all of us to keep her mother's memory alive." He laughed at the memory. "And to keep us out of trouble. I just don't want Emily to forget. Those stories are all she has left of her family."

"You're her family," I reminded him gently.

He shrugged. "And I've done a wonderful job of that, haven't I? I'm just a distant cousin. I'll never be able to fill in the hole her parents left behind."

I bit the inside of my lip. Amazed at the words that were fighting their way out. "My cousin was my protector and my closest friend."

Something sparked his attention, and he watched me

intently.

"He never took my parents' place, but without him..." I couldn't continue. The ache in my throat was too much. I felt my eyes stinging.

"What happened to him?"

I cleared my throat. "Brice shot him on the riverbank. He died putting Emily and I into that skiff. I owe him everything."

"Then I suppose I do, too."

There was a long silence, each of us alone with our thoughts. Then a question came to my mind. "Why didn't you tell that farmer the truth?"

"Because one question leads to another, and there's a good chance we're being followed. There's nothing suspicious about a 'charming family' passing through town." He winked at me, standing to his feet.

"But we're not a family," I said, still feeling the need to say the truth aloud for conscience sake.

He bent down, lighting a second candle with the flame from the lantern, then headed toward the door, turning at the last moment with a smile. "You're right. We're not," he said, letting the door swing closed behind him, as he headed for the work shed.

• • •

"God's faithfulness is clear to me,
He breathes life into this sod
And for this sorry heart of clay,
He gave His own heart's blood
The saints and sinners all alike
Saw Him answer faithfully,
So tell me, child of His grace
When did He abandon thee?"

Reverend Durham sang under his breath, as we worked,

side by side. "You look troubled," he observed when he'd finished.

I smiled, trying to shake off the look, but there was no fooling him.

He halted his work at the printing press and sat down on a stool by his desk. "Perhaps we ought to take a break."

"I'm not tired," I insisted, turning back to the press to continue working.

"Katy."

I halted, knowing that gentle, loving tone all too well.

"What's troubling you?"

I turned to look at him. "It's that song."

"I wasn't aware my singing irritated you so much." His eye gleamed with amusement.

"No, not you. It's the song. I just…" I bit my lower lip. "I know I should sing it, and believe it with all my heart, but sometimes…"

His smile softened, compassionately. "Sometimes we feel abandoned, don't we?"

I nodded. "I worry for you," I confessed. "I worry for all of us, but it just seems foolish to place all of our trust in Someone Who can do whatever He wants. Sometimes I'm not willing to stake my life on that."

He stood from his spot, and walked over to me. "Kate, do you remember how you came to me?"

I nodded again.

"When did God abandon thee?"

I stared at him in confusion.

"Was it on that ship?"

Looking down at the floor, I felt tears filling my eyes.

"Was it along the road?"

I shook my head, unable to answer.

"Was it in the storm?"

"No," I gasped between shaky breaths.

"Tell me, Katy. When did He abandon thee?"

"Never," I said, softly.

He tilted my chin up to look at him. "Never is enough to stake a lifetime on, wouldn't you say?"

The lowing of a cow was so incredibly close it startled me awake. I rolled over, opening my eyes, the dream fading so fast I could hardly grasp the memory of it before it was gone. In the early morning light, I saw the cow still in her milking pen, Emily sleeping beside me. As I relaxed in the bed of straw, I fought desperately to hold onto my dream. I'd nearly forgotten that day in the print shop. It had been just days before Reverend Durham had been taken. It had been our last conversation.

I didn't want to stand, didn't want to get up. I knew what today would bring. I knew where we were going. There would be someone there, just like the first time I'd arrived on the back porch of the parsonage. Miss Durham had called it a sacred spot, because that's where she had found James and I dirty and half-dead without the slightest remembrance of how we'd gotten there. The last thing either of us remembered was the helplessness of the road in the rain. She called the place sacred because she said that's where the angels had left us. Today there would be someone waiting there for us. I wondered who. Thomas Rowton? Mate Connors? Or Simon Cephas himself?

Then, with a sudden stab of grief, I remembered what all of this was leading up to. I would say goodbye to Emily today. Jackson would leave too. The thought produced an empty ache inside me. They would leave with whomever came to meet us, and I would be alone. This thought upset me even more than the thought of being in Riversend. What would I do? Where would I go? Back to London? I felt sick at the notion. I couldn't bear that place. I had determined that when we'd stayed at the Seven Stars. Should I head north to where all of this had started? There was nothing there, no inheritance, no family, not even memories. Until now, I hadn't even considered what I would do when Jackson and Emily left.

An idea came to my mind, so unbidden and ridiculous that I nearly laughed aloud.

I could go with them.

My heart was breaking at the thought of letting them leave me behind. I loved Emily. She was the reason I had started all of this, but now in the solitude of my thoughts, I knew she was not the only reason I wanted to continue.

I thought of the way Jackson had held her in his lap, the way he smiled at her when he forgot I was watching. I saw the man he was at heart, and I had come to cherish his friendship, but what if the bond we had formed was deeper than that? I would never know unless I saw this journey through to the end.

The door creaked open and I sat up. All of a sudden I was more excited than nervous for this day to start. It was a new beginning. I saw Jackson and my heart sped up. I had made the right decision.

"Are we ready?" he asked in a hushed voice.

I nodded, leaning over Emily and gently shaking her awake. I felt a warmth inside me as I realized all over again how deeply I loved her. I wasn't afraid anymore. She rolled over, still fast asleep. I laughed, and scooped her up in my arms, letting her head rest on my shoulder. Jackson held open the door, and we stepped out into the early morning. It was cold, and I held Emily tight as we walked. My new beginning would start today, but before it could, I knew I had to face my past, along with all of the memories and wounds that lay in Riversend.

• • •

The sky was a murky shade of gray as the few farm houses came into view. I set Emily down to walk beside me.

The long curtain of willows to the right of the road

brought the first memories that took my breath away. I could almost see James and I as children darting in and out between them. I swallowed hard, not wanting to let my grief stop me. It would only make things worse. The song of the swishing leaves echoed behind me as we walked into the deserted town. It was as silent as the day I'd left. I could feel Jackson's eyes on me, watching me for the pain he knew was there. I gave him a reassuring nod. With a deep breath, I held Emily's hand a little tighter. "This way."

We stepped around the church building through long, unkempt grass. I jumped at the sound of scraping stones, as the sudden flight of birds sent several bricks from the chimney tumbling to the ground behind us.

Tears stung my eyes when I saw the house. *My house.* It was filthy, crumbling, neglected. The garden Miss Durham had tended all her life was grown over with weeds. I remembered promising her that I wouldn't let that happen. I remembered all the hours we'd spent, planting and weeding and watering. Her rocking chair creaked on the porch. I stopped in the middle of the path to the front door.

"Is this it?" Jackson asked.

I nodded mutely.

"What are we supposed to find?"

The memory of the letter broke through my troubled thoughts. I needed to focus.

There will be someone waiting for you, just as there was the first time you arrived.

Without a word, I climbed the front steps and opened the door. It groaned in pain as it swung open.

"Do you want us to wait here?"

I shook my head at Jackson's question. I didn't want to be alone. I wanted the comfort of knowing someone was here with me as I walked through the darkened house. Without looking down, I reached for Emily's hand. I found Jackson's instead. He closed his fingers around mine. It gave me enough strength to step forward into the den of memories.

Books were scattered on the desk. A broom lay in the middle of the floor. Dishes were uncleared from the dining table. It had been a day like any other. The doors to the bedroom and the Reverend's study lolled on their rusting hinges. A rustling sound caught my attention, and I glanced at the table by the window. A single tear slipped down my cheek. Letting go of Jackson's hand, I stepped toward the table. There was the Bible. The opposing breezes from the front door and the open window were sending the pages back and forth. I laid my hand down on the fluttering pages before one more could turn, and a verse caught my eye.

Little children I write unto you, for your sins are forgiven you for His Name's sake.

The words *little children* were circled. Picking up the Bible, I flipped through the pages, the smell of evening prayers and memorized verses filling the air. I clutched it close to my heart, then set it back on the table. I had a job to do. Turning back to Jackson and Emily, I moved toward the back door, opening it and stepping outside. It was still. Looking all around, I felt instantly that something was wrong. Then, I noticed the folded sheet of paper that lay at my feet. The word "Kate" was etched in the center. I bent to pick it up, and broke the seal, my heart pounding.

"What's wrong?" Jackson asked.

I couldn't speak above a whisper. "We're too late."

CHAPTER 20

Her name is Hopewell. She's from London. And if you have any hope of meeting her you must be at the dock before the chapel bells sound. We waited for you until the last moment, but I had to get my people to safety. We're bound away to a City Upon a Hill by the grace of God. If you miss us once more, you must hide yourself and the girl until I can come for her. I will come for you as soon as I can.

Durham would have been so proud of you.

There is one more favor I must ask of you. It's time to let go of what's been done. This will not be an easy task for either of us. It's in the print shop. Your deepest regrets. Your darkest fears. Mine are there as well. For years I have left them buried there with all the other treasures I couldn't keep safe. I want you to go to the shop, and no matter what happens, don't pry open the coffin of regrets. Destroy it. Don't leave until you have uncovered and destroyed the guilt you find there.

You are forgiven. You are made clean. Washed in the Blood of Christ! In Him you are a new creation. All that is old is passed away. All things have become new. He has seen you at your worst and

*at your darkest and He loves you still. You cannot
live the rest of your life holding onto the shame and
bitterness. In Him you are set free. Go in peace.*

*When you have read this and understood its
meaning, destroy it.*

*In Christ forevermore,
Edward Jackson*

"Edward Jackson?" I said aloud.

"Simon Cephas," Jackson answered. "Same person."

I showed him the letter. He studied it hard, and as he did I
saw the words scrawled on the back of the parchment.

*Disturb us, Lord, to dare more boldly,
To venture on wilder seas
Where storms will show Your mastery;
Where losing sight of land,
We shall find the stars.*
~Sir Francis Drake

"She's a ship. The Hopewell," Jackson said, breaking into
my thoughts, as he folded the letter.

"A ship to where?"

He didn't answer, still studying the parchment. "Chapel
bells," he mused, his eyes widening. "That's Sunday. That's
tomorrow."

"Will we make it?"

"We don't have much of a choice. We've got to try."

"But where are they going?"

"I don't…" Jackson paused again, his eyes focused on one
phrase. "Winthrop." He stared at me, a look of shock on his
face. "They're going to the New World."

"How do you know that?"

"I'll explain later. We need to go." Handing me the letter,

he picked up Emily and walked through the house to the front door.

"Wait," I called after him. "There's something I need to do."

. . .

"Do you want us to go with you?" Jackson asked.

I shook my head. "I need to do this."

Emily was at my side, her face against my skirt.

Lowering to my knees, I looked into her dark, shining eyes. "Will you pray for me?"

Her head bobbed up and down eagerly.

"We'll be waiting for you," Jackson said as I stood to my feet.

With a deep breath, I turned to the dark, forgotten shop.

The moment I stepped in the shadows of the room, my heart began to pound. The memories were so strong, they brought me to my knees on the sunken earth floor. I stopped holding back, stopped trying to forget. My fear melted away, giving way to guilt. I let every choice, every thought, every recollection play in my mind as I sobbed. Then my guilt slowly turned to anger. Digging my hands into the earth, I burned with hatred for Lindon, for Fortune Cole, for the stranger who had murdered my parents. It wasn't right. They had all walked away without the slightest recompense. I cried until my tears and my energy were spent. Then, in the silence, I heard a voice, small and still.

When did God abandon thee?

I could hear his voice, as if he were still standing there, in front of me.

Was it on the ship?

I closed my eyes, letting the words soothe my burning heart.

Was it along the road?

I shook my head.

Was it in the storm?

"No."

Tell me, Katy. When did He abandon thee?

"Never," I said softly. Slowly, I looked up, staring through a crack in the ceiling, at the sky beyond. "And never is enough to stake my life on."

He had never left me. He had always been here. He was deeper than my deepest fears and doubts. Stronger than every sinful act. More powerful than any bitterness. He burned with holiness, while I burned with hatred. He loved me even though I'd turned my back on Him. He had seen me in my secret heart. I had hated Him, rejected Him, feared Him. Now, I felt His loving arms around me, as I poured my heart before Him.

I had no right to hate when Christ had loved me so much. I had no reason for guilt, when He had taken the blame for all my sin. I had nothing to fear, when He was on my side. I felt His presence strengthen me. I stood from my spot. The coffin of my regrets had been destroyed. The place around me no longer frightened me. It had been redeemed, and so had I.

• • •

We walked all that day and through the night, Jackson carrying Emily, not stopping to rest, never complaining. I smiled, remembering how his quick pace had irritated me the night we had walked to the widow's. I laughed softly, thinking how odd it was to go from being enemies to passing ourselves off as husband and wife all in little more than a week.

"What's so funny?" Jackson asked, breathless from the long walk.

"You."

"Me?"

"You're so different. Are you the same sailor who wanted to have me hanged?"

"I don't know. Are you the same lunatic who tried to kill me...twice?"

"Three times," I corrected.

"Three?"

"Well, in the prison, I didn't actually try to kill you. I just tried to leave you for dead. I'm not sure if that counts."

"Oh no, of course not. That's completely...wait. You tried to what?"

"We were in a hurry," I defended, wishing the darkness would hide the laughter in my voice as well as it hid my smile.

"You must have been. Might I ask what changed your mind?"

"Do you even need to ask?" I motioned toward the little girl in his arms.

He looked down at Emily. "My good luck charm."

I laughed, then gave a long sigh. I found myself staring at them. The family he and Emily shared was still a mystery to me. "What is your connection with Simon Cephas? I know he's Emily's grandfather and that you're related somehow, but I'm having trouble sorting it all out."

"He's my uncle," he said without hesitation.

I nodded, still trying to set the questions of my mind in order. "Which would make him..."

"Scot's brother."

I stopped in the road, unable to hide my surprise.

"Hard to believe, isn't it?"

"How is that even possible? They're nothing alike." I asked, falling in step beside him.

"Actually, they're very similar."

"Really?"

"They're both passionate men, who believe in the cause they're fighting for."

"With Cephas, I agree with you, but Scot?"

"When I was little, my father told me stories about men like William Wallace and Robert the Bruce."

"The Scottish Rebels?"

"Men that stood for something, stood against the corruptness of their leaders. He said that in the three hundred years since their deaths, no one has ever taken a stand like that. He said it was what this country needed."

"Did Cephas agree with him?"

"Maybe at first. It would take a blind man not to see the fact that this country needs a reform of some sort, but Cephas saw the problem as a spiritual one. He wanted to purify the country, not start a revolution. That's when their fighting started. For hours my mother and I would listen to them argue about politics and religion."

"Sounds unbearable."

"It was until my father left."

I heard the brokenness in his voice. "He left you?" I asked.

He nodded, clearing his throat. "Well, they both did. I was eight. Times were hard. They both needed a way to feed their families. They went north because Cephas had found work on a ship and told my father to come with him. I think it was his way of trying to set aside their disagreements."

"What happened?"

"I only know what I was told. There was an accident. Most people said it was some sort of scandal, and my father was involved. My uncle came back. My father went to prison. It was what finally drove them apart. Neither of them will talk about what happened, and neither of them were ever the same."

I could only listen in stunned silence.

"When my uncle came back, he said he'd promised my father that he would look out for me, and he did. He was a better father to me than Scot ever was. He was always there when I needed him, especially when my mother died. He tried to keep my faith in tact, but that's when I stopped listening. I didn't want to hear about the God who let my father leave and my mother die."

"I know what that's like," I said softly.

"I remember my uncle that God's timing is perfect, but the Devil's is pretty good too. Just when I started to question everything, I got a letter from my father. He told me he'd been released from prison for lack of evidence and had become successful through sea trade. It was years before I found out that he'd escaped from prison, hence the name change from Jackson to Scot. He'd gone to sea as a crewman, then mutinied with the crew's support. His letter had sounded so sincere. He told me he was so sorry for never being a part of my life. He said he wanted a second chance. I went to meet him without telling my uncle. I went to a tavern he'd specified in London, but my father wasn't there. Brice was. He said my father was on his way. He invited me to have a drink. The next thing I remember is waking up on the Defiance, on my way to the Indies."

"He kidnapped you?"

He nodded. "What made it worse, is that my uncle and all the others thought I'd abandoned them. In their eyes I just disappeared one day, and there was no way for me to get word to them. I never got the chance to tell him that I didn't run."

I remembered the night of the explosion, and finally understood the importance of the message. Timothy was coming home, and he hadn't run. "He had to know you wouldn't do something like that."

Jackson shook his head. "I'd been troubled ever since my mother died. I'd talked about leaving and going to sea all the time. It was one of the last things I said to him, before I left. That's part of the reason I didn't want to come back. I'd only planned on being gone a couple of days, but after two years I wondered if they would see me as the enemy. I hated every second on that ship, but it was there that I remembered everything Cephas and my mother had taught me. I tried to hold onto everything I knew was right. That faith I'd grown up with was all I had on the other side of the world, but after enough time, I started to believe the lies. Scot told me that Cephas would never accept me again, that he'd been trying to control me my whole life. By the time we got to London, I was convinced that I'd been liberated by Scot, not kidnapped. I let Scot control me." He glanced down at his wrist. "And I'll bear the mark of it forever."

In the darkness, I reached over and took his hand, running my thumb down the scar left by the mark. *Ferox.*

"You know," I said softly. "It doesn't just mean defiant."

"No." His voice was low. "It also means arrogant, headstrong, and wild."

"It also means courageous."

I felt his hand grasp mine, and my heart skipped a beat. The night air was sweet as we walked on in comfortable silence.

"You haven't even seen Cephas in two years?" I asked.

"I haven't spoken with him," the pain was evident in his voice. "But I saw him. In Newgate prison he was sick and starving. I had to watch him without his notice, waiting until midnight when I could set him free."

I was suddenly touched, remembering how many times Jackson had asked the question that had so annoyed me that night. *Did he get out?* It was all he'd wanted to know, even when his own life had been unsure. "What changed your mind?" I asked. "On the Defiance, I mean. What changed you?"

He cleared his throat. "This lunatic we found in the River Hull tried to kill me."

"Stop it!" I laughed, giving him a playful shove. His teasing suddenly reminded me of being with James, and I grew desperate to change the subject. "What do you think the New World will be like?"

"Untouched wilderness I suppose."

"How do you know that's what the letter meant?"

"A City Upon a Hill," he quoted. "That's the phrase John Winthrop used when he left five years ago. He and Cephas were close friends. Winthrop tried to convince us to come with him and the seven hundred others that were headed to the New World so we could create 'A City Upon a Hill.' He saw the persecution coming, when none of the rest of us did."

Now I remembered why the name was familiar to me. "I remember Reverend Durham mentioning a similar offer. I've often wondered how different things might have been if we had listened to him."

"Now we get a second chance."

I smiled to myself. "I could use a second chance."

He looked at me, then looked back at the road. "You don't have to stay here. You could come with us."

I smiled. "Maybe if Emily asked me very sweetly I'd consider it."

"Well, not that I'm any substitute, but Emily is currently unavailable."

I started to laugh, but cleared my throat, attempting an authoritative voice. "Then proceed and make your plea on behalf of her Highness."

He shifted Emily's weight to his other arm. He didn't answer for some time, and I wished for the smallest bit of light to better read his face. "I'd miss you, Kate."

I felt my cheeks grow warm, and my heart started pounding, at the first time he'd ever used my name.

He forged on. "I know I was hard on you for everything that happened on the Defiance, but the truth is, if you hadn't come I'd be completely lost. All that time on board the ship, I'd been asking God to send me a sign, to show me that He still cared about what I did with my life. I finally just assumed He didn't care. You proved me wrong. That's the reason I hated you, but I never thought it would be the reason…" He halted, clearing his throat.

I laughed. "Don't stop."

He returned to his playfully pleading self. "The reason I humbly ask you to join us

I looked at the path in front of me, wondering if that had been the original end to his sentence.

"And it's not just me. Emily needs you. She needs someone to watch out for her, care about her, understand her. Her mother's gone. You're all she has."

"Don't give yourself so little credit."

"Well, we do make 'a charming family,'" he attempted his best impression of the farmer we'd met along the road.

I let my laughter spill over, feeling suddenly happier than I had in years.

The sky was lightening and dawn was coming. We knew we still had at least another few hours before we reached London.

"Do you think we'll make it in time?" I asked.

"We should. If I know Cephas he'll hold that ship until the last moment."

We walked in tired silence during the last miles of our journey. As we neared London, I found myself fighting to keep my eyes open as we walked.

"Staying awake?" Jackson asked, as I steered myself in a straight line.

"Of course," I yawned.

"I want you to stay at the hut by the river with Emily."

"But we're in a hurry."

"I know. Scot knows it too."

"You're afraid he's there waiting for you."

He nodded, his jaw tight. "There are still plenty of things that could go wrong. I just want to make sure we're not walking into a trap."

I felt a pang of fear as we neared the hut by the river.

"Give me an hour. If I'm not back…"

"Go to the dock and ask about the Hopewell," I finished.

"No." He halted and turned to look me in the eye. "If I

don't come back, I want you take Emily, and I want you to run."

"Where?"

"Anywhere. Back to Riversend. Back to the widow's house. Anywhere safe."

I nodded, mutely, knowing my voice would shake with tears if I tried to answer.

He gave a reassuring smile. "Don't you trust me?"

"Of course," I said, without hesitation. The thought that he would abandon us here hadn't even occurred to me. "Be careful."

Glancing at me over Emily's head he nodded. "And I *will* come back."

"I know. I trust you."

In front of the cabin, I laid a hand on Emily's back, and she stirred in Jackson's arms, reaching out toward me sleepily. Shifting her, slightly, Jackson tilted her in my direction, and I took her in my arms. I knew now that she and I wouldn't have to say goodbye. I held her close, knowing she was mine to love. I glanced up to see Jackson, watching me, with a look in his eyes that was something like awe. Our gazes met. He took a breath as if about to speak, but turned away, clearing his throat. "Will you be all right here, alone?"

I gestured toward the city. "We got along just fine before you showed up, didn't we?"

"Is that actually a question you want me to answer?" he called over his shoulder.

"Just go," I laughed.

Laying Emily on the cot inside, I rubbed my raw freezing hands together. I had noticed a fire pit in front of the cabin, and decided to put it to good use. Placing the satchel over my shoulder, I bent down to strike the flint. Once the fire was burning, there was nothing to do but wait. I shivered as I thought of how my life was about to change. We were leaving everything. The thought of living on a ship for two weeks made me sick inside, but the thought of living alone was ten times worse. I had expected to be more afraid of the sea than ever before, after my experience on the Defiance. Instead I found myself less frightened.

I had been chained in the hull of a ship for three days, tortured by fears. I had weathered a storm and come out safely on the other side. Anything I experienced on the way to the New World could not be worse than that. I pulled out Cephas' most recent letter. *A City Upon a Hill.* I liked the sound of that. With a certain peace I couldn't explain, I folded the letter, and placed it back in the satchel. James would have never wanted to go to the New World, and would have fought me on it at every turn, but he'd told me to get Emily home. I found myself aching, wishing for his blessing on my decision. I smiled, remembering how often I'd despised him for ordering me around. Now I longed for it. "I wish you were here," I whispered softly, "So you could tell me what to do."

I felt something dig into my back. "I'll do my best," a voice hissed behind me. Before I could react, there was a knife at my throat and a hand over my mouth. "Get up!" He wrenched me to my feet, dragging me backward toward the stream. Pinning my back against a tree, he leaned over me, pressing the knife against my throat. I saw the face of Scot's spy who'd distracted me while Emily had been kidnapped. I instinctively glanced toward the cabin.

"Cry out, and I will kill you."

CHAPTER 21

He slowly removed the hand from my mouth, but not the knife from my throat.

"What do you want?" I asked, barely above a whisper.

"It's time to make good on your promise."

I took a deep breath, my mind spinning. I'd forgotten about my promise completely, but I couldn't let him know that. I had to stay calm. Glancing up at him as he leaned over me I shook my head feigning relief. "Is that all?"

He eyed me, unmoving.

"I'm sorry to disappoint you, but I didn't find it."

"What?"

"The lock. I never found it. You can tell Scot..."

"He doesn't care about that!" he cursed me, tightening his hold on the knife. "Where's Cephas? Don't lie to me. I know he told you."

"That wasn't our deal," I choked.

The knife pressed closer again. "I'd save your breath. I saw the letter. I know he told you."

Keeping my eyes fixed on him, I reached in the satchel, feeling for the parchment. Once I was sure I had a hold on the loose, unfolded pages, I withdrew them.

Using his free hand, he snatched the letter from me.

"It's all there," I promised.

"Oh no you don't." He shoved the papers toward me. "I want names and I want dates and I want a map. Everything I need to know."

"I can't."

"Is that right?" he asked, pushing the knife closer.

"I don't have a pen."

He muttered something under his breath, then stared hard at me. "Then give me the message."

I couldn't do it. I knew that my words wouldn't be enough to convince him.

"Did you hear me?"

I fought to keep from screaming. "Wait! I can send him the message. Just let me sit down."

He stared at me in confusion.

"Please," I begged.

Watching me, with a suspicious eye, he let me lower to the ground, never removing the knife from its place at my throat, as he lowered to his knees.

"Everything I need to know," he reminded me, as I bent down over the letter.

As I struggled to keep from shaking, I brought my fingers to my lips, and spit on them.

He eyed me.

I ground my moist fingers into the earth beside me until they were brown and muddy. Then, I used the mud to highlight my message within Cephas' epistle, marking a letter here and there, until they spelled out my missive to Scot.

Riversend.

"Is that all?"

"That's everything you need to know," I assured him.

Once again, he pulled me to my feet, nearly ripping my arm out of joint. He shoved me against the tree, the knife clutched in his fist. Leaning closer, his foul breath surrounded me as he hissed in my ear. "He'll be watching you. Every second he'll be watching you."

"That's everything I know." My voice broke as I tried not to listen to his threats.

He motioned his head toward the hut. "For her sake, it had better be. He's asking nicely this time, but if he finds out you lied to him, he'll drop her on the road before you can run, and then he'll get the information he needs. Let me ask you one more time. Is this everything I need to know?"

I nodded.

He leaned back. "Don't doubt that he'll do it. He'll kill her without a second thought."

I couldn't listen to another word of his threats. "We wouldn't let him touch her."

A question came into his eyes. "Who's we?"

My mouth dropped open, realizing what I'd just given away.

"It's Jack isn't it?" The knife was tight against my throat. "You're working with him, aren't you?"

I fought hard to keep my composure. I had to make him believe me. "That's what he'd like to think." My voice was calmer than I'd expected.

He turned away, muttering and cursing. With knife finally removed, I had the urge to run, but knew my plan hinged on staying here, and staying calm.

"Why so upset?" I asked. "I'm leading him right to you."

The sailor's eyes lit up, and my smile wasn't altogether fake. He believed me.

"Follow the instructions of that letter, and we'll meet you there. You get Jackson. I get the little girl, on one condition. I had nothing to do with it. Are we clear?"

He didn't argue with those terms. A sly smile slid across his face as he sheathed the knife, and shook hands with me. "Pleasure doing business with you, Miss." He turned disappearing into the trees.

I nearly collapsed from fear, and put a cold trembling hand against my throat.

"What do you think you're doing?"

I screamed, and jumped back, at the sound of Jackson's voice. He stepped out from behind the tree I'd been leaning against, his jaw set, his eyes burning.

I couldn't answer as the frightened tears came to my eyes.

He took a step closer. "What kind of game are you playing?"

"I—I'm not."

"What else would I *like to think*?" he asked.

"No," I fumbled. "You don't understand."

"Then explain it to me!" he cried. "Because when I see one of Scot's men here I'm assuming you're in trouble. Then I get closer and stop long enough to hear you." He paused, the words falling from his lips like shards of glass about to shatter. "Selling me to Scot?"

"It's not like that," I promised. "I…" Something rustled in the bushes, and the sailor's words came back to me. *He'll drop her on the road, before you can run.* I couldn't explain. We were being watched. I couldn't tell him what I'd done, how I'd sent Scot in wrong direction, unless I wanted to see him shot right in front of me. "I can't explain it to you."

He gave a bitter laugh. "Why doesn't that surprise me?"

"I mean I can't explain it to you *yet*!"

"Oh no! Let me give you a few days to come up with a convincing story. What else did you give him? The letter?"

I stared at the ground.

He exhaled. "Perfect. Now he knows exactly where we're going."

"I didn't know what else to do!" I cried. "I forgot he was coming for the information."

"Wait!" Jack stopped me. "You knew he knew he was coming?"

"I knew he wanted the information, but I didn't think…"

"Why didn't you tell me?"

"I forgot! In London I needed that letter from Scot and I

had nothing left to trade for it, so I told him I'd give him any information he wanted."

"You made a deal with him?"

"I didn't have a choice!"

"You couldn't have told me about this?"

"I didn't remember! Besides what could you have done?"

"I would have moved faster. I wouldn't have left you out here alone. I wouldn't have given him time to ..." He stopped, staring at me the way he had the first time he'd seen me. His eyes were cold and filled with hate. "I'm such an idiot."

"What?" I asked, not understanding.

"Was any of it true?"

I stared dumbly at him.

He just shook his head. "The delay. You were stalling, weren't you? All of that about the memories. You were just waiting for him. Giving him time to catch up."

"No!" I cried, my heart breaking.

"Why did you do it?" His voice was dead of emotion.

"I didn't!"

"You didn't make a deal with Scot?"

"I did, but—"

"You didn't know he would come to collect? You didn't promise to hand me over?"

I couldn't answer. How could I explain without getting him killed?

"Anything to save your own skin. Is that it?" His voice was weak. "What did he promise you?"

The tears spilled down my cheeks. "Nothing." I looked up at him, taking steps toward him, until I was right in front of him. "Jack."

He wouldn't look at me.

"I know it doesn't make sense, but you have to trust me."

"Until when?" he looked down at me, his face nearly touching mine, as he gripped my shoulders. "Where do I draw the line? When do I stop trusting you? When I'm watching

Scot pay you off?"

His words cut me so deep that my knees nearly buckled.

He turned away from me. "I can't let you come with us."

"What?" I panicked, feeling terrified. "No! Don't leave me here. Please! If we hurry—"

"I can't risk Emily's life."

"You won't! I promise. Please! You've got to take me with you! If you don't Scot will catch up with me."

"Which is exactly what you've wanted this whole time, isn't it? It's exactly what you deserve." His voice was emotionless.

"No." I moved forward, putting a hand on his shoulder. He flinched at my touch like it was a hot iron, and I pulled my hand back. I didn't know why, but I was aching to tell him that I had cried over his death in the prison, that my tears had come in torrents, and been based in something far deeper than I had understood, until now. I found myself wondering if he would cry for me when he found out that Scot had killed me for giving him false information. Or would he still say that I was getting what I deserved? My heart felt as though it would crack in two.

"We need to leave." There was iron in his voice. "The ship will only wait so long." He started for the cabin.

"Wait!" I begged.

He stopped, not turning to look at me.

"Don't tell Emily. I'll explain it to her."

He gave a stiff nod, then ducked into the cabin. As soon as he was inside, I reached in the satchel, felt for the other letter, the one that pointed us to the Hopewell, and drew it out of the bag. I dropped it in the fire, watching through blurry tears as it shriveled into ashes.

It was done.

· · ·

He wouldn't put her down long enough for me to even embrace her. "You're going to go on a ship," I told her, unable to keep the tears out of my voice. "Then you're going to have a new home."

She reached out her fingers to mine. "Why are you crying?"

I glanced up at Jackson who looked away, his jaw tight. "Because I can't go with you."

She squirmed and wiggled out of Jackson's arms until he couldn't hold her any longer. I reached out for her, catching her, and clung to her.

"You have to come." She buried her face in my shoulder. "We're a family. Jack said so."

I felt my cheeks burn as I realized she hadn't been sleeping through that conversation in the night. "Emily, I love you so much."

"Then come with us," she begged.

"I can't." I could feel the sobs shaking my body. Looking up, I saw Jack, watching the exchange with a hard expression. I stared directly into his eyes. "Someday it will all make sense to you."

He looked away.

I loosened my hold on Emily so I could look into her eyes. They were shining with tears. "You've got to be good for Jack. He's just doing what he thinks is best for you. You listen to him, all right?"

She nodded.

I leaned forward pressing my forehead against her and looking right into the sparkling eyes that had given me so much hope. "That's my girl."

She threw her arms around my neck. "I love you, Katy!"

"I love you too."

• • •

I watched from the hillside as the Hopewell pulled away from the dock and pressed its way down the Thames. They were gone. My heart beat so hard I thought it would burst. I had done the right thing, hadn't I? I had scoured my brain for any way to send the message to Jack, but I had lost him completely. I was now the enemy. The only thing that kept me from giving up hope was knowing that in breaking his heart, I had saved his life and Emily's.

Someone had been watching our conversation. Someone knew that they were on the Hopewell, but they obviously hadn't reached Scot with the news in time, since the ship was slipping down the river and out of sight. I knew what I should do. I should find a place to hide, in the hope that I could go to the dock and find a way to pay my passage across the ocean. Once in the New World, I could explain everything to Jackson. That is, if he would listen to me. I knew that it was as good a plan as any, but I couldn't move from my spot. I watched as the ships came in and out of the harbor. The ones I loved were safe. They were all safe. That was what mattered.

"You thought you could fool me, didn't you?" The deep rumbling voice sent chills down my spine, but I turned to face Captain Scot, unafraid.

His eyes blazed. In his hand was the letter with the one word I had created by marking the letters. *Riversend.*

CHAPTER 22

"You thought you could send me all the way to Riversend and back." The captain's voice was low and menacing.

I stared at him without answering. My emotions were spent.

From behind, I felt two sets of hand, clamp down on me like sets of iron shackles. I glanced from side to side, seeing Brice and the man I'd given the letter to.

Scot leaned over me, his eyes piercing me, searching me. "I told you not to betray me."

"Incorrect," I replied. "You told me not to do anything I might regret, and betraying that girl's family to you would be the darkest regret of my life."

"But you didn't always have such high ideals, did you?"

His words twisted my stomach.

"You never told me your name."

I watched him, my heart pounding.

He smiled. "I had to do some digging to find out just who you were, and do you know who I found?" His grin was one of absolute glee as he turned to look behind him.

I followed his gaze, and my knees buckled under me. The grip of the two sailors was all that held me up.

From behind Scot walked my worst nightmare. He gave his wolfish grin and winked at me. "Hello, Katy."

"No," I breathed.

Charles Lindon laughed. "Is that any way to greet an old friend?"

How was this possible? After having caught the notorious pamphlet writer on behalf of the bishop, Charles Lindon was now one of the most powerful men in the country. What would he have to do with a man like Scot?

"Ah," Scot grinned. "So you remember. Touching."

A helplessness overcame me. "What more could you want, Lindon?"

Scot was chuckling, enjoying every moment of this. "I'll let you in on a little secret, if you'd like. Lindon wasn't a Puritan hunter. He didn't work for the Bishop. He worked for *me*. I knew Durham was my Puritan brother's closest friend. I sent Lindon to find a weakness, anything he could use to convict Cephas, and he'd compiled quite a heap of evidence. He wasn't looking for pamphlets in Riversend."

"But you led me right to them," Lindon laughed.

Scot shook his head. "He thought it would be more profitable to report the pamphlets to the Bishop than it would be to report the evidence to me."

"And so it was." Lindon's grin was unbearable. "I saw a promotional opportunity, and I couldn't resist."

Scot sneered at Lindon. "Without so much as a thank you. You even lost the evidence." He turned to me. "You know, he won't even hardly acknowledge me anymore. It's as if he doesn't even know me. However, I caught his attention when I mentioned you." He smiled at me, his eyes seeing every weakness, every fear. "I think I finally understand you. This isn't about religion, but it is about redemption, isn't it?"

I stared at the ground, with no words or tears left.

"You know what the saddest part is? You didn't save anyone. Not Cephas, not Emily, and certainly not Jack."

I stared into his eyes, unbelieving. "There's nothing you can do, Scot. They're already out of your reach."

I expected him to turn dark red with rage, but instead he threw back his head and laughed, a terrible, cruel laugh.

I watched him in confusion.

"Not killing you was one of the best decisions I've ever made. You're so entertaining," he cackled, then turned to Brice. "Ready the men." He turned to leave.

"Sir?"

Scot looked back as Brice handed me over to the other sailor.

"Ready them for what?" he asked.

The captain smiled. "For an armed pursuit. Her name is *Hopewell*."

"No!" I cried, struggling under the grip of the sailor. It was pointless. I couldn't fight my way out. Scot neared me once again. I lifted my head, ready to resort to begging. "They just want peace."

He stood to his full height. "There will be peace. There is always peace when the guilty are punished."

"What have they done to be punished?"

The cruel smile returned to his face. "You mean he never told you? What a pity. I'll tell him you said goodbye. Oh, and I heard about your lovely little display of betrayal with my son. Beautiful job. Couldn't have planned it better myself. You've done it again." He waved his hand toward Lindon. "She's yours."

• • •

The darkness was something that could be felt rather than seen. I couldn't tell if the cold heaviness I felt was a result of the prison cell's lonely interior or the fear that fairly dripped down the walls.

I gripped the iron bars. It couldn't end here. Someone had to warn them. I thought of the way I curled up in defeat on the Defiance. I couldn't give in this time, yet even as I fought against it, the reality of where I was set in. I sank to my knees, resting my forehead against the cold metal bars, thinking of Jack. I could just see him in the sunlight, out on the ocean, perhaps holding Emily in his arms or letting her sit on his shoulders. They would see a ship in the distance. They might try to outrun it, but there was no chance of that. The Defiance would overtake the Hopewell. There would be cannon fire. There would be pleas for mercy. Then there would be silence as Scot shelled the ship and it slipped beneath the waves. Jackson would die hating me, and I would never have the chance to explain.

If there were any other occupants of the cells of Newgate prison where Lindon had left me, they didn't make a sound. I might as well have been alone. This was the section closest to the site of the explosion and only a few of the cells were in working order. The place felt more like a tomb than a prison.

The words came slowly and brought me no comfort, but I whispered them anyway.

> "God's faithfulness is clear to me,
> He breathes life into this sod
> And for this sorry heart of clay,
> He gave His own heart's blood
> The saints and sinners all alike
> Saw Him answer faithfully,
> So tell me, child of His grace
> When did He abandon thee?"

The tears fell softly, soaking into the earth. "When did You abandon me?" I asked. Had it been when I hurt Jackson so deeply, or when I said goodbye to Emily?

Had God left with them? Why had He abandoned me here? "I was trying. I thought I knew what You wanted me to do. I thought I finally understood Who You were. Why? Why would You bring us this far to let us die?"

"Kate?"

I started, my skin prickling at the sound of my own name. My heart pounded as I wondered if God Himself were here with me.

"Is that you?" the voice echoed.

My gaze swept the darkness of the prison. I backed into the cold metal bars that separated my cell from the one beside me. I needed something at my back, where no one could sneak up from behind. "Who's there?"

There was no answer, save the echoing drip in the darkness. I listened for the slightest sound. Nothing.

Something cold brush against the back of my neck. With a shriek, I scrambled to the opposite side of the cell.

"Kate," came a weak voice.

I crawled, cautiously back toward the bars, staring into the darkness. The gaunt hand that had brushed against my neck reached out, gripping one of the bars in a weak grasp. I watched for several moments, seeing only the dark eyes that stared back at me, but I knew them so well. "James?"

He made a sound that was somewhere between a laugh and a sob.

I reached out for his hand and held it in both of mine.

"You're real," he moaned. "You're real. I thought I was dreaming."

"No," I sighed. "Just living a nightmare."

His hand felt so fragile, as if I could break it by simply holding it too tightly, but it was all I had of him. "What have they done to you?"

"It's not too bad." A cough rattle through his chest.

"I won't let them do it again. I'm here." I was suddenly seven years old again, huddled with him on the floor of Fortune Cole's cabin. There was nothing I could do, no promise I could make that would keep him safe.

"Today was the last time," he gasped as the coughing subsided.

"I thought you were dead," I said, my voice breaking.

"So did I."

"What happened?"

"I thought it was over. I knew I was going to die and after suffering here for days, with no relief from the pain, it was all I wanted. But there was an old man imprisoned in this cell. He called me by name. He told me you were safe. He said God was still with me."

"Did you get his name?" I asked, without the slightest question in my mind.

"Edward Jackson. He bribed the jailers to get me food. He talked to another prisoner who was a physician, and convinced him to help me. He said God had spared me. That lead ball should have killed me, but it went right through my shoulder. I started to heal. The man knew everything about me, Katy. I told him I didn't believe there was a God, and he pointed out every time in my life that God had been there for me."

"And what did you say to that?"

He gave a weak laugh. "I told him to mind his own business. I thought he was some sort of fortune teller or circus magician. Then they started to question him. Day after day they would take him out and torture him. I watched him, waiting for him to curse God, or at least ask why, but he never did. I couldn't argue with it. Most of the men in the prison were allowed to at least have their hands and feet free, but he was put in chains. He was suffering more than any of the rest of us, but he insisted God was here, that God had a plan. He'd saved my life, but there was nothing I could do for him. He told me to pray." He laughed again. "I thought I'd forgotten how."

"I did too."

"I dared God. I told Him that if he could make Edward Jackson a living, breathing, free man, anything was possible." He stopped, the story exhausting him, and I waited, giving him time. "That day, one of the jailers took me to a separate room.

I thought he'd come to question me, but instead he told me that he'd come to free Edward Jackson, and that if I would help him, he would set me free. I didn't believe him, but he didn't act like the other jailers. He said he knew what it was like to live like a prisoner, to be treated like an animal. I laughed at him, until he turned and I saw the blood on his shirt from a whipping. I couldn't argue with that either."

The pieces began to fit together. "Jackson."

"He was Edward's nephew. He gave me the key to unlock the old man's chains. Then he told me to be ready at midnight." He stopped, a weak pain coming into his voice. "I did everything I was supposed to do, but something must have gone wrong, because he never came."

"There was an explosion," I explained.

"I felt it. Right at midnight. Then someone I'd never seen before came from the back of the prison to free the old man. When I told him about my deal with the jailer, he shut the cell door and laughed at me. He said I was lying, and that I deserved to be here like all the rest. Then he left, and that was the end of it. The next morning the other guards questioned me. They found the key and the unlocked shackles. They knew I'd been part of the plot, and they've questioned me every day since."

"James." I shivered at the thought of their cruelties and tortures.

He laughed. "Well, God still answered my prayer. I guess I should have asked for just a little bit more."

We sat in the silent darkness together, our hands entwined through the prison bars.

"So what happened to you?" James asked finally.

I took a deep breath. What *had* happened to me? I told him my story, sparing no detail, leaving nothing out. As I told him about losing Emily, and my conversation with Brice on the bridge. What he'd said finally made sense. He had told me he had connections in the prison, and that he could get anyone

226

released for me. He hadn't been talking about Cephas. He'd been talking about James. As I neared the end, I was unable to stop the flood of tears. When my story finished he said nothing, and I wondered if my tale had put him to sleep, but I kept talking. "I feel it's been years since I've seen you. So much has happened. I'm so tired. I feel more like I'm seventy than seventeen."

"Eighteen," he whispered.

"What?"

"You turned eighteen two days ago. I thought about you all day, wondered if you were safe, wondered if I'd ever see you again."

Had my life been so turned around? I didn't know how old I was anymore. "It never even crossed my mind. How did you know?"

"Edward always knew what day it was. He was counting down to May fifteenth. He said there was a ship due to leave that day, and he'd hoped to be on it. After he was gone, I just kept counting. I suppose it was one way I tried to stay sane."

I rubbed my eyes. "I suppose that means I haven't even tried."

"Were you going to go?"

"To the New World? Yes. No. I don't know. I wanted you to tell me what to do."

"You need to go. There's nothing left for you here."

I gave a short, cold laugh. "Thank you. I'll get my coat and be on my way. Why don't you join me?"

"I'd like that," he said genuinely. "Do you know what I think?"

"What?"

"I think that sailor loves you."

"It doesn't matter anymore."

"Don't give up yet."

"Have you looked around? This is the perfect place to give up. There's nothing left to do. There's nothing here."

"There's hope."

"Is that what's in your cell? Because they didn't even give me a cot."

"Katy." The intensity and urgency in his voice silenced me. "I didn't understand it either. I'd given up too, but that old man never did. He told me God was here. He was right. For the first time, I know it's true. God is here. Can't you feel it?"

"I want to," I said, my heart breaking. "But we're in prison," I reminded him.

"I've been in a prison most of my life, too afraid to let myself out, thinking my fear and my bitterness were all that kept me safe. Now, here I am, trapped in the dark day and night, but I'm free."

"I don't understand."

"That old man gave me a little book. There's a crack in the wall of this cell, and every morning for an hour or so, the light comes through that crack, and I read that book."

"And what does it say?"

"*Fear not I have redeemed thee. I have called thee by name. Thou art mine.*"

The knot in my throat choked back a reply.

"He never left us Kate." In my hand he placed the little book. "Promise me you'll read it."

"I will."

"And promise me something else. Promise you'll go to the New World, get married, have a dozen boys, and name one of them for me."

I couldn't help but laugh through my tears at his optimism, or perhaps delirium was a better word. "I'll do my best, but you're coming with me, aren't you?"

He didn't answer.

"James?"

"I'm not afraid, Katy. I know what's coming. He's setting me free."

"No. No, I can't lose you again." I begged, my breath

shaky with fear.

"You're not losing me, Kate. We'll just be apart for a little while."

"No." I shook with sobs.

"Promise me you won't stop short of what God's got in store, Kate. Promise me. Promise me you'll keep running."

"I promise."

"That's my good girl."

I tried to wipe the tears from my cheeks. "You're always telling me what to do," I said fondly.

"Someone has to." He gripped my hand. "Read something to me?"

"It's so dark."

"Kate," he said softly. "You practically have the whole thing memorized."

Through the rest of the day and into the night, I recited every Scripture I knew by heart. Just when I thought I had come to the end, I would remember another. Just when I would start to feel alone, James would give my hand a squeeze, letting me know to keep going. As the bells struck midnight, I finished with a passage from the gospel of John. "*In my Father's house are many dwelling places; if it were not so I would have told you. I go to prepare a place for you.*" I choked back a sob. "I know we never really had a home here. I'm sure ours is beautiful. My parents are there. I'm sure yours are too. James, I never told you this, but you're my best friend. You never left me. You stayed with me no matter what I did or how I failed. I love you so much."

The prison was silent his hand limp in mine, and I knew then, that he was free.

Tears coursed down my cheeks as I lifted up the little book he'd given me, pressing it against my lips, as if it would somehow bring me closer to him.

I heard footsteps echoing down the hall.

"Hello, Katy. Did I wake you?" Charles Lindon's words

may as well have been in another language. They meant nothing to me. I heard my cell door open. I didn't care. It didn't matter what he did. It didn't matter if he killed me. He could take nothing more away from me.

He yanked me to my feet.

"Why the tears? Wouldn't you like a little diversion from your cell?" He cackled, pulling me toward the door.

I looked into the darkened cell beside mine. "I promise," I whispered, the fire inside me igniting once again.

Lindon unlocked the door at the back of the prison. I remembered the night of the explosion how it had swung wildly on its hinges. Whoever it had been that released Cephas from his cell had been too flustered to close the door. I remembered how the prisoners had been shouting about a prison break. None of it had even made me stop to think.

As he opened the door, a chilling night wind filled the corridor. Holding my arms behind me, he pushed me forward, into the darkness. I could see the whipping post ahead of me.

It was time to learn from my mistakes.

"Hands in front of you," he instructed.

"All right." I swung around, hands in front of me, clutching the pistol I'd just removed from the his belt. "Like this?"

He started toward me, but I cocked the hammer back.

"Don't make a sound," I warned.

He seemed to shrink in size, and for the first time, I saw him for the coward he had always been. "Y-you wouldn't," he stammered. "I mean…you couldn't. You don't have what it takes to pull that trigger."

From behind him, I saw a figure emerge from the shadows and was tempted to run. What if Lindon wasn't alone? Then, in the dim lantern light, I recognized the bulky form coming toward us. Looking back at Lindon, I held his gaze. "Not only do I have what it takes, I have every right to do it. You have taken everything from me. There is no reason I should spare your life, no reason I should show you mercy, but I want my freedom."

He turned away, wincing. "You have it. Shoot me, and go."

I lowered the gun. "The only freedom I have ever found was in forgiveness."

He glanced back up cautiously, then laughed. "I knew you didn't have it in you." He stepped toward me, but the figure behind him was finally in place. With a loud crack, Charles Lindon fell unconscious at my feet.

I looked up at First Mate Connors, who cracked his knuckles after dealing Lindon the blow. He laughed at my shocked expression. "I'm sorry. He was getting on my nerves, and I don't have time to tie him up. We need to move."

CHAPTER 23

Taking me by the hand, Connors led me into the shadows down a series of side streets.

"I need you to warn Cephas and the others."

I couldn't answer, still overcome by shock. "They're dead," I managed bluntly.

"Not yet."

"I don't understand."

"They had cargo to retrieve, up north in Ipswich. Scot can't shell that ship until it's out at sea. He has to bide his time, until they head back down the channel and go into open water."

The information was coming at me too fast. I was still trying comprehend the fact that Jack and Emily were still alive.

"Scot's looking for something. Says he can't leave without it."

"The lock," I said, more to myself than to Connors.

He halted. "Do you know what he's looking for?"

I shook my head, still trying to make sense of it all. "Not really, but I know it will ruin Cephas."

"That sounds about right."

He led me around a corner into an alleyway. Just when everything was still, I heard the stamping of horse hooves against the cobblestone street. In the darkness, I could see the animal's breath as it pranced nervously in the alley.

"What more could Scot need to ruin Cephas?" Connors went to untying the rope that was keeping the horse in place.

I froze. *His deepest regrets and darkest fears.* "I know where it is!"

"Where what is?"

"The lock! It was right in front of me."

He wasn't listening as he motioned for me to mount the horse. I did so with his help.

"You need to warn them. Now you'll have to pace yourself some, Ipswich is eighty miles north of here."

"I'm not going to Ipswich."

"Are you listening to me?"

"Connors, if we don't get to that lock before Scot does, it will all be for nothing. I'll get the lock and head to Ipswich from there. You'll have to stall the Defiance. You know that ship better than anyone." I took the reins in my hands, but he still held the animal.

"Are you sure you know what you're doing?"

I let out a shaky breath. "Not really."

He laughed. "Godspeed." He slapped the horse's flank, and the animal went shooting forward. It charged into the street and it was all I could do to keep it racing in the right direction.

The night wind whipped past me as I rode. I struggled to see what was ahead in the strange light of the stars. The letter I had burned echoed in my mind. *Your deepest regrets.* The breeze stung my eyes with tears. *Your darkest fears.* I held onto the reins with all I had. *Mine are there as well.* "Please, Jesus," I begged with every hoof beat. "Please don't let me be too late."

• • •

It was still dark when I reached Riversend. I slowed the horse, tying it near the river to rest. There was still a long way to go.

Winded from the ride, I sprinted through the town, ducking into the print shop. *For years I have left them, buried there with all the other treasures I couldn't keep safe.*

Treasures. The pamphlets. No one could keep the pamphlets safe. Stepping into the middle of the room, I saw the hole where the men had ripped away the flooring that terrible day and taken every pamphlet. The wood surrounding the pit formed a splintered frame around the exposed soil.

Buried. I fell to my knees and started plowing up the earth with my hands. It was here. It had to be here. I couldn't be too late. *Don't leave until you have uncovered and destroyed the guilt you find there.* I searched the earthen floor, digging my hand into the soil every few feet. Where was it? I didn't even know what 'it' was. What was I looking for? A lock? A coffin?

My fingers brushed against something deeply rooted in the soil. It was a smooth surface. Ripping through the hard packed earth, I felt my way in the dark. The surface was not large, but stuck fast in the moist ground. I dug around it until it came loose, and I pulled it from the dirt. It was a small wooden chest. In the dark, I couldn't make out more than that. I needed a light. Then I remembered where I was. Standing to my feet, I rushed across the room, opening the door to a cupboard.

It was all still there, the candles, the tinderbox, everything I needed. Unpacking the little box, I thought how odd it was that with all that had happened, these tools had remained unscathed and untouched. Striking the flint, I watched the sparks catch on the char-cloth I'd piled on the ground. I blew them into a little flame, then lit a tallow candle. Turning back, I waved the candle over the chest. It didn't appear big enough to hold whatever evil was inside. It didn't look like I had expected. I reached for the lid to open it, but the memory of the letter made me stop.

Don't open the coffin of regrets. Destroy it. What could be inside the chest? *Regrets...*

I remembered the cruel smile on Scot's face when he'd spoken to me on the hillside just that morning. *You mean he never told you?* What hadn't Cephas told me? What could he possibly have to regret?

"No." I placed a hand firmly on the chest. I wouldn't open the coffin. I would trust Cephas. I would destroy it.

But how? I looked down at the tallow candle in my hand. Burning it would be exactly what Cephas would want. I was sure. I leaned the candle toward the chest, but before the flame touched it the light revealed something I hadn't noticed. It was nothing more than a round, indent, about the size of a schilling, carved into the front of the chest. Holding the candle closer, I gazed inside the indent. The wood was patterned and engraved. The pattern looked familiar. I recognized it as the seal of the signet ring.

"A lock without a key," I mused to myself.

"Actually, the lock *is* the key."

In a panic, I scrambled out of the earthen hole and pressed my back against the wall, holding my candle against the darkness like a tiny dagger against a legion of armed troops. I waved it around, unsure where to look. Where had his voice had come from. I clutched the chest under my arm.

"Please," he said with a laugh. "Don't try to run. I've come alone."

I didn't believe him for a moment. I would have run if there had been any other exit, besides the doorway in which he was standing.

He stepped through the doorway and bent over.

"Don't come a step closer!" I warned, moving forward away from the wall.

He halted, his hands spread apart. "I'm at your mercy. Wouldn't want to risk you smashing another ale glass, or holding me hostage with an empty pistol."

"I know why you're here." My voice trembled like the flame of the candle.

"Oh? Well, then, I won't waste time explaining, but let's not try to fool one another." He took a step forward, entering the small, rippling pool of light. "I know why you're here, too."

It was Captain Scot's tone, more than his words that made my knees feel weak. Before I could respond, he stepped back into the darkness again.

"Come, Miss Elyot. Let us be honest with one another." His voice was directly behind me now as he moved silently on the earthen floor. I knew I should run, but what if he had men posted at the door? "You aren't in this for the girl."

Don't play into his game. Run.

"Are you?" His hand rested on my shoulder. My chance was gone.

I turned my head, looking up at him.

"You're here because of what he promised you."

I turned my gaze straight ahead. "Your son gives you far too much credit. You're not nearly as clever as he thinks."

He made a disgusted sound and stepped around me, planting himself in front of me once again, arms folded across his chest.

I gripped the candle tighter to stop it from shaking. "Cephas hasn't promised me anything."

"Is that right?"

"Yes."

"He didn't promise you worth? He didn't promise you hope? He didn't promise you a second chance?"

I felt my stomach turn, and I looked at the ground.

Scot laughed. "You forget, Miss Elyot, how well I know your enemy."

My head shot up. "You are my enemy."

He glanced down at me, his smile slightly cock-eyed like

his son's. "Am I?"

I felt myself beginning to question everything, and held my breath, trying to focus.

He laughed at my obvious frustration. "Am I the one you should be running from?"

"You kidnapped Emily. You tried to have me hung. You would murder your own son." I wasn't sure if I was listing these things off to remind him, or to remind myself.

He sighed. "Jack has painted an ugly picture of me, hasn't he?"

"He didn't have to."

"Did he tell you I whipped him? Did he tell you I kidnapped him, threatened him?"

"Yes."

"Did he tell you I favored him?"

I didn't reply.

"Did he tell you that I only wanted him to excel, to be a man? I know I pushed him too hard." There was something like remorse in his voice. "All his life I wanted the best for him. I pushed other, more qualified men aside to let my son succeed and make something of his life."

I had tried not to believe a word that came from Scot's mouth, but it was the look in his eyes made me catch my breath. He was not the cold-hearted captain. He was a father.

"I was only trying to free him from the enemy that you should have been running from. Instead you've played right into his hands."

I felt a chill sweep over me.

"You never even suspected that it was Cephas who was out to harm you. In fact, you thought he'd come to rescue you."

I took an instinctive step back. Wanting him to fade into the darkness.

"He called you by name. He told you he trusted you. Cephas gave you your second chance. That's why you're here.

You had to know. Why would he choose you? Why would he pluck you out of obscurity?"

I fought back tears. I had to get out of here before he said anything else. I dodged around him, aiming for the door.

He didn't try to stop me as I darted for the doorway. I was nearly out, nearly free.

"It's in there."

My feet stopped without my permission.

He turned to face me in the doorway. "The answers you've been searching for. The questions that keep you awake at night. The explanation to every 'Why?' you've ever asked. It's in that chest."

I could only shake my head in denial, too weak to even think of an argument.

"Cephas is liar and a murderer who let me pay for his crimes. He stole my son's heart and turned him against me."

"I don't believe you," I shook my head, trying to fight my way through his dizzying words.

"Who killed your parents?"

"They died...in an accident."

"But you always knew, didn't you?"

"No."

"You always knew it wasn't an accident." He stepped toward me. "I was there, Kate. And I can assure you, it was no accident."

I felt powerless against his words. How could I refute them? I had been only a child.

"He started a mutiny among the ship's crew."

"That's not true."

"He convinced them that we could take the ship, hold your family hostage. Then when we'd gotten the money from your estate, he was going to kill all four of you. I tried to stop him. I informed the local authorities of his plan. When he saw that it was no use, he set fire to the ship, still hoping that he could somehow claim your inheritance when you were dead.

He never counted on the fact that you might survive. So he hid you and abandoned you with that old woman, where no one would ever find you."

"You're lying!"

"Oh, Kate," he reached into his coat pocket, and withdrew a golden signet ring, holding it out to me. "I only wish I were."

I reached forward, taking it from his outstretched hand, my fingers numb and trembling. I stared at it. The words of the letter echoing back. *No matter what happens, don't open the coffin of regrets. Destroy it.* I wasn't supposed to open it, but I had to prove Scot wrong, had to prove Cephas' innocence. He hadn't killed my parents. He hadn't. It couldn't be.

"Do you remember the day you met him?"

I looked up.

"Do you remember the Northern Tavern, where an old man told you and your cousin that the Elyot estate was no more? If I'm not mistaken, that was right before you received your first letter. You see, if you had stepped forward and claimed what was yours he would have been ruined. His lies would have been undone, so he sent you a letter."

"No."

"And another and another and another, trying to keep you away from everything that's rightfully yours."

I could hear the blood pounding in my head. It was all too much to take in.

"And look at you now. Why, you're ready to lay down your life for him. All because he offered you a second chance."

"No!" I fell to my knees, clutching the chest in my arms. "I don't believe you," I whimpered.

"I never asked you to. Open it, and see for yourself."

I looked down at the lock and key in my hands.

"Go ahead," Scot coaxed.

"I trust him," I said, looking up at Scot.

"Do you really?"

The question brought a smile to my face. It was Jack's question to me. It was Cephas' question to me. It was God's question to me.

Don't you trust Me?

I looked back up at Scot, the answer finally clear.

I had to move carefully. Standing to my feet, I glanced at the thick forest that sprawled for miles behind the print shop. It was the perfect place to hide. All those years of tree forts and imaginary lands I'd created in those woods were about to save my life. I made my way toward the print shop doorway again, turning at the last moment to face Scot. "You cannot turn me against him." With that I turned, flying into the thick brush.

I could hear his deep voice echoing like thunder behind me. "So be it."

I plunged through the woods, my every step giving me hope that perhaps Scot had come alone as he'd said. Glancing behind me, I didn't see him pursuing. It didn't make sense. This was Scot's last chance. Where were all his men?

The shrieking whistle of an arrow made my blood run cold and my skin prickle. With a gut-wrenching thump, I heard it stick in a tree, and saw it just above my head. They were all around me, hidden from sight, yet drawing closer. I started to run in a panic, heart thrashing, feet pounding. The whistle of arrows sounded closer and closer every time like the howling of pursuing animals. I looked down at the chest, clutched in my arms, the ring in my fist. I had the power to stop what was coming. I had to keep running. The thick dewy grass clung to my legs. I couldn't stop. Ducking under branches, shoving my way through the trees, I stumbled into an open clearing. Unable to catch myself, I hit the ground, but sprang up again, wild with fear. I was trapped. I couldn't go forward. I'd be an all too easy target. I couldn't go back.

Kate...

Suddenly the sound of my own heartbeat was all I could hear. I'd been here before. I knew this place. My recurring nightmare...Where had He been standing in my dream? I saw the hill on the other side of the field. I could make it. I had to make it. I turned to check my pursuers. I turned too late.

The trees behind me erupted, two sailors streaking out of the dense forest. They were upon me before I could run. One crashed into me, knocking the chest from my hands as I fell to the ground. I struggled, stretching toward the chest just out of reach, but the sailor gripped my shoulders, wrenching me to my knees.

"Did you think it would be that easy?" Scot stepped calmly into the clearing. "Did you really think you could just take this with you? You didn't even ask."

I stared up at him, fighting against the sailor's grip.

"And I suppose you were headed to Ipswich. Life's just not that simple, my dear." He turned to the man who'd taken the Lock from me. "Get the key."

I started to fight, even though I knew it would do no good. He wrenched my wrist around, twisting it until I could do nothing but watch as he pried my fingers open and ripped the ring from my grasp.

Scot leaned over me. "This is the last time you will stand in my way." He turned walking toward the trees with the sailor who carried the lock and key, but he looked back at the man gripping my arms. "Kill her."

The sailor released one arm to reach for his knife, but before he could get it I twisted around to face him. I strained against him with all I had until I couldn't withstand his hold any longer. I let go allowing his strength to drive me into him. The unexpected force knocked him off his feet and we both hit the ground. His grip loosened for only a moment and I wrenched my arm away. The other sailor had seen us and broke through the trees as I leapt to my feet, racing for the hill.

I heard one shot go off as I reached the foot of the hill. As I tore up the incline another shot exploded. I swerved at the sound of the pistol, losing my balance at the crest of the hill. I fought for control, but skidded down the opposite slope, rolling toward the riverbank at terrifying speed. As I reached the bottom, I threw my hands out reaching for anything that would slow me down, but found nothing. Digging my hands deep into the muddy earth, I slid to a stop right on the river's edge and looked behind me. They had just crested the hill. Struggling to my feet, I stumbled toward my horse, still tied in his place. They were out of shots. Their only hope was to catch me.

I sprinted breathlessly toward the animal without checking my pursuers. They were gaining. I could hear them as I reached the horse. The reins were tied to a branch and my fingers shook violently as I undid the knot, constantly checking behind me. They raced toward me along the river bank. The rope came loose. I scrambled onto the horse's back just as one of them reached me. I dug my heels into the animal's sides and he surged forward. The sailor caught a corner of my skirt, but couldn't keep his grip as my horse pounded forward, down the forgotten path leaving them far behind.

A cold, white sun pierced the mist as we thundered down the dirt road. Dawn had come. I would never make it to Ipswich in time.

The Hopewell would pull out of Ipswich Dock completely oblivious to the danger waiting for her. If only I could get word to them. If only I could reach them before Scot did.

The thought hit me with such force that I slowed my horse. There was only one way. I glanced back over my shoulder where Riversend lay on the distant horizon. "No. It was not the last time. But this will be."

Chapter 24

I watched the men scattered over the dock like a colony of ants. They were everywhere. The Defiance loomed in London's harbor, surrounded by people. This was going to be harder than I had anticipated. I remembered my reaction when Jackson had told me he was going back to the Defiance, and laughed to myself.

If only he could see me now. The laughter was quickly replaced by an ache. If he could have seen me, he still would have thought I was a traitor, but this would make things right. I only prayed that he would live to see it.

Ducking behind a stack of enormous crates I could hardly breathe, seeing how close I was to the ship I feared so much. Every second there were people up and down the plank. There was no way to sneak aboard.

"What am I paying you for?!" Brice's words were slurred as usual. I froze, my heart pounding. It suddenly hit me how foolish this was, how dangerous it was. What was I thinking?

"All of the crates go on!" He let loose a stream of profanities at the dockworker.

I heard the scraping of wood against wood as one of the crates was lifted by several men on the other side of the stack. I couldn't lose my resolve. This was my only chance. *All the crates go on...*

• • •

The dockworker picked up an end of the massive crate, then dropped it with a crash. "John!"

"What is it?" The other voice was tense and strained.

"Come on!"

"Too heavy for you?" he mocked.

"Shut up! It's the last one."

They heaved up the crate, jostling it from side to side. It tipped upward as they wobbled with uncertainty up the plank, and onto the ship. They set it down on the deck for a moment's respite, then proceeded down several sets of stairs. Reaching the hull, they dropped it with a thud on the ground.

"Watch it! Do you know how much powder could be in there?"

"Black powder?"

"Enough to blow us to Kingdom Come."

"Captain's not the cautious type, then."

The piercing shriek of the door closing never sounded so sweet. I waited in the darkness for a long time, until I felt the ship lurch, lolling from side to side as it left the harbor. It was time to move. Pushing up on the lid of the crate, I peeked out at the hold of the Defiance. I was in.

Climbing out of the wooden box, I stretched my cramped joints. The door clanked as someone started to unlock it, and I dove into the shadows behind boxes and barrels. From my crouched position I watched as a sailor came in with a small barrel on one shoulder and noticed the open crate. With a string of obscenities regarding the dockworkers, he set down his barrel, slammed the lid on the crate, then turned, pulling the door closed behind him.

I started breathing again. I needed to find a hiding place closer to the door. I leaned back, in order to push myself to my feet, when my hand brushed against something warm. My heart froze. It was another human hand. Before I could scream, his hand covered my mouth. He had his other arm around me, pinning my hands to my sides. "What are you doing here?" came the harsh whisper.

I stopped my struggling at the familiar voice. "Connors," I breathed as he released me, taking the hand from my mouth.

"You're supposed to be in Ipswich."

"I ran out of time. I found the lock."

"Where is it?"

I hesitated. "Probably in Scot's cabin."

He groaned.

"I'm sorry. I tried."

"What are you doing here?" he repeated.

"I still need to get the lock. If Scot's telling the truth—"

"Which isn't likely."

"What's inside that chest could get Cephas hung without so much as a trial."

"If he shells the Hopewell, a hanging won't be necessary."

"He must be planning to take Cephas alive, or he wouldn't have gone back for the lock."

"What are you going to do?" he asked.

"The last thing Cephas told me to do. I've got to destroy that chest."

"And what about the Hopewell?"

"I don't know!" I buried my face in my hands. "We have to get word to them."

"Impossible."

We sat in silence, the ship rocking back and forth. I leaned forward out of the shadows.

"What happened to you?" he asked in surprise.

I looked down at my hands and arms. They were black with gunpowder. "There are only so many ways to get on this ship," I answered.

"Even less ways to get off." Connors gave a low laugh, starting to his feet.

"What?"

"That's it. That's our way off."

"What is?"

He turned to me, a smile looking unnatural stone-like features. "Black powder."

I stared at him dumbly, waiting for the rest of the joke. "Pardon my hesitation…"

"Don't worry. Just trust me."

I stood to my feet, still not sure what the plan was. We moved to the shadows by the doorway. "What are you planning?" I asked, when we were settled and waiting.

"You sound worried," he chuckled, rubbing his hands together. "This stuff has gotten me out of plenty of scrapes."

The thought of the blinding explosion in the prison flashed through my mind. "Was one of them recently at Newgate Prison?"

"Actually yes. Why do you ask?"

"Just wondering." I could feel my stomach winding itself in knots as I remembered the dockworker's words. *Enough to blow us to Kingdom Come.* "Anything I should know?"

"Get rid of that chest, then wait for me."

"Anything else?"

He looked at me evenly. "If I run you should probably run too."

I felt my mouth hang open, but no words were forthcoming. This was a horrible idea. I had to say something before…

The door shook as someone unlocked it from the other side. The sailor who'd found the open crate earlier marched in, letting the door swing behind him as he headed into the hold. Connors caught it, and I darted through with him right behind me. The door swung shut and he gave me a nod to continue on. I took the steps two at a time, halting at the top to see who was on the gun deck. It was deserted, just as it had been the night Jack and I had escaped. We heard the door to the hold screech open behind us. Connors and I glanced at each other.

"Go, go, go," he mouthed, motioning toward the far set of stairs.

I sped toward them, stopping only to look back when I reached the first step. Connors had vanished into hiding. I still didn't like this plan.

The sailor was plodding up the steps from the hold. I leapt up the last few steps and found myself on another gun deck, meant for the lighter cannon. I could hear the pounding footsteps behind me. There was no time to pause. I saw a ladder leading to a hatch and ran for it, grasping the spokes and frantically reaching for the hatch. Relieved that it wasn't locked, I shoved it open, climbing through and letting it fall closed behind me. I stopped to catch my breath and take in my surroundings.

"You don't need to slam it!"

My heart stopped.

"People are trying to rest." Brice lay in a hammock several paces in front of me, his back to me. I was in the officers' quarters. Brice was the only occupant. I searched desperately for a way out. There was a door on the far side of the room. He already knew someone was there, and that sneaking around wouldn't do me any good. Instead, I took long, heavy strides, trying to sound like the drumming of a sailor's footsteps. Reaching the door, I found myself thinking of how Jack would have laughed at my stomping.

"Did you hear what I said?" Brice shouted, just as the door swung closed behind me. I was in an empty room, another section of the officer's quarters, but this one was different. It was several moments before I noticed that the difference was light. The officers' quarters, as well as all the subjacent decks, were lit by lanterns or candles. Clear, cold light streamed in from beneath a door at the end of the room. I was getting closer. Hurrying toward the door, I laid my hand on the latch and opened it, cautiously.

Light stung my eyes, coming from an entire wall of

window panes. It fell on the luxurious surroundings. The door latch clicked closed behind me. As I stood in awe of this room, I became aware of a soft ticking. My attention fell to the desk, stacked with maps, books, a quill, ink, and a gold watch. I was in the captain's cabin. The rhythmic ticking and soft sound of waves were all that could be heard. I stepped forward, somehow unable to hurry. Beside the books there sat a miniature portrait that attracted my notice. It was a painting of a family. A somber couple stared back at me. In front of them there was a little boy, whose mouth tilted in a familiar, cock-eyed smile. I shook myself. I was wasting time. On the desk, the chest lay open. Without giving myself time to think, I looked inside.

Edward Jackson

I looked straight up out the window. The pages inside the chest had gripped me so suddenly that I hadn't had time to prepare myself. No. It couldn't be true. My eyes drifted downward, landing on a filthy, aged piece of parchment. The ink had faded, but I could make out a few of the names written in a ring. I remembered Jackson's words. *Most mutinies start with a piece of paper.* Two names were clear on the parchment, side by side.

Anthony Jackson Edward Jackson

No. Scot couldn't have been telling the truth. It wasn't in his nature. The man couldn't help but lie. I flipped to the next page in the chest. Agreements of money, payment for four fares. It was all there. Then the handwriting changed to an all too familiar slant.

To his Lordship, Henry Lane,
    It is with great regret that I inform you of the

death of four passengers aboard the Faithful...

I felt the tears prick my eyes.

> *I cannot compensate for the loss of the Elyot family. Their death, and the death of their posterity, is no small thing.*

I found myself gasping for breath as my eyes searched the letter for any sign of hope.

> *Since the number of those who would seek to inherit the Elyot fortune are as abundant as the rumors surrounding this tragedy, I have sent this to confirm to you that the Elyots have no surviving descendants, and therefore cannot claim their portion.*

> *Sincerely,*
> *Edward Jackson*

All of my strength was gone. I was bereft of feeling, lost for words. I knew my knees were about to give way. With all of my purpose, all of my running, I had simply played into the hands of my parents' murderer. He'd believed in me. He'd trusted me. He'd treated me like my life mattered. In the end, I was just a tool. Yes, Simon Cephas had known me well. He'd known just how gullible I was, what an idiot I was, and just how easily I could be fooled.

"You didn't believe me, did you?"

I waited for the jolt that Captain Scot's voice always brought with it, but felt nothing. There was nothing left to feel. He'd been right. It was all a lie. "Why didn't he kill me?" I asked staring out the window at the stormy gray ocean.

"You'd have to ask him," he answered. "But if my brother

is anything like me, he simply underestimated what a problem you would be."

I turned to face the captain.

He smiled confidently. "I tried to tell you." Stepping around me, he scooped up both lock and key.

I started to look for an escape, but the captain caught me by the arm. "Why fight when there's nothing left to fight for?"

· · ·

The wind-whipped rain soaked through my clothes, pulling my heavy dark curls over my eyes. I didn't mind. This way I wouldn't have to watch. There was little I could do about it anyway with my hands pinned to my sides by the ropes that lashed me to the foremast. My back ached after only a few minutes of the torture.

Captain Scot's laughter caused me to look up. When he saw my face, he mocked surprise. "What? No tears?"

I didn't answer, staring at the murky skyline. The Hopewell had come into view as the land mass behind us disappeared. I could see people moving back and forth on the deck, little suspecting what was ahead. Suddenly, my heart began to beat faster. They weren't just people. They were people I recognized, people I loved. I thought of the Rowtons' little boy, Jacob. He'd spoken of a sailing ship. Were they aboard the Hopewell? What of Widow Lawrence? Had she finally found the courage to leave? I knew that Jack would be at work, climbing the rigging, doing whatever the captain would let him. And somewhere on that ship, was a seven-year-old girl whom I loved, whom I had sworn to protect. Scot was wrong. I hadn't done this for myself. I hadn't done this for Cephas. I had done it for a little girl who loved me, trusted me, believed in me. And she would always be worth fighting for.

"Are we in range yet?" The captain asked Brice who was heading down to the gun deck.

"Nearly there, sir."

I turned to the hate-hardened man beside me. "Scot, don't do this."

He smiled, a patronizing grin, holding the chest under his arm like a cherished pet. "your fears to rest, Miss Elyot. Cephas isn't worth protecting."

"This isn't about Cephas."

He studied me. "After the lies he's told you, why would you spare him now?"

"There are innocent people on that ship. They're good people. Some of them are children."

"There is a price to pay for the blind that follow the blind."

"And that price is innocent blood?"

"They are on that ship because they have been deceived by his hypocrisy. I cannot change that." He turned, the fateful drumming of his boots pounding down the first few steps that led from the forecastle to the main deck.

"Your son is on that ship!" I cried in desperation, appealing to any shred of his heart that would listen.

He halted, setting the chest on the top step, and turned back to me. The look on his face was one of shock and grief and pain. "If that is so," he said, his voice weaker than ever I had heard it. "Then he will betray me no more." He turned, marching down the steps with purpose. "Give the order to fire."

"No!" I shrieked. Struggling and tearing at the ropes. They wouldn't budge.

"I said fire!"

I screamed, wishing my cries could carry over the water, where the innocent Hopewell glided along the waves, thinking the Defiance was nothing more than a passerby. "God please," I whispered. "Please."

The ship rolled and rocked with cannon fire. I couldn't hear my own screams as blast after blast shattered the air with sound. I waited, unable to take my eyes off of the Hopewell.

Nothing happened. The Defiance roared, and shook with the lethal explosions, but the Hopewell remained unharmed.

Scot ordered the barrage to halt. "What happened?"

The crew on deck didn't answer.

A sailor stumbled up from the gun deck, struggling for air, and covered in soot. "The cannon, Sir, they've misfired!"

"What?"

"They were packed down with powder. We've got fires on both the lower decks."

I bit my lip. *Connors.* This was his work. I felt the tears of relief forming in my eyes.

"Captain!" It was Brice's voice, echoing as he came from one of the lower decks, also showing signs of the catastrophe. "There are twenty men trapped on the lower decks. The fires are beyond our control. If we have any hope of seeing land, we need to turn about now, and head for the dock." He stumbled toward the ship's wheel, gripping it to guide the Defiance back to shore.

Scot took Brice by the front of his shirt. "The only hope you have of seeing land again, is aboard the Hopewell. Is that clear?"

"But Captain!"

Scot shoved Brice aside, then turned to grip the wheel. "The Defiance has no cowards."

I watched, wondering if the crew would rebel against their leader, but not a man protested, as they steered the vessel toward the Hopewell. Brice got back to his feet and slunk to work with the other men.

The smaller vessel had been warned by the failed shots, and was attempting to pick up speed, but it was too late. With Captain Scot at the helm, the Defiance moved easily into position, alongside the Hopewell. Sailors were perched on the side of each vessel, prepared for the fray.

The crew of the Defiance carried grappling hooks, and as

the ships drew parallel to one another, launched them into the air. The much crew of the Hopewell dove for cover. The grappling hooks held, and the men drew the ropes in, pulling the smaller ship closer. Many of them drew swords and pistols, waiting for the captain's orders. Scot positioned himself at the stern and held up a hand halting them, as though he had all the time in the world. There were sounds of cracking beams and splintering boards beneath us. This ship was sinking under him, but he would not be denied this moment.

"State your business!" cried the commanding captain of the Hopewell. "We have no quarrel with you!"

"Then release to me your passenger Edward Jackson, or perhaps you know him as Simon Cephas!" Scot's voice carried over the water.

A rough voice whispered in my ear. "There you are."

I searched frantically, unable to turn around to see the speaker. I felt hands brush against mine as the ropes behind me were loosened. With the mens' attention on the other ship, he had snuck up behind the foremast.

"Was the plan that hard to follow?" he asked.

"What are you talking about? You said to wait, and I've been here…waiting. Quite the show with the black powder."

"Did you like that?"

The captain of the Hopewell looked puzzled. "We have no passenger by that name!"

I strained to see the men on the deck of the Hopewell. Most of them I didn't recognize. Then, I saw him, burning eyes fixed on his father. "Jack," I whispered under my breath. Cephas was aboard somewhere on that ship. Why didn't he show himself? Men were about to die, and he wouldn't even show his face. "Hurry," I urged Connors.

"Nearly there." I could feel the tension of the ropes releasing one by one behind me.

Scot turned to his crew. "Prepare to board."

A wild cry erupted from the crew of the Defiance.

"Done." Connors said, the last rope releasing. My knees buckled at the unexpected snap of the rope just as the first few crew members leapt from the Defiance to the Hopewell.

Connors pulled me to my feet. "Time to go."

Scot looked on as his men jumped from one ship to the other. Had not a third of his crew been trapped beneath the gun decks, the struggle would have been over in mere moments, but the Defiance had little advantage in the hand to hand battle that ensued.

Connors led me to the ship's railing. My gaze swept the deck of the Hopewell, searching for Jack. He was locked in a fight with Brice, who was desperate to end their years of rivalry with a final victory. I looked across the gap at the deck of the Hopewell. It wouldn't be a long jump, but the smaller ship was a good distance below us. The space between the two ships felt suddenly insurmountable with the ocean roiling below.

"You can make it!" Connors shouted, reading my mind. "Are you with me?"

I gave Connors a nod, and he released my hand, climbing up on the railing.

I started to follow his lead, until my eyes landed on Scot, poised at the stern of the Defiance. His gaze was fixed on Brice and Jackson. Brice was losing in the combat. The captain's words ran through me. *He will betray me no more.* I knew what he was planning. Jack wouldn't see him coming until it was too late. I couldn't warn him in time.

Connors jumped, and I realized I was supposed to have jumped with him. He landed on the deck of the Hopewell, stumbled, but regained his footing. I turned away from the rail, and ran for the stairs where the chest sat on the top step.

Just as I reached them, a thundering crack split the air, causing the ship to shudder from the impact. The tremor knocked me from my feet just as I reached the stairs, and I stumbled forward, gripping the stair railing. The chest toppled down the stairs, scattering the documents. I glanced up, and saw what had caused the ship to quake. The base of the mainmast was weakening. The fires on the lower decks were finally eating through the levels of the ship. The mast would fall at any moment.

I looked to the stern, hoping I wasn't too late. Scot was the only one who hadn't leapt to the deck of the Hopewell. He was poised to jump, just as I reached the main deck. I fell to my knees beside the scattered pages, and cramming them inside the chest.

"Scot!" I screamed, trying to raise my voice over the din of chaos.

He turned in time to see me gather the pages into the chest. His eyes went wide. I'd needed to get his attention, and now I had it. It was time to move. Scot pounded across the deck, charging toward me, drawing his pistol as he ran. He only had one shot, but it was all he would need. As I hurried toward the railing, I saw that Jack had Brice on the ground, his blade positioned just above Brice's neck, when he looked up and saw me. I could see his lips form my name, and he seemed to forget Brice altogether. He ran to the forecastle to stand beside Connors, who was directly across from me. Reaching the railing, I glanced behind me. Scot was racing over the deck toward me, but I wanted to look him in the eye. Without breaking my gaze with him, I threw the chest over the side of the Defiance. It plummeted, splashing into the water below. Scot went white. My death was written in his eyes.

The cracking sounded again. I looked up in time to see the mainmast falling toward the Hopewell, like an enormous oak being felled. I braced myself as it crashed downward. Scot looked up too late. With a sound like thunder, it collapsed on top of him, tearing through the netting and the sails of the Hopewell, nearly splitting the Defiance in two as it rocked back and forth in the water. When the rolling ceased, I stared in shock. Scot lay still and lifeless, trapped beneath the mast.

"Kate!"

I turned at the sound of my name, staring down at Connors and Jack waiting for me on the other side. Climbing onto the railing, I took a deep breath. I was going to make it.

The shot rang out.

It felt as though someone had pierced my side with a hot fire poker. I couldn't breathe. I saw Jack, his eyes wide with horror. I looked back to see Scot. He lay pinned beneath the mast arms stretched tight, in front of him, smiling in triumph as he lowered the pistol. His final shot had found its mark.

I heard Jack scream my name as my knees buckled, and I collapsed forward, unable to stop myself. I plunged down toward the water. Suddenly everything was silent. I was surrounded by water. Quiet, peaceful water. I opened my eyes, seeing the two ships floating just above me like dark clouds. The fire in my side continued to burn, but soon blackness and silence began to shroud my consciousness. I thought of how the water had always frightened me, but it was peaceful here, beneath the waves. I'd always imagined myself having peace at this moment, when I knew there was nothing I could do, when I knew I would die.

CHAPTER 25

Heaven was warm, like a summer's evening. Heaven was soft, the way I'd always imagined the clouds. Heaven was safe. I couldn't even imagine what it was like to be afraid. I opened my eyes. Heaven was perfect, white light. The light shifted and changed, becoming shapes and colors.

I had never imagined Heaven having windows with lace curtains, but then, I'd never really thought about it. I turned my head to look around me and blinding pain made the world flash white again. This wasn't right. I struggled to breathe.

"Now, now." A cool hand rested on my forehead, and I felt water trickling down my burning throat.

"Who are you?" I asked, the shapes coming back into focus.

"Your servant, Miss," came the soft reply.

I strained to look at her, still dizzy with pain. "Where am I?"

She laughed. "In your home."

My heart began to pound. I didn't have a home. The lovely, cavernous room that surrounded me wasn't familiar.

"Do you not know it?" she asked, her voice laced with concern.

"No," I said in a shaky voice. "No. This isn't right." Where was I? I tried to make sense of it, but the memories of all that had happened were slipping away like a forgotten dream.

"There, there," she soothed. "It was all just a nightmare. You always were prone to nightmares, Miss Katy."

"No!" I sat up, the pain in my side so fierce, I found myself fighting back unconsciousness. "It was real," I gasped.

She laid her hands on my shoulders. "Miss Katy, you're not well. You mustn't get up."

"How do you know my name?" I cried, struggling against her.

"This is your home. I am your servant. Why should I not know your name?"

"You're lying!" I pushed her hands away, throwing aside the blankets that covered me. I tried to stand, but the pain made my head spin, I fell to my knees, fighting away the black shadows at the corners of my eyes. Her hands fussed about me. I looked up at her. "Jane, stop!"

She froze, taking a step back. I knew her name. How did I know her name?

I pushed myself unsteadily to my feet, stumbling through the heavy wooden doors, trying to get away from the room that was looking more familiar every moment. I gasped for breath. Where was I? This hallway. I knew this place too. I had to get outside. Without hesitation, my feet seemed to know the way. As I stumbled down the corridor leaning against the wall for support, I couldn't stop the pictures and memories that broke into my mind unbidden. There were stairs to my right. Without stopping to count, I knew that there were eleven of them, and they led up to three bedrooms. As I passed a set of heavy double doors to my left, I knew they led to the parlor. No. It couldn't be true. This was not my home. I had never been here before in my life.

It wasn't a dream. It wasn't a dream. It was all real. If anything, *this* was a dream, or rather the nightmare. Jane was calling after me, but I didn't stop. I had to get outside. I had to know for sure. The corridor turned right up ahead, but there was a window just in front of me, draped with lace curtains. I halted. Handcrafted lace, made to fit this specific window. I remembered the day it was hung. I remembered the way her eyes sparkled. This was her favorite window. I reached out and touched the lace, my fingers slipping through the loopholes and resting in the curtains. I could see the view outside. The green hills stretching upward, cloaked in mist.

Can't you see it Katy? God wraps the hills in His cloudy blankets, so they won't be cold on days like today.

"Lady Elyot?"

I turned from the view to look back down the hall. A woman stood at the end of the hall. Her appearance was so regal she could have been a queen. I gaped, searching for words.

She reached out a delicate hand toward me. "Please don't be afraid. We mean you no harm." I took a step toward her, but could no longer battle against the pain in my head. My side was burning, and the shadows were prevailing. I fell to my knees, unable to fight any longer as the blackness surrounded me.

• • •

The woman gazed into the fire, looking ethereal in the glowing light. She was tall. Her very presence would have made the most graceful being feel clumsy. Her hair was gathered up, but even from a distance I could see the silver strands here and there. The scarlet of her skirt seemed alive as the flickering shadows of the fire played upon the silken fabric. Her arms were folded in front of her, as if to ward off a chill.

"Who are you?" I asked softly.

She turned, surprise breaking her calm for only a moment. "Elizabeth Lane."

I stared in confusion, waiting for the explanation.

She didn't offer one.

"Should I know you?" I asked.

She kept her eyes on the hearth in front of her, and gave a warm, low laugh. "No. I don't suppose you should."

"This is my home, isn't it? This is the Elyot Estate."

She nodded, still not looking up from the fire.

"Why are you doing this?"

"Your mother once did me a kindness I could never repay."

I opened my mouth to ask another question, but she roused herself, moving toward the bed where I lay. "I promise I will tell you all I know, when you are strong enough to hear it."

Her words were not comforting. "I'm strong enough," I insisted.

She smiled, laughing the same gentle laugh. "Soon."

"Please," I begged as she turned to go. "What happened to them?"

"Whom do you mean?"

"Jack." I gasped for breath. "Emily. The Hopewell. Where are they?"

"I would tell you if I knew, Child."

The door closed behind her, leaving me in the silence, to let my questions rock me to sleep.

· · ·

Elizabeth Lane's version of soon was not nearly as soon as I was expecting. It was days before I saw her again. My questions grew stronger at the same rate I did, but there was little I could do about it. The only people I saw were a private physician and Jane the chambermaid who waited on me incessantly. It wasn't until I could stand up and walk for myself without trouble, that Elizabeth Lane came to see me again, offering me a walk through her garden. I accepted, following her outside. The memories flooded back as we walked. I remembered the climbing of every tree. I knew where I had chased butterflies and jumped in the puddles. After only a few minutes, I had completely forgotten the woman walking beside me and was surprised when she started to speak.

"My father took over this estate more than ten years ago, when he received word of the accident. We received a letter telling us that there were no survivors to claim this estate or receive the inheritance."

I felt the knowledge prick me like a brier thorn. I knew where that news had come from, and who had invented that lie.

"Our family estate was farther north, but rather than see the land divided, he wanted to preserve it. He was a good friend of your family. He died the following winter. My brother and his wife took over our family estate, and I came here after my husband died. I never dreamed that anyone would come back."

"Neither did I." I shook my head. "I still don't understand. Why am I here?"

She didn't reply. Her dark eyes were facing forward. I followed her gaze and saw that she was looking at the little graveyard in the shade of the trees. I remembered it, but hadn't strayed there often as a child. "I want to show you something," she said moving toward the entrance.

I felt the slightest apprehension in following her. What could she have to show me?

The grave stones were not many, but some were ancient, time having eroded the words from the markers before I was even born. She walked over to where two gravestones, more erect and less faded than the others, were placed side by side. I knelt down next to them.

Anne Elyot
Healed and safe from all harm.
1601-1625

Edward Elyot
Rewarded and beloved.
1596-1625

The tears filled my eyes. There were no graves in the shadow of the markers. There had been nothing to bury. I ran my hand over the lettering.

"Placing these memorials was the first thing my father did when he arrived."

I nodded. "Thank you for bringing me here," I said, without turning to her. I could see why she had waited so long to show me these things. It was not an easy thing to take in.

She was silent for a long time before she spoke. "That's not what I came to show you."

I turned to look at her. She was gazing at two more gravestones which I hadn't noticed. They were smaller, each inscribed with only a name and a date.

James Elyot
1617-1625

Katherine Elyot
1618-1625

"This is where he told me to bury you."

I heard her words, but they made no sense. I watched her as she looked down at the gravestone bearing my name, her arms crossing in front of her again, as if to guard her against the cold.

She looked up at me, her gaze so intense and mystified that I was paralyzed beneath it. "There was no hope for you."

She waited for my reaction, but I could only stare at her. "You were dying. That's why he brought you here. He said to bury you with your family. He said that he needed to make things right."

"Who?"

"The old man that brought you here. He said to give you all I could, and offered to pay me for the expense. He told me to let you die in comfort and in peace, as you should have lived, then to bury you here."

I brushed away the tears as I tried to let her words sink beneath the surface. I looked down at the marker. I was here among the trees and the birdsong. I should have been there.

"I called for my physician. He's a brilliant man, but I never thought he could save you. I only called for him because I had promised to do all I could."

I was lost for words. My mind raced. Question after question vied for a place in my thoughts. "How did you know who I was?"

She smiled, stepping forward. "I knew it was Anne's daughter. You favor her. She was the closest thing I had to a sister."

Her compliment touched me and I turned away, looking at the vast, expansive landscape. There was no doubt in my mind that Simon Cephas had brought me here. "Why did he care what happened to me? Why now, after all that's happened, after all he's done?"

"I don't know any more than I've told you."

"Was he alone?"

"Yes."

"Then what about the rest of them?" I didn't expect an answer, but the questions wouldn't stop.

She stood beside me. "If you'd like, I can find out."

"Would you?"

"Give me the names of the people you're searching for if you have any idea where they might have gone."

Finding would be a difficult task. "I can't ask any more of you."

"Actually, there was something else I was going to offer you. Although I see the resemblance, you have nothing to prove who you really are. Legally, you're more dead than alive. You can't take back the estate, but I have lived here all alone for so long. I would be honored if you would stay here."

I stared at her in disbelief. "Here?"

She nodded. "All of this would eventually be yours. I would leave it to you, as my heir."

I was lost for words. I gazed at everything in front of me, the land, my family home. I thought of how James and I had searched this countryside for our estate, and here I was. I thought of my parents smiling down on me as I took back their title and kept up their land, living the life I had been born to live. I thought of how long I had walked, how much I had struggled. This would be the perfect ending.

. . .

I was choking. I couldn't breathe. The darkness, the cold, the pain, they were all closing in. I couldn't hold on, but he was pleading with me. I could hear him, begging me to breathe. I was trying, but it was as if a great weight was on my chest.

"Please, Kate. Please stay with me!"

I felt the weight lift, replaced by a sharp, unbearable pain, like a knife in my side, every time I took a breath. I could see him, right above me, his face twisted in anguish. I saw his lips move, but I heard nothing. I could offer him no hope, no comfort. With every drop of strength I had left, I reached up, running my fingers down his cheek. He knew. He knew I had done it for him. He gripped my hand in his own, leaning over me until his forehead pressed against mine.

"Don't leave me."

I sat up in the darkness, my heart pounding. Trying to

calm myself, I leaned back on the pillows behind me. Just a dream.

No, it wasn't a dream. It was a memory. They came back in frightful, terrible sequences. Night after night, I would remember something different. In some dreams, I was in the dark, unable to move. I could hear Jack's voice, but could do nothing to respond. Sometimes, he was talking to me. Other times he was praying. I hadn't seen his face in any of these dreams until tonight. I felt the tears on my cheeks and buried my face in my hands, exhausted.

I tried to go back to sleep, but my thoughts would not allow it. Seeing his face, knowing the way he had stayed with me, rescued me. When would my loneliness end? I wiped away fresh tears, as I remembered that wherever Jack was, he thought I was dead. I had tried to right things, tried to send them word, but every time I sat down to write the letter, I would only stare at the blank parchment, not knowing what to say, or how to say it.

What if I was mistaken? What if these were only dreams, and not memories? What if he still hated me?

From everything Lady Elizabeth had been able to find, it appeared that the Hopewell had returned to London, and that the passengers I wanted to find had boarded another ship, *The Planter,* sailing for the New World. They had also returned with several prisoners in their possession. These prisoners, Brice among them, were all being put on trial for betraying the crown by attacking one of His Majesty's commissioned ships. The Defiance had never returned to the dock, but had disappeared beneath the water, taking her captain with her.

There were other things that bothered me in these long night watches following my nightmares. I was unhappy here, and I didn't know why. I lacked nothing. Lady Elizabeth had spared no expense on me. She would not be satisfied until I had everything my heart desired, but as time wore on I knew that my heart's desire was not in any dress shop or parlor. He was across the ocean in the New World.

Already Lady Elizabeth was mentioning the young men of court who would be suitable for me. I had no doubt that her intentions were kind, but my stomach lurched whenever she mentioned it.

I wondered if he was ever awake at night thinking of me. It was cruel not to send word to them. It had been months, but I simply couldn't put it into words. I had to see him, had to look into his eyes and explain the truth. Yet how could I leave? I had everything I had ever wanted here. For once in my life, I wasn't afraid of going hungry, being left destitute, or being found out. It was the life I'd always wanted, wasn't it?

The dreams were not the only thing haunting me. While my sleep was filled with memories, my waking hours marched on to the rhythm of the words I could not forget.

Disturb us, Lord when we are too pleased with ourselves,
When our dreams have come true,
Because we dreamed too little,
When we arrived safely,
Because we sailed too close to the shore.

They were the words of the poem Cephas had scratched on the back of his letters. They pounded in my mind day after day.

Disturb us, Lord, to dare more boldly,
To venture on wilder seas
Where storms will show Your mastery;
Where losing sight of land,
We shall find the stars.

No. That wasn't right. I was finished with wild seas. I was not about to dare anything boldly. I just wanted to live a simple life, uninterrupted, and undisturbed.

Disturb us, Lord.

"No," I said aloud.

Throwing aside the covers, I got up to light a fire in the hearth. The warm flicker was my only companion in the lonely cavern of my room. I huddled in a chair beside the fireplace.

Promise me you'll keep running, Katy. If he could have seen me, seen where I was, what I had found, would James have still told me to keep running? He had told me to go to the New World. The recollection of his other instructions made me want to laugh and cry all at the same time. What would he say if he could see me now?

The knock at my door made me jump. "Come in."

I was surprised to see Lady Elizabeth Lane, a shawl wrapped around her nightgown, her hair flowing down her back.

"I didn't mean to wake you," I apologized.

She only smiled. "Do you think you're the only one who has trouble sleeping in this cave?" Pulling up a chair beside the fire, she sat down, the posture of habit, making her look every bit the lady she was. "The silence has stolen more hours of my sleep than I can count."

I nodded, knowing exactly what she meant. "It's so empty," I said, my voice echoing off of the walls.

"Not half so empty as it was before your arrival."

We sat in the silence of the firelight, each with our burdens, each with our thoughts, each wanting nothing more than the solace of the other's company. "You look troubled," she said at last.

I shrugged. "Here I am. All I've ever wanted is at my fingertips. What do I do now?"

"Other adventures await." Her smile was so expectant, that for a moment, I was carried away in her enthusiasm. "You have so much to learn, so many people to meet. Why, in time, I'm sure I could get you an audience with the King himself."

My smile faded as I imagined meeting the man who had overseen the death of Reverend Durham and countless other Puritans. Everyone from the King to the King's Fool would gape as I gave King Charles himself the lecture of his life. My execution would follow shortly after.

Lady Elizabeth was laughing.

"What?" I asked.

"That was quite a face. Is court life boring you already?"

I managed a good natured smile. "In all honesty, I worry I can't do it. I fear that I'll humiliate myself, fear that I won't be everything I need to be."

She turned to me, her smile reassuring. "My dear, you cannot let fear keep you from being who you were meant to be."

Her words brought sudden clarity to my mind. "You're absolutely right."

CHAPTER 26

It was not until the dirt crunched beneath my feet that I regretted my decision. What was I doing here? The scenery before was wild and untamed. I wanted to turn and hop back into the longboat that would row me to this ship. What had I been thinking?

"Do you need help, Miss Elyot?" the cabin boy asked.

Yes. Yes, I needed help. I should have been labeled insane for ever thinking that this was a good idea. But if Elizabeth Lane had taught me anything, it was that outward confidence went a long way. I let out the breath that was making my chest ache and squared my shoulders. "Thank you, but no. I'm quite capable."

"Indeed you are." He gave me a wink. This particular cabin boy's wink was so awkward and forced that for the first week aboard ship I'd thought he had an eye condition. However, upon observing that this eye condition only afflicted him around the ship's female passengers, I concluded that it was his subtle attempt at charm.

I looked around me, dazed. Fifteen days of waves, wind, and sea-sickness for this. I was a fool. I should have listened to Lady Elizabeth. My decision to come had sparked many heated arguments, all of which spun through my mind now.

Her voice pounded in my head as I walked along the

shore. "Leave and you'll starve to death or freeze to death or be murdered by a savage!"

I had argued that everyone I knew and loved had gone to the New World, and that I would not be deterred with rumors and stories.

"*A New World.* What, might I ask, is wrong with the old one?"

The list was too long. I knew I would never belong there. I knew it would never change.

"You're making a mistake. When you get there and see that all of these *rumors* and *stories* are true, I'll be here waiting, and I won't say that I told you so."

She had been right. This was a mistake. Here I was. Rough houses hewn from the wilderness stared back at me in challenge. Pointed, cone shaped tents dotted the landscape here and there between the dwelling places.

So this was Boston, the City Upon the Hill.

I caught the stares of passersby and looked down at my dress. It had been the simplest one Lady Elizabeth had sent me with, and still I felt ridiculous. The embroidery down the sleeves and the silver stitching on the bodice were such tokens of vanity. I would have given anything for simple, black linen, but silk and satin was all I had.

I took a shaky step forward, realizing I had no idea where to go. It could take days to find them. Hesitating, I wondered if I should just turn and board the longboat again, but then I recognized that slithering whisper of fear.

No. I would not be controlled by it any longer. If fear told me to go back, I would move forward. That was why I had come. I knew from experience that a life of fear would be a more terrible fate than any winter, any starving time, or even any…savages. I was resolved to move forward, but in what direction? I was lost, and I hadn't even started out yet.

"Katherine?"

I jumped at the sound of my name, and turned to see a

man coming toward me on the road. It was Scot. The jolt of fright paralyzed me. I couldn't move. I couldn't run.

He came toward me slowly, gently, as if I were a frightened animal. "Katherine." As he got closer, I stared in amazement. It wasn't Scot. He looked so much like him, but he was thinner, and he said my name with a fatherly tenderness. After the terror that had just filled me, I wanted to cry, but my fear was instantly replaced by anger. Tightening my grip on my bag, I sent him a sharp look, and began to march down the road.

"Kate."

I turned back to him, unable to disguise the ice in my voice. "I didn't come here to speak to you, or to hear any of your excuses."

His pained eyes were gray, just like his brother's. I knew he could see right through me, but he wasn't searching me for fear. "Of course. You're here to see Emily."

I fought back tears, staring at the sky, hoping they wouldn't spill down my cheeks. "Not just Emily." My voice trembled.

"We started a settlement outside of Boston. I'll take you there."

I nodded in agreement, not sure what other choice I had.

We walked in silence, but the battle against my tears didn't stop. Here he was, beside me. Simon Cephas. The man who killed my parents, the one who left me with Fortune Cole, and the coward that wouldn't show his face on the Hopewell.

"You opened the lock," he said quietly, without a hint of anger or disappointment.

"No," I answered. "I didn't open the lock. Just like I didn't stop defending you, just like I didn't abandon your granddaughter." I couldn't bear it any longer, and stopped on the road to look at him. "I did everything you ever asked me to do! No, I didn't open that chest, but I saw what was inside. I saw your name in that ring of traitors. I saw the letter you

271

wrote to Elizabeth Lane's father. I know what you did, and I tried so hard not to believe it." I stopped, waiting for him to answer, but he only looked at me as if his heart was breaking. "Go ahead!" I cried. "Tell me how it's all a lie, and how Scot made the whole thing up."

He said nothing, but his eyes were so sorrowful I couldn't bear to look at him anymore.

I turned and started to walk down the road, having lost the battle against my tears.

"I have no defense."

I halted, turning back to look at him.

"I did everything he said."

My throat ached with tears as he took a step forward.

"I have no excuses. There's no reason you should trust me or believe me. That's why I stayed so far away, why I never tried to explain it to you."

"You started the fire on the ship?"

"It was all I could do to stop Scot."

"Scot?" I knew where this was going and was ready to refute him. "So *he* was the one who wanted to kill my parents?"

He took another step forward. "His plan was so much bigger than your family. You were just the beginning."

"Of what?"

"A resistance against the royalty, against the wealthy, against power in general. Scot was determined. Nothing would stand in his way. He knew he could fund the resistance with a ransom for your family. Then, he planned to make a public example of all of you."

I shook my head. "Your name was in that ring with all the others. Did Scot write it there?"

He stared at the ground. "No. The captain that ruled us was a cruel man. Scot convinced me that the plan was to keelhaul the captain once we got out to sea, leaving him stranded with provisions on an island off the coast of Africa. I signed it, trying to put an end to the cruelty and the violence. I didn't know what he was planning until it was too late. When I stepped in, trying to keep them from killing the captain, I was imprisoned in the hull, just below the gun deck. If I did nothing, Scot would have killed countless people, but I couldn't stand against them alone. I started the fire, hoping I could get to your cabin before the flames reached the powder. I was too late to save them, Kate. They died by my hand, and for ten years I've lived with that. I have no defense, no excuses."

I could tell by the guilt and the fear etched in his features, that he was telling the truth, but beyond that, his story made sense with my memories. I remembered him now. I remembered the man who had burst into our cabin, picked up James and I, and saved us from the fire. He had tried to save us. "You told them we were dead."

"Every man on that crew survived. I knew they would come after you. You were the symbol of every wealthy royalist. It didn't matter to them that you were children. I had let your parents die. I wasn't going to take a chance with you."

"So you left us with Fortune Cole?"

"Where no one would ever find you."

My mind was racing.

"I waited until things died down before I came to get you."

I bristled at his words. "No one came to get us. We were forced to live there until we ran."

"I was there, Kate. You never saw me, but I was there."

"Where were you?" I cried, angrily. "Where were you when she tried to beat him to death? Where were you when we were starving and terrified?"

"Who unlocked the door, Kate? Who followed you through the storm? Who carried you when you could go no farther? I had to leave you with Fortune Cole. My brother was in prison. My family had no idea where I was, but I came back for you, and I carried you the rest of the way."

I choked back a sob, remembering the figure following us on the road in the storm. "Did Reverend Durham know you brought us to him?"

He smiled fondly. "He did, but he never said anything, not even to his sister. I didn't ever want you to know I was there. I knew you would be happy with them. I knew they would teach you the things of God, and that was all I ever wanted for you."

I felt suddenly exhausted, as if the anger and fear of ten years was suddenly released, and I didn't even know how stand without them. "You know, Lindon wasn't looking for pamphlets. He was looking for you."

"I know. Durham wrote me after he stole the evidence from Lindon and hid it beneath the print shop, but by the time I got there it was too late. Kate, I tried everything to get him released from prison. I offered myself in his stead. I did all I could do, not just because he was my friend, but because I couldn't bear to watch you lose your family because of me again. The last time I saw him, he gave me the signet ring and told me where the Lock was."

"And the letters? Emily? What of them?"

"I lost track of you after Durham's death. I couldn't find you. Then I saw you in the tavern, up north. It was my last attempt. I knew Scot had come back. I knew he was searching for me. I had to keep you away from your inheritance. What if Scot had come looking for that as well? I had to keep you safe. I wanted to give you a home with us. I gave the letter to my daughter along with the key. Then we received a warning. Scot knew where we were. We had to flee for our lives. I couldn't ask you to be a part of that. The letter was forgotten in its hiding place." His eyes grew misty. "You know the rest."

I was at a loss for words. I stared at the man in front of me, the letters, the promises, the Scriptures all making sense.

"Why didn't you show your face on the Hopewell?" I

didn't know why I asked. I wasn't angry about it any longer. I knew there was an answer for that, just as there had been for everything else.

"I wasn't on the Hopewell. I was in London, planning to leave on the next ship. I was there when they brought you back." His voice broke. "They said you were dying, that there was nothing that could be done. Timothy wouldn't leave you, but there was nothing he could do. He allowed me to take you North to your home. I just wanted to make things right."

I felt my heart begin to race. They had been more than dreams.

"Kate," he held out his hands. "I fell so short. I tried to keep you safe. I tried to set James free, but I only succeeded in failing you again and again. I wanted you to know God was there, that He hadn't abandoned you."

I stepped forward, holding his gaze. "You did protect me. I'm standing here. You did set James free. He told me. And God is here. No one could have taught me that. I had to see it, I had to choose Him. He was always there, watching over me and so were you."

He looked up, his eyes glistening. I understood his tears. They were the tears of being forgiven. The tears of a second chance.

• • •

"Wait here." There was a sparkle in the eye of Simon Cephas as motioned for me to sit down on the steps of the modest sanctuary.

I nodded, understanding his meaning and feeling a nervous anticipation. "I'll be waiting."

"I won't be long."

He turned, hurrying down the road. I wanted to laugh at myself. How much had she changed? It had been nearly five months since I'd seen her last, and I found myself nervous. I knew it would be a few moments before her grandfather found her and told her that there was a surprise waiting for her at the church. I stood in front of the sanctuary, vibrating with so many emotions. I was exhausted from the journey and from my conversation with Cephas. I was nervous and excited to see Emily at last. Whenever I thought of speaking to Jackson, my heart started to pound so hard I thought it would burst. What would I say? How could I explain? It was the thought of seeing him that had moved me to make my decision to come to the New World.

Walking around the church, I shivered in the glowing autumn sunset. It was not a large building, but they would expand it after they'd built houses for everyone. I felt like I was in a dream. I was finally here. I waited for the feeling of home to surround me, but it hadn't yet. I felt a prick of fear that this would be just like England. Perhaps there was simply no place where I would feel at home.

"Thought I might find you here."

I jumped at the deep, familiar voice, when I noticed open window above me. The voice was coming from inside the sanctuary.

"Anne and I have been talking, and we think Emily should come to live with you." That was Thomas Rowton's voice.

"If she's a problem, I'll make other arrangements." There was another voice I recognized, but the fight and the passion I loved so much in it was gone.

"It isn't that." Rowton sighed. "We love the girl, but she's so sad and so lonely. Not even Jacob can cheer her up. She's always falling into fits of tears and..."

"What do you want me to do?" Jack cried, his voice so broken it brought tears to my eyes. "What can I offer her? I can't comfort her, can't console her, can't bring back anyone she's lost. She doesn't want me."

"She needs you," Rowton insisted.

There was no response.

"Timothy, how long will you blame yourself?"

Silence.

"Until you feel you've been adequately punished? Until Emily loses you too? How long, Timothy?"

"Who else is there to blame? For once, I was trying to do the right thing, the selfless thing! I was trying to push everything I wanted aside to keep Emily safe."

"It was a mistake."

"Is that what I'm supposed to tell myself for the rest of my life? That it was a mistake? Sometimes, I lay awake at night, and all I can hear is her voice, begging me not to leave her there. She did, you know. She begged me. Do you know what I told her? I told her she was getting what she deserved."

My heart was breaking, my love for him so strong in that moment that I began to run toward the door to the sanctuary. He had to know. I had to see him.

"Katy?" The breathless little voice stopped me in my tracks. I turned and saw her down the road, a silhouette against the fiery sunset.

I ran toward her, racing over the path, closing the distance between us. Falling to my knees, I caught her up in my arms. She melted into my embrace, her little body shaking with sobs.

"You're here," she gasped.

"I'm here! I'm here." Words beyond those failed me. "I love you." I never wanted to let go of her, but I held her at arm's length to look at her. The sunset turned her tears to gold as they slipped down her cheeks. She laughed, her beautiful, innocent, perfect laugh and wiped the tears from my face with her little fingers. I leaned closer pressing my forehead to hers, laughing as we rubbed noses. We were together, and nothing could ever rip us apart again. She suddenly turned to look back toward the chapel and I followed her gaze.

Jackson was standing outside the doors, shielding his eyes as if trying to see us clearly. "Em?" he called.

I stood, and his eyes went wide. He didn't move. It was as if he didn't want to hope, didn't want to believe it was me. I tried to think of something to say, anything that would let him know that this was real. I stepped forward. "Jack," I said his name softly, but I knew he heard me. My heart began to pound. Nothing, not even fear, had made it beat this hard before. It was thundering as he broke into a run toward me. As he raced over the path, I could hardly breathe. He didn't slow down, running right into me, catching me in his arms, refusing to let go.

"Kate! Oh, Kate, I'm so sorry. I'm so sorry!"

I sobbed into his shoulder. "I know. I know, it's all right!"

He held me, every fear, every doubt disappearing like mist in a warm breeze. "I love you," he whispered. "Kate, I love you. I never got to tell you."

I pulled back looking into the face that I'd seen in my dreams, hearing the voice that had pleaded with God for my life. "I knew." I fell back into his embrace. "I knew." I was so thankful for his strength and his love. This was the happiest moment of my life. "Thank You. Thank You, God."

"Kate?" he asked, softly.

"Hmm?"

"Promise me you won't leave."

I stepped back, unable to stop the warm laughter that spilled out of me, as I looked up at him. "Why would I leave? My family is right here."

Both of us glanced down at the same moment, where Emily stood looking up at both of us. This had probably been her plan all along from the way she was beaming. Jack bent down, scooping her up and balancing her in one arm, while pulling me toward him with the other. We stood in the glow of the sun's fading light, holding each other.

I was finally home.

EPILOGUE

I look around me tonight as the winter winds howl outside. This house has stood for ten winters now, some much harsher than this. The fire crackles cheerily in the hearth, lighting up the faces of my family. *My family.* The words never cross my mind without nearly bringing me to tears. There are many who take such words for granted, but I count them as a gift every time I speak them.

Beside me on the hearth, sits my husband. I laugh softly to myself as I realize that no one else looks at him and sees the cocky adventurous boy I nearly shot the day we met. Very few people know the past of the Reverend Jack. They see a man passionate. They don't see his scars, only the courage God has wrought from them. I pray that is true of me as well. It has not been an easy road for us, yet God has brought together two very broken people and made something wholly beautiful.

Beside him sits a young woman whom I will always see as a little girl. She has grown so tall and lovely as many people, young Henry Rowton especially, have noticed. She has called me Mother from the day Jack and I were married, and came to live in this cabin and raise her as our daughter. She has been my comfort and my joy.

Baby Anne stirs in my arms, her ruddy little curls shining in the firelight. She took her first steps today, and I caught her up in my arms, amazed that something so small could delight me so much. I think I understand now, how our Heavenly Father feels when we take our tiny steps of faith.

Simon Cephas, or Edward Jackson as we all know him now, sits in a chair by the fire staring at the sparks, as though he is far away. I feel a little pang of worry, wondering what he will think of the surprise I'm going to share.

Two forms lie on their stomachs before a prized picture book. For being twins, they don't look much alike. James is a lanky, troublesome replica of his father. And Timothy, with his shining black eyes and dark curls, resembles a family member that does not sit around the fire with us, but is with us in many ways.

The happy images around me blur with tears as I hope that he is proud of me. I have done everything he told me to. I haven't stopped running. I have found so much hope. I'm married. I have children, though not quite a dozen. I even named one for him.

My heart is so full I can hardly speak, which of course is why at this very moment the wise Simon Cephas looks up at me.

"I wonder, Kate, what you have there in your lap."

"I have something to read to you all." I fight to swallow back my tears, without success. They come spilling down my cheeks one by one.

Jack gives me a crooked grin. My heart still pounds at the sight of that smile, reminding me of the day I arrived on these shores. He alone knows what I am about to say, as he takes the slumbering baby girl from my arms.

"I want you all to make me a solemn promise."

My boys look at each other, then at me, mischief clearly written on each face.

"I don't ever want this story to leave this family."

"What story?" Emily asks, her eyes sparkling.

"Our story. I want you to have it. I want your children to

have it." I can't help laughing at myself. "But I don't want anyone else to have it."

"You wrote it down," Emily breathes in amazement. "I'd always hoped you would."

Little James vibrates. "Is this the story of when you tried to shoot Papa?"

I send my husband a look, to which he raises his hands in innocence, glancing slyly toward his son. "Where did you hear about that?"

"Are we in it?" Timothy asks.

"Yes."

James jumps up, his eight-year-old curiosity unable to be suspended. "Where? Where are we?"

I lean forward nose to nose with my little boy. "You are the happy ending."

His father tells him to sit down, and I look down at the words I have penned and again find myself fighting tears.

"What's wrong, Mama?" Emily's voice is sweet and gentle, just as it was the day I met her.

I struggle to think of words that explain my tears. "It's...it's more than I ever asked for."

I feel Jack's hand on mine, and I am overwhelmed by God's goodness and His grace. With a deep breath, I take up the stack of pages in my lap and begin to read.

"'I'd always imagined myself having peace at this moment, when I knew there was nothing I could do, when I knew I would die.'"

I tell them the story, which, if they all keep their promise, will never leave the safety of our family. I have here inscribed it for one purpose, the purpose God gave the Children of Israel at Gilgal.

"'That this shall be a sign among you that when your children shall ask their fathers in time to come saying, "What mean you by these stones?" Then ye may answer them, that the waters of the Jordan were cut off before the Ark of the

Covenant of the Lord…'"

To whichever of my children or grandchildren has read this Chronicle, know this: God has not given us a spirit of fear. Neither has He forgotten us. Never will He abandon us, not when we struggle in the storm, not when we cry in the darkness, and not even when we slip beneath the waves.

Listen for His voice. He is calling you by name.

"But now thus saith the Lord, that created thee, O Jacob:
and He that formed thee, O Israel,
Fear not: for I have redeemed thee:
I have called thee by thy name, thou art mine.
When thou passest through the waters, I will be with thee,
and through the floods, that they do not overflow thee.
When thou walkest through the very fire,
thou shalt not be burnt, neither shall the flame kindle upon
thee."

ISAIAH 43:1-2

AUTHOR'S NOTE

One of my favorite parts of weaving together historical fiction is choosing what threads of history to use in order to complement and contrast the threads of fiction. Please enjoy a look at the colors and textures that set the tone of this novel.

The events of this story take place in the spring of 1635, nearly fifteen years after the Separatists settled in Plymouth, and ten years before the English Civil War.

All of the characters in this story are fictitious, except for the following historical figures which are mentioned only briefly.

King Charles I was the reigning monarch of the time and carried on the persecution of the Puritans that had been instigated by his father, James I.

The Bishop Laud was the Archbishop of Canterbury at the time and an adamant persecutor of the Puritans. Both men were executed as a result of the Glorious Revolution led by Oliver Cromwell.

John Winthrop was a Puritan lawyer and the founder of the Massachusetts Bay Colony. It was his desire to create a self-governing colony that would be a "City Upon A Hill" and an example to the rest of the world. The original Winthrop Fleet that was made up of eleven ships and about eight hundred Puritans was followed by thousands more, seeking religious and economic freedom.

William Wallace and Robert the Bruce are heroes of Scottish history. Fighting for Scottish independence, they won her the freedom that both Scotland and Ireland longed for. (interesting fictional fact: Captain Anthony Jackson chose his alias surname "Scot" as a result of his worship of these Scottish heroes.)

There are also several locations that find a place in our world, as well as Kate's.

All of the towns and cities mentioned in the book are real places, except for the small Puritan communities, such as the home of Widow Lawrence, and the village of Riversend.

Over twelve ships in the Royal Navy have borne the name the Defiance. Though the sixty-six gun galleon in this story was a trade ship not a navy Ship, I did attempt to pull facts from the ships that really did sail. For example the HMS Defiance that sailed from 1664-1669 was destroyed by being "burned by accident," much like the ship in this novel.

The Hopewell sailed from London in April of 1635 carrying at least sixty eight passengers. There is no record of them ever being chased down, shot at, or boarded by a power-hungry captain and his crew. Perhaps they simply forgot to mention it.

The Seven Stars in Holborn London was built in 1602 and survived the great fire of 1666. Today it stands as a public house and historical sight.

The Devil's Tavern was originally known as the Pelican and was built in 1520, making it possibly the oldest Riverside Tavern on the Thames. The name *Devil's Tavern* was not given to the pub, but rather it was earned by reputation. It was notorious as a meeting place for sailors, smugglers, and cut throats, and has even played a part in many English legends. It was burned in the 19th century and rebuilt as the Prospect of Whitby. All that remains of the original building is the stone floor.

Newgate Prison still stands at the corner of Newgate

Street and Old Bailey Street. It was built in the twelfth century and was destroyed and rebuilt countless times in its history. Prisoners were able to bribe the jailers (or as it was spelled then, *gaolers*) for food, blankets, and even their release. It often held criminals awaiting their executions, and there are several accounts of prisoners escaping which I used as the framework in writing Cephas' midnight escape.

Several practices that were from the pages of fact rather than fiction also graced the pages of this story.

The "ancient heathen practice" Master Owens speaks of in Chapter 2 was called Tatau. It was a Samoan custom which we know today by its Americanized name; Tattoo. Sailors were the first from the western world to discover it and employ it.

The piece of paper that began a mutiny came to be known as the Round Robin. The use of this form of mutiny was recorded as early as 1714, but may have been in practice before that. It assured that every sailor involved in the plot shared the blame equally, as their names were all written in a circle. The account that Jack shares with Kate in Chapter 19 is a true historical account which took place under Captain Nathaniel Uring in 1714. He suspected a mutiny, and demanded the Round Robin to prove it. When none was forthcoming, he beat the suspected leaders until a man not involved with the mutiny stepped forward with the document in hand. Captain Uring did not prosecute the men, or punish them further. Their mysterious disappearance is a thread of fiction I created for this story.

The Geneva Bible was printed in Geneva, Switzerland in 1560 and was a collaboration of the efforts of many scholars. It is still thought of today as "the Bible that shaped America," as it was used by the Pilgrims in Plymouth, Boston, and by many of the Founding Fathers. The covers of these volumes were simple and black, so as not to draw attention. Some were inscribed with the dates, names and illustrations referenced in

Chapter 11. The Puritans used only this translation because they believed the King James Version to be corrupt since it was commissioned by King James, their enemy. I chose to use this version for all the Scriptures quoted in this novel, not because I agree with this belief, but for its historical accuracy. I admire the Geneva Bible Translation for its desire to correctly display the heart of God. Rather than being translated from the flawed Latin Vulgate as both the Wycliffe and Tyndale versions had been, it was one of the first translations to be taken from the original Greek and Hebrew texts. It was also the first to insert Biblical commentary.

The poem *Disturb Us, Lord* was written by Sir Francis Drake in 1577. I had never heard of it until a friend, who'd read it at a youth camp, shared it with me. It has moved me and reminded me of God's constant calling to us as His children to move into wilder seas where we will draw closer to Him.

And lastly, what of the Puritans themselves? The greatest confusion that arises is the difference between the Separatists and the Puritans. What is the difference? Fifteen years, one hundred and thirty-three miles, and perhaps an extra ounce of stubbornness. The Separatists believed that the Church of England was corrupt beyond saving and therefore separated, founding Plymouth in 1621. The Puritans, on the other hand, believed that the Church of England, though flawed, could be purified from the inside out. They were proved wrong in the 1630s when King James I began arresting and executing them. This persecution forced them to the New World in droves. They were led by John Winthrop and founded the Massachusetts Bay Colony in 1630. It is estimated that over thirty thousand English emigrants settled in the New World before the start of the English Civil War in 1642. The reasons for the persecution were based in their constant rejection in the King's religious practices. They refused to set up their altars in the assigned places. They didn't use the translation commissioned by the King. To irritate them further, King James published his *Book of Sports.* In this book, he laid out the games which all the people of his country were *commanded* to participate in on Sundays. Since the Puritans believed in upholding the Sabbath, they constantly defied this law, and were therefore fined or imprisoned. The true reason for, persecution, however was the secret printing and distributing of the Puritan pamphlets. They condemned the King and defied the Church of England's authority. Those found guilty of printing the pamphlets were branded on the cheek with the letters *S* and *L* for *Seditious Libeler.* Those caught writing the pamphlets could be convicted for treason and executed.

Often the Puritans are misrepresented as cold, legalistic rule followers, and certainly that is what the Puritan branch of Christianity became. But we must understand that at its beginning the Puritan faith was a courageous stand against corruption, and a bold leap into the unknown. We owe our country's infantile years and strong heritage to these saints and martyrs. They laid the foundation for a nation that could stand as a "City Upon a Hill." Their stand against corruption must not be forgotten, as the "City Upon a Hill" flickers and dims in the New World they found. What they began must not be lost in history, but treasured and appreciated and carried on.

ACKNOWLEDGMENTS

Special thanks to Darien Gee for guiding me through the editing and marketing process and for giving me the motivation and work load that I needed to get this thing finished!

Much thanks to Karen and Katrina who edited my work, corrected my grammar, and slashed out comma after comma. Your encouragement has fueled my creativity for this final stretch.

To Emily, and all of the girls in my Thursday Dance Class who unwittingly were the inspiration for the character of Emily Blake. You are all a part of her, even if you didn't know it. Thank you for inspiring me!

Thank you to my amazing family for letting me write. Thanks to my parents for making me stop writing when I need a break and to my brothers for bursting into my office and tackling me. You guys keep my life so real, and inspire me day after day. I love you all!

Never-ending thanks to my Lord and Savior, the Author and Finisher of my faith, and the Writer of every story: Jesus Christ. May my words honor You and bring glory to Your name. I love You.

Hannah Duggan is a young woman fervent about God's grace and His Will in the young people of this generation. As a worship leader, dance instructor, and Bible study leader, she is constantly pouring into the lives of young people. Her passion for writing stems from her desire to spread the powerful gospel message through both fiction and non-fiction. She has two younger brothers and is an active part of her parents' ministry at Calvary Chapel Hamakua on the Island of Hawaii.

To learn more about Hannah, her books, and her ministry visit www.hannahrosed.com.

Or write her at hannahdugganauthor@gmail.com.

41660595R00179

Made in the USA
Middletown, DE
19 March 2017